John Strange Winter

The Strange Story of My Life

A Novel

John Strange Winter

The Strange Story of My Life
A Novel

ISBN/EAN: 9783337032296

Printed in Europe, USA, Canada, Australia, Japan

Cover: Foto ©Andreas Hilbeck / pixelio.de

More available books at **www.hansebooks.com**

The Strange Story of My Life

A NOVEL

BY

JOHN STRANGE WINTER

Author of
"Bootles' Baby," "Army Society," "Cavalry Life"
"Beautiful Jim," "Garrison Gossip," "Red Coats"
"A Born Soldier," "A Magnificent Young Man"
"The Same Thing with a Difference"
"The Truth Tellers," etc., etc.

FOURTH EDITION

LONDON
F. V. WHITE & CO.
14 BEDFORD STREET, STRAND, W.C.

———

1897

TO

MY LITTLE GIRL,

NANCY,

WHO WAS BORN ON THE DAY ON WHICH THIS STORY
WAS FINISHED, I, WITH MUCH LOVE,

𝔇𝔢𝔡𝔦𝔠𝔞𝔱𝔢

"THE STRANGE STORY OF MY LIFE."

JOHN STRANGE WINTER.

Dieppe, 1896.

CONTENTS

The Strange Story of My Life

CHAPTER I

GOING BACK TO THE BEGINNING

It may sound rather an odd thing to say, but I had never been home in my life. The truth was I had been born and brought up in India, and the far-away country which we English people always called "home" was as a sealed book to me. I knew nothing whatever about it. Sometimes, when I was little, I used to ask my mother what home was like, and then she would describe a far-away, quiet, sleepy kind of existence in which church-going played a great part—church-going and the poor—and when I would say to her, "Yes, but that is not what I want to know. What about London? What is London like?" then she would answer, "My dear, I never saw London but once, which was for a week after I was married, when it was all so new and strange and confusing that I really can hardly tell you what London is like. I have a recollection of buying a great many things and of looking in a great many shop windows, and of going to theatres, which was a very new experience to me, and of how your father laughed at me when I wanted to see picture-galleries and churches and other sights. But he was very good, he took me to see as much as he could before we sailed;

A

but it is so long ago, dear, and it was such an unrestful time that it is more like a dream to me than anything else. Some day we will take you home—we shall all go home together—and then we will make a long stay in London, and you and I will do it, and learn it thoroughly."

But alas for the mutability of human hopes and desires! We never did go home together, for, long before my father had even begun to think of a couple of years' leave, my pretty mother had gone to another home from which there is no return, on a journey for which we may make no arrangements for companionship by the way; when I was nearly fifteen, she fell a victim to cholera and died.

My mother's death made a changed man of my father. Theirs had been a most passionate love match—a love which began on the day that he, staying at the squire's in the little north-country village of which her father was rector, had fallen in love with her when his eyes first fell upon her under the spreading chestnut trees which shaded one side of the Rectory garden. I have never seen that old garden, but my mother described it to me often and often.

My father was twelve years older than she was, and at that time of day she was only eighteen. Her whole life had been bounded by her father's parish. The most prominent person who had ever come into her existence had been her father's squire, Lord Rivers. She had never in her life ventured from under her mother's wing, but had grown up sweet and simple and shy as a wood-violet, surely the last girl in the world that one might imagine would be called upon to leave home and kindred and to make her own the utterly and entirely different

life which is lived in the shining East. And yet,
how wonderful love is! One glance of a stalwart
soldier's brave blue eyes was sufficiently magnetic
to draw the simple young girl completely away from
all the ties and associations of her whole life. He
proposed to her within a few days of their meeting,
and six weeks later they were married in the little
country church wherein she had been christened,
married by the father whom she was leaving, never
to see again. And so the two turned their backs on
what to her had been her world, and set their faces
toward the unknown.

I can safely say that my mother never repented
the step which she took that day. From first to last,
my father was her lover and her king. She worshipped him, and he, for his part, idolised her.
Lovers they were always; an ideal husband and
wife, they existed for each other, and I, their only
child, was ever and always a something outside
their perfect life. Not that I had ever to complain
of lack of love—oh, no, no. I can never look back
to the day when my mother seemed to be fettered
by my presence, or my father to be impatient of
my childish questionings. I had the most devoted
ayah who ever existed, and perhaps it is true that
Indian mothers do not have very much trouble
with their children, but still, I never in my life felt
shut out, although I was always conscious of only
coming next to my father or mother in the estima-
tion of either.

My father was never the same after my mother's
death. When the time came for him to take his two
years' leave, he resolutely declined any idea of going
home. I was most bitterly disappointed. I was very
young, but just sixteen years old, and the ambition of

my life had been to pay a long delicious holiday to the old country, to go home. My father, however, absolutely set his face against any such idea. "No," he said resolutely, "if your mother had been still with us, it would have given me the greatest possible pleasure to take you and her home again ; but to go without her, leaving her out here all alone, to go to visit such of her people as are still living, to go to all those places which we last saw together, is more than I can endure. It is quite out of the question, Dottikins. You must not ask me to do it. One of these days you will go home without me, and you will understand then exactly what I am feeling now."

I felt the hot tears gush into my eyes as his meaning broke upon me. "Dear Father," I said, slipping my arm round his neck and holding him very tightly, "don't think that I want you to do anything that will hurt you or make you think too painfully of what might have been. I shall be quite content wherever you are. I wish I had said nothing about it."

"Oh, my dear," he replied, "you are young—very young—and young things happily do not quite understand the sorrows which come to older hearts. Yours will come, child, soon enough. Don't think that I want you to be any different to what you are. You remind me more of her every day."

So it came about that my father and I never went home together, and the long, dreamy, delicious wanderings which dear mother and I used to discuss with such pleasure of anticipation never came to fruition.

We did not waste our leave—oh, by no means! We took it out as it were in patches instead of enjoying it all in one lump. First we went off to Cashmere for six months; then, when Father had put in a few months' more work, we went in the opposite

direction and made Japan our Mecca; and so we got
change of scene and of air without reminding Father
too painfully of the holiday to which he had so long
looked forward.

I had spent most of my Indian life at Simla, and
had been at school there for some years. With our
journey to Cashmere my school-days came to an end,
and by the time we returned from Japan I was, to all
outward appearance, quite a woman grown, although
I was but just seventeen. By then my father had assumed the command of his regiment, and on my return
home to take up my position as mistress of his house,
I found myself a person of considerable importance.

I think, on the whole, that my father felt my
mother's death less after I came home for good. Of
course, he must naturally have been terribly lonely
during the time that I was still at school, for all that
we spent of the whole year together was the time
when he was able to get leave, or I was able to go
down to the plains. He did not say much about it
—he was never a man to mope, but remained a gallant, upright soldier to the very end of his life—but
others told me how bitterly he had felt his loss. There
were ladies in the garrison who were most anxious
to mother me on all possible occasions, and they one
and all united in telling me that my father was quite
a different man now that I had come home altogether.

For myself, I was perfectly happy at this time. Of
course, I should have been more happy if I could
have had my mother, as I had naturally expected to
have, but I was young, and young people do forget
—at least, they do not go on feeling as older ones do.
I have often thought since that it is middle-aged
people who suffer intensely from bereavement. Old
folk bear the loss of those they love with comparative

equanimity. They seem often to feel that it is no use giving way to their grief, that, after all, it is but for a time, or, as some poet puts it, "A passing out of this room into the next." And young things, although their grief may be very poignant at the outset, soon learn to find other interests and to make the best of what is. But middle-aged people—men in the very prime of life, as my father was—it is they who feel grief and sorrow with intensity. Still, he did feel it less after I went home, and it is almost impossible for me to express how great was my satisfaction when I realised beyond all doubt that such was the case.

Of course, it would have been but a dreary and monotonous existence for me if my father had been a man to mope and shut himself up with his grief. Fortunately, he was one of the cheeriest and most pleasantly domestic men that one could meet with in a year's march. He was always interested in my little projects, always ready for me to take the smallest bit of pleasure that happened to be on foot; he would cheerfully go, night after night, to dances or some other festivities, and stay till all hours watching me enjoy myself, when I daresay he would often much rather have stayed quietly at home.

"You are staying late to-night, Colonel," I heard someone say to him one night.

"Ah," replied my father, "my little girl is enjoying herself. I like to see young things happy while they have the chance of being so."

"Miss Massingham is enjoying herself," rejoined the other voice with a laugh, "that is very certain."

"All the better, all the better!" I heard my father say. "She won't enjoy herself too much for me."

And then I stole away, and neither knew that I had heard a single word.

CHAPTER II

MY LIFE CHANGES

I was sitting at tiffin one day with my father, when he looked across the table at me with a glance which was one half of apprehension and half of anxiety. "Dottikins," he said, speaking rather abruptly, "I think you ought to get off to the hills as soon as possible."

"Off to the hills!" I exclaimed. "But why?"

"Well, you know, you have had a long spell of this place, and it is getting fearfully hot. You are looking very pale and peaky, far too much so for your age. I think you won't be able to wait for me. I shall have to make arrangements to send you off to the hills by yourself."

"Oh, but I can't go without you, Father," I replied.

"I think it would be better."

"Oh, no, dear, I really could not leave you down here. You are ever so much happier when I am with you, you know that."

"Yes, I know that," he said, smiling, "but, at the same time, if you get run down a shade too far, that won't make me happier."

"Oh, but I am not ill!" I exclaimed.

"No, you are not ill, but you may get ill at any moment. You know, child, you are not seasoned as I am, and every day now the weather will get worse,

7

not better. The heat will get more oppressive and
the atmosphere more stuffy."

"But Mother always stayed down with you?"

"Not the first year or two," he replied.

"Oh! didn't she?"

"No. She wanted to do so, for she was just as
unselfish as you are; but it became so very plain—
patent to the meanest observation, indeed—that she
could not stand heat as well as I could, that she very
sensibly gave in after trying it for part of one hot
season. I really think you had better go up as soon
as possible, and I will follow you later on."

"But I cannot go by myself, Father!" I exclaimed.

"No, no, of course not. Mrs Sheepshanks is going
up."

"Oh, I couldn't go with Mrs Sheepshanks and all
those crying babies! No, Father, I really could not.
I would rather stay here, even if I died."

"That is talking nonsense," said my father. But
he laughed under his moustache, and I knew that
Mrs Sheepshanks was, under no circumstances, to be
my companion if I should be compelled to leave him
at Muggrapore.

Finally I turned my back upon Muggrapore and
set off for Simla in the company of Mrs Hamilton, a
gay little woman, whose husband was in the artillery.
She had only been out three or four years, and had no
idea of burying herself for love's sake in a down-
country station during the hot season. I am not
sure that my father was not a little doubtful as to
her efficiency as chaperon for me. She was young,
and distinctly of a gay turn, one of those blonde-
haired, blue-eyed, insouciant little women who take
life as it comes, and as easily as human nature and
circumstances will allow. She was undoubtedly ex-

tremely fond of her husband, and would infinitely
have preferred that he should be going to Simla likewise, but as he was not able to go to Simla any more
than my father was, she made the best of the fact that
she had to go alone.

My father and Captain Hamilton both came to see
us off on our journey, and as the train steamed out of
the Muggrapore station, leaving the two standing together on the platform, her gaiety and brave airs all
melted into a perfect passion of tears.

"It is awfully silly of me," she said, dabbing fiercely
at her eyes with a little wisp of a handkerchief which
she had rolled up into a tight ball in her nervousness,
"because, of course, Jack is coming up as soon as he
can possibly get away, but' (choking) ' I always feel
like this when I leave him first. It is awfully silly.
You will think me a perfect fool, child. Some day
you will be married yourself, and then you will know
what it is. Poor old Jack! I almost wish I hadn't
come. But, of course, he insisted on it, and, after
all, it would be an awful bore for him if he were to
have me ill on his hands, and the doctor said I should
get ill if I stayed down in stuffy Muggrapore. Horrid
place! I don't know why they wanted to quarter us
in such a hole! How lucky we got the carriage to
ourselves!" she added presently, in a different tone,
"because I do hate crying before people and making
a fool of myself. There, you needn't look at me with
such pitiful eyes, Dorothy. I am all right now."

And then she whisked open her bag, whisked out a
little dressing-glass, which she stuck up on the window-
ledge, and began to dab at her face with some cooling
lotion. "One cannot afford to cry in this country,"
she explained to me. "That is what Jack said when
we first came out—'Don't cry about things, little

woman. Nobody can afford to cry in India. It takes too much of your vitality out of you.' I must say that I have always found the poor dear old fellow perfectly right."

She had spoken truly when she declared that she was not going to cry any more. Not another tear dimmed her radiant blue eyes so long as I was with her.

It was a hideous journey, and I felt sometimes as if I should hardly live to reach my destination alive. True, we had our diversions as we went. We had a carriage reserved for us—that is to say, reserved for our exclusive use—and as there were several officers whom we knew travelling by the same train, Mrs Hamilton made a great show of her good-nature in inviting them to pay us little visits. She did not make them free of our carriage—oh, dear, no! But at the first stopping-place, when a couple of them came to see how we were getting on, and to inquire if we were comfortable, she graciously informed them that they might come in as far as the next station if they liked. "After that," she said, "we shall be resting, and you will be glad to get back into your own compartment."

Still, even relieved in this way, the journey was a most tedious one, and glad we were when the last tiresome part of it was over, when we had left the hot and stuffy train and found ourselves carried along like so much baggage.

Looking back from my present standpoint, I often feel that it was just as well that my father had not realised how very young a chaperon Mrs Hamilton was. We stayed at an hotel only for a few days, and then moved into a charming little bungalow which the Hamiltons had rented from some friends who lived at Simla altogether. She was young — she was really much younger than I, although she was three-and-twenty, and I was not yet eighteen—she was gay, she had plenty of money, and she denied herself nothing. Every indulgence which she granted herself she set down to the score of Jack's wish that she should not mope. Surely Jack must have been the most complacent husband to be found in the length and breadth of India—of the world, for that matter. She had the smartest dresses, the most gorgeous liveries, gave the most cheery little tiffins and dinners, and she went here, there and everywhere, knew everybody, and was a universal favourite. Being her house - companion, I, too, went everywhere and knew everybody. I was not, perhaps, such a universal favourite, because I lacked her wonderful flow of spirits, and her tremendous amount of enterprise; but, all the same, I managed to have a very good time, and in every letter that I wrote to my father, I sang my little hostess's praises, and begged him to hurry along as quickly as he could that he might come up and share our fun. He always wrote back in the same strain—"Enjoy yourself all you can. Delighted you are having such a lovely time. Don't stint yourself. I trust to your good sense and discretion not to overrun the constable too much."

But he always put me off about his leaving Muggrapore. At last I asked him plainly how it was that neither he nor Captain Hamilton were able to come up at anything like the time which they had expected. In answer to this question

he replied that things were not going very well
at the station, that we were neither of us to worry,
but that it would be impossible for any officers to
leave just at present.   "There are rumours of
trouble in various quarters," he wrote; "the health
of the troops is not very good, and we may be
wanted at any moment. You need not make yourself at all uneasy, only you must get along without
me for a little time longer."

How Mrs Hamilton's Jack contrived to satisfy her
I never quite knew. She used to seize his letters
eagerly enough to have satisfied the fondest husband
in the world, glance them down, utter an exclamation
of disgust and dismay, saying, "There now! Jack's
leave put off again! It is iniquitous! I believe it
is nothing but that horrid old Lady Lonsford, who
has always been disagreeable and detestable to me,
and who hates me like poison. I daresay she's being
horrid to Jack now just because of my flirting a bit
with the old General. But I'll flirt with him when
I go back again; you just see if I don't pay that old
lady out!"

"Perhaps she is flirting with your Jack," I suggested.

"Yes, perhaps she is. And perhaps my Jack is
flirting with one of his own chargers," Mrs Hamilton
flashed out.

Lady Lonsford was rather like a horse, and I could
not help laughing at the implied simile.

However, she put the letter away in the drawer
where she always kept those from her husband, and
after a minute or two said,—" Well, it's no use our
wasting our time grizzling here all day, Dorothy.
Let us get ready to go to the Macdonalds."

To have seen her an hour later, the gayest of the

gay, surrounded by at least a dozen of the best men
in the place, nobody would have believed that she had
ever been troubled even by a passing cloud. For
myself, I was, of course, intensely disappointed that
my father had not been able to come as I had expected
and as he had arranged, but I could not help seeing
the wisdom of her suggestion that we should make
the best of a bad business, and be as happy as we
could without our men folk.

I remember that it was at that party at Mrs Macdonald's that I first met a man who possessed any real
interest for me. Men I knew by the dozen, offers I
had had in plenty, partners—why, I could have had
fifty of them at every dance I went to. It was no
unusual thing for me to find the Viceroy's A.D.C. at
my shoulder with an intimation that His Excellency
wished for the next dance. I was very young, and I
took it all as it came, enjoyed myself thoroughly
from morning till night, and wished with all my girl's
heart, at the end of every entertainment, that it could
begin and happen all over again. Until I met Captain
Hamlyn I had thought of all men as being one as
good as another, and had been absolutely impartial
in my behaviour towards them. But from the first
moment of meeting him things were different with
me. I do not know why it was. He was not especially
good-looking; in fact, a good many people thought
that he was rather ugly. He was the regular type of
a cavalry officer, long of limb, lean without being
skinny, walked with a swinging, soldierly gait, had
brown curly hair, cut so close to his head that you
could see no more than a wave in it, and a very sun-
burnt face, about which there was nothing at all
in particular excepting a pair of very blue eyes and
a carefully-trained, reddish moustache. He was the

kind of man that one sees about a military station every day of one's life, a man with nothing especially distinctive or particularly individual about him. He was well dressed, like every other man of his station, his manners were good, as the manners of men of his class always are, perhaps his most noticeable characteristic was a singularly smooth and pleasant voice, and an easy, friendly sort of manner, about which there was not the very smallest trace of affectation.

He was introduced to me by Mrs Macdonald herself, and as there was dancing going on he asked me to honour him with a waltz just then beginning. He danced to perfection, and before we had taken two turns round the big marquee, which had been erected on the lawn for the occasion, he told me that he had not met with any lady since he came to India whose step suited him so well as mine did. This led, naturally, to my asking him how long he had been out. He told me that he had not been in India quite a year; then, when the dance was over, he drew me away down a secluded walk of the charming garden, and found me a very comfortable seat, where we were able to talk in complete retirement.

He had, I learned, come out to India with the 23rd Dragoons, and chiefly with an idea that he would find his reward in the way of sport. On the whole, he had been disappointed, both in India itself and in the sport which it afforded. "I shall exchange as soon as I reasonably can," he said.

"But you like Simla?" I exclaimed.

"Oh, yes, I like Simla very much. It is a fine place. Very go-ahead, you know, Miss Massingham."

"Oh, I don't know that it is," I replied. "Is it more go-ahead than any other places that you have been in?"

" Very much more. Compare it, for instance, with London."

" I can't," I said, with a laugh, " because I have never been in London in my life."

" You have never been in London? You have never been home? But you were not brought up in India ? "

" Yes, I was."

" Really ? " He turned and looked at me with the utmost surprise. " You astonish me," he said.

" But why ? I don't see that there is anything to be astonished at. I was brought up in Simla, or almost entirely so."

" You don't mean it ? And do you live in Simla all the year round ? "

" Oh, no. I am only staying here with Mrs Hamilton," I told him. " I am most of the year down at Muggrapore with my father."

" Oh ! Your father is at Muggrapore ? "

" Yes. He is in command of the 110th Native Lancers at Muggrapore."

" Yes. Oh, that is the place where they have got the cholera so badly." He blurted the words out and then looked at me apprehensively.

" I don't think they have cholera at Muggrapore," I replied.

" Oh, but they have. The men are dying like sheep there. Is it possible you didn't know? I— I—ought not to have told you. Oh, Miss Massingham, I am so sorry. Perhaps I muddled the name of the place. You know these Indian stations are not very familiar to me as yet. Don't think about it until you have made sure."

I knew from his manner, however, that he was right, and that suddenly explained to me the reason why my father's leave had been put off so many times; indeed, he had said in his last letter to me that the health of the troops was not very good. Probably, if he had spoken the whole truth, he would have said that the health of the troops was exceedingly bad.

Captain Hamlyn made the most heroic efforts to prevent my thoughts from dwelling more than was necessary on the information which he had let slip. He told me a great deal about himself, about his home and his own people. He described London to me very graphically, far more so than either my father or mother had ever done. He told me all about the wide streets, with the ceaseless stream of human life ever moving to and fro, he described some of the great palaces and mansions, and told me a great deal about the wide, swift river flowing silently, yet full of life, through the great city. He tried to make me picture some of the churches and historic buildings, and then he told me of the parks and the endless strings of perfectly-appointed carriages moving up and down the Row. "Of course, here," he said, "where one meets the same people over and over again, where everybody has exactly the same interests, and everything goes by officialism, where one old Johnnie is jealous of another old Johnnie because he happens to have been three days longer frizzling out in the sunshine, and all the old Johnnie's wives are ready to fly at one another's throats for no earthly reason whatever, it does seem rather petty and small compared to a really big population full of so many and such varied interests as London. For myself, I like London," he said with a half sigh. "I came out to India, and found it all rather a delusion and a snare. Big sport? Yes, but it costs such a heap of money, and is so difficult to get at, and such a little thing spoils the whole show. Gorgeous climate? Well, it may be gorgeous to have the cholera, and to have a sunshine that blisters your fingers if you happen to trust them outside your verandah for five minutes. It may be gorgeous to have beastly insects crawling about you day and night, and it may be gorgeous to have twenty servants where three would do the work better, but I think it is rather a comfortless kind of existence compared with what one gets at home. No, Miss Massingham, India is all very well for those who do not get a good time in England, but for those who have got enough to live upon and a decent position to fill, believe me, England is the place of places, and London the centre of civilisation. Now there are some fellows," he went on, "in the Service at home who grumble and growl from morning till night because they find themselves quartered at Aldershot. I never could see myself what there is to grumble at in Aldershot, for in the first place one gets a chance of work—of intelligent work—learning something about one's profession; no soldier ought to grumble at that. Then one has a chance of making a mark, that every soldier who is a soldier ought to value. Then one gets a blessed season-ticket, and one goes off to London whenever one gets a chance."

"And how far is London from Aldershot?" I asked.

"Oh, thirty miles. You can slip up to town when your day's work is over, get your dinner and do a theatre and be back again in time for a decent night's rest. After all, what can any man want better than that?"

I looked round at the quiet, enchanting view which

spread itself on all sides of us. We were seated on a flat ledge at the extreme end of Mrs Macdonald's garden. The bungalow itself stood on a plateau of rock, so that the trees and brush which covered the hill rose beyond it, making a charming background. Behind it the garden, which was very long, stretched away in a sloping direction along the side of the ghaut. The seat which we had found was at the extreme end of the garden, quite a long way from the bungalow, and we could look down hundreds of feet below us.

"And is London pretty?" I asked. "Is it as pretty as this?"

Captain Hamlyn laughed outright. "It is not anything like this," he replied, "and yet when you see it and know it I have little doubt that you will prefer it infinitely to Simla."

CHAPTER III

A SIMLA LOVE STORY

I DID not like to tell Mrs Hamilton anything that I had heard about their having the cholera badly at Muggrapore, but during the course of that evening I happened to find myself talking to a Mrs MacAndrew, who was our nearest neighbour, and I asked her if she had heard the report, and if she thought there was any truth in it.

"Oh, my dear," she said, "if your father has not told you anything about it, I should not worry myself if I were you. You know these unfortunate natives are so dirty and so unsanitary in their habits, they are always getting cholera and things. After one has been in India for a while, one gets to take no notice of rumours of that kind. Probably if you were in Muggrapore at this moment, you would not know that there was a single case of cholera in the entire station. Now, I have a sister out in China, her husband is a sort of mandarin out there—"

"What! Did she marry a Chinaman?" I exclaimed.

"No, no," replied Mrs MacAndrew, with a laugh, "but he has got a very good appointment, and he gives himself the airs of at least a dozen mandarins. We always call him 'the Mandarin' at home. Well, the other day I wrote to her and said that I was so fearfully sorry to see by the English papers that they had the plague so frightfully out in Canton, and I didn't sleep for nights, I couldn't get my sister and her dreadful position out of my head. My dear, she wrote back by return mail and said, 'Don't upset yourself about the plague in Canton. I made inquiries after I received your letter, and I found they had had the plague rather badly down in the native quarter, but until then we did not know anything about it.' So, my dear," Mrs MacAndrew went on, "I don't think you need upset yourself about any cholera they may be having down at Muggrapore. What does Mrs Hamilton say about it?"

"Oh, I didn't tell her that I had heard anything," I replied.

"Well, if I were you," said Mrs MacAndrew, promptly, "I would not do so, because, you see, she has not been very long out, and she might worry herself to fiddle-strings."

In my own mind, I did not think Mrs Hamilton was at all a woman who would worry herself to fiddle-strings from any cause, but it was no use saying so to anyone else. So I allowed Mrs Mac-Andrew's remark to pass in silence.

I did mention the cholera to father when I wrote to him again. I mentioned it in a casual kind of way, told him that I had heard that the cholera was rather bad at Muggrapore, and asked whether it was true. His reply was extremely reassuring. "I hope you have not been thinking too much of this cholera rumour," he wrote. "There is cholera in the native lines, but then that is no new thing, it would be much more unusual if there were none. Pray don't allow yourself to get nervous about it. Tell Mrs Hamilton that her husband is looking very fit and well, and that we shall probably come up to Simla together when we do manage to get away."

I did tell Mrs Hamilton. She gave a sigh, and a cloud came over her blue eyes. "Poor, dear old Jack!" she said. "It is hard that I should be enjoying myself up here and he be frizzling down in that hateful old Muggrapore. I don't know why, if we have got to India, and to serve half our time in such a hateful country, that they could not quarter us in decent stations. It seems so stupid to pick out all the most horrid and unhealthy cities in India to plant the troops in and make military stations of!"

The next moment she asked me whether it was not time to dress, and all signs of a cloud had absolutely vanished from her laughing face. For myself, I may as well confess that I never gave the cholera another thought. My life seemed from that time forward to be filled up with the personality of one individual; that individual was Captain Hamlyn of the 23rd Dragoons. It was natural enough, as he said at first, that we should meet everywhere. You cannot get out of anybody's way in a place like Simla, and as I did not try to get out of his and he unmistakably did everything he could to get into mine, it was equally natural that we were together morning, noon and night.

I think, on the whole, that the mornings were our best time. Mrs Hamilton and I always rode through the cool and pleasant air. She was an excellent horsewoman, and generally used to lead the way with two or three devoted squires in attendance upon her. I began with a variety of attendance, but after Captain Hamlyn came upon the scene, they gradually dwindled away until he was the only one to be found at my saddle-bow. So we used to lag behind, just keeping my gay little chaperon in sight, sometimes barely that; and it was during one of these rides, when he had been up in Simla nearly three weeks, that he suggested to me that we should cast in our lot together and make our morning companionship into a compact for the rest of our lives.

"You know," he said to me, leaning over to lay his hand upon my horse's neck, "I have never been really hard hit in my life before. That was one of the reasons why I did not mind coming out to India for a year or two. My people were distinctly against my doing so, because my father has not been dead very long, and my mother hated the idea of my being out of England. She wanted me to marry and settle down; but, as I told her, a poor man cannot very well marry on nothing—no, don't look like that. I am not asking you quite to share nothing. I have a few hundreds a year besides my pay, and I shall have more at my mother's death, but I am not what you would call well off. I thought I was perfectly safe in coming to India; that I should never meet any lady out here to fall in love with, but you see I was utterly wrong. And somehow, as you have been all your life out here, I do not feel that it is the same hardship to ask you to stay out a little longer for my sake. There, I have put it very lamely. I know it; but, Dorothy, can't you see what I mean? I am not much of a catch, dear, but I am desperately in love with you, and I would stay out here for the rest of my life quite cheerfully and contentedly if I thought that you would be willing and content to stay with me."

I did not directly answer this, for I had nothing to say. I liked him, oh, yes! The sight of his blue eyes and bronzed face was enough at any moment to put my whole heart in a flutter. The touch of his hand made my heart thrill and thrill again. I liked everything about him—his heart-whole laugh, the flash of his white teeth, the turn of his well-cropped head, the set of his shoulders—everything about him pleased and satisfied me. After all, I had not been accustomed to much luxury or to great wealth, and what was I, to look for so much in a husband? I was no beauty, or, at least, I had never thought so.

"Haven't you anything to say to me?" he asked wistfully, after a moment's pause.

"I don't know what to say," I said half-shyly.

He laughed outright. "Then don't say it," he rejoined promptly. "I will say it for you. I know what you mean. You are just as fond of me as I am of you; isn't that about it?"

And then I admitted that that was exactly it, and somehow we lagged farther and farther behind the others, and when we got back to the bungalow, we had quite made up our minds as to the future.

For the first time, Captain Hamlyn came into the house with us. "Mrs Hamilton," he said, half-hesitatingly, as we reached the door, "you might give me some breakfast this morning."

"Why, surely," she replied. "Does that mean that you have been pining for breakfast on other mornings and that we have neglected to ask you? If so, that was exceedingly remiss of Dorothy."

"I certainly have never asked him!" I exclaimed.

"Dorothy, my dear," said Mrs Hamilton, "you will find out by-and-by that men things are always the better and more complacent for being fed."

"I don't think that I wanted Captain Hamlyn to be more complacent," I rejoined.

"Oh—oh! I see. Well, come in, Captain Hamlyn. If she won't make you welcome, I will."

He followed her into the pretty drawing-room— and it was a pretty room; looking back after all these years, I still carry in my mind's eye the charming picture of its snowy draperies, its wealth of flowers and the profusion of green plants with which my hostess had decked it.

"The fact is, Mrs Hamilton," I heard him say, in a very confidential tone—and then I scurried out of hearing, because I realised that he was going to tell her how things were between us.

I was already out of my grey habit, and into my fresh white muslin gown before she came to my room. "Why, Dorothy, you sly little witch," she exclaimed, as she entered, "who was to know that you meant serious business all this time? He has told me all about it, my dear. I congratulate you with all my heart. He says he is not well-off, but I don't know that that makes much difference. His family is good, and he himself is charming, and I should think your father will be very much pleased indeed. I should be if I were in his place."

"I think that Father will only be pleased because I am pleased," I said with a half sigh as I remembered him, for truly, I had not given him a thought up to that moment.

"Well, dear, well, it is what men with pretty daughters in India must expect and look for; at all events, if they neither expect nor look for it, it is what they will get—that other men shall come along and appreciate them."

"But I am not pretty," I exclaimed.

"Oh, is that your genuine opinion, Miss Modesty?"

"Yes, indeed it is," I cried.

"Well, I don't agree with you, and I don't suppose your father would agree with you, and I feel quite sure that Captain Hamlyn would not agree with you either. It is delightful to think that so pretty a little person should have such a modest opinion of herself. I like you better for not thinking yourself at all attractive, Dorothy." And then she drew me to her, kissed me several times with a motherliness which I did not think she had in her, and, pushing me away with a laugh, declared that she must fly to change her habit. "Do you go along and play pretty hostess to that nice young man," was her last laughing admonition.

I finished my toilet and then went back to the little drawing-room, where I found my impatient lover awaiting me. "What an unconscionable time you have been!" was his greeting.

"Oh, no! I have been very quick indeed, a very short time," I replied airily. "You will often have to wait for me much longer than this."

"Then," he said promptly, "you cannot care for me half as much as I do for you."

"Perhaps I don't, then." He caught hold of me.

"But you do, Dorothy; you do, you know you do. You know you are awfully in love with me. If you are not, you ought to be, because I am so tremendously in love with you."

"I would certainly give you time to change your clothes," I persisted. "Besides, Mrs Hamilton came in to give me her version of the situation."

"And she said—?" he asked eagerly.

"Oh, she seems to think you are all right."

"Of course she thinks I am all right; anybody but a match-making parent would think I was all right," he declared stoutly. "But, Dorothy, only one thought troubles me—Is your father anything of a match-making parent?"

He put the question to me so solemnly, and in such

evident good faith, that I could not help laughing aloud. "My father," I said, "married, himself, for love pure and simple. I do not think that he will ask whether you are rich, his first question will be whether I care for you."

CHAPTER IV

DOREMY

"I THINK," said Captain Hamlyn, during that first joyous little breakfast, "that I shall go down to Muggrapore and see your father myself."

"Oh, I wouldn't do that," said Mrs Hamilton. "I think if you write it will be quite as much as Colonel Massingham will expect or wish for."

"Well, perhaps that is so," he said doubtfully, "but to my mind, one interview is worth a hundred letters."

"It is a long way to Muggrapore," said Mrs Hamilton, warningly, "as we know by bitter experience—eh, Dorothy?"

"Yes, it is a long way to Muggrapore," I returned. "And my father is not the kind of person who insists upon out-of-the-way attentions."

"Why don't you write fully and offer to go down?" suggested Mrs Hamilton. "It would look pretty and attentive, and as if you were anxious to do the right thing."

"I am," he said stoutly.

"Of course, you are, I know that you are, but it is no joke going down at this time of the year to Muggrapore and coming back again. It is such a waste of time and money; and you have to think of ways and means now, you know."

'Yes, that is so," he admitted, with a rather rueful glance at me."

"If you offer to go down, that will be all that is necessary. Colonel Massingham will then see that you are really desperately in earnest. And, ten chances to one, he is just on the eve of coming up for his own leave, so your journey and your money and your time, and your patience and your strength will all have been exhausted for nothing. Oh, believe me, you had better write. Tell him everything there is to tell about you, and say that if he wishes it you will be delighted to go down to Muggrapore and—show yourself."

Eventually this was the course he took, and when his letter had gone we set ourselves to await with such patience as we could my father's reply and decision.

"What do you think your father will say, Doremy?" he asked me at least twenty times during the course of the next few hours.

"Oh—I think he will say that I am much too young to dream of marrying or even of being engaged."

"Do you really think so?"

"Yes, really. Then I think he will say that in addition to not thinking much of my age as qualifying me for matrimony, he does not think very much of you as a prospective son-in-law, and that as a matter of fact he has some hideous old nabob up his sleeve to whom he intends to sell me as soon as I go back to Muggrapore."

"Doremy," said my sweetheart, sternly, "you are laughing at me. Doremy, it is very wrong to laugh at your husband."

"It is very wrong of you to give your future wife nicknames," I retorted.

He caught me nearer to him. " I like to give you a name all of my own," he said, suddenly dropping his teasing tone and speaking very tenderly ; " I like to feel that there is something about you, even your name, which nobody but I can share, which belongs to me, to myself alone. I like your sweet, soft-sounding name of Dorothy ; it is the prettiest name in the world, but everybody calls you Dorothy, everybody who knows you—Mrs Hamilton, Mrs MacAndrew with the red hair and the teeth, she calls you Dorothy. I am sure your father calls you Dorothy, too."

" No, my father never calls me Dorothy. He calls me Dottikins."

" Dottikins ? That is an insult."

" Ah, but you see he doesn't think of me as you do."

" No, no, but Dottikins ! It is a profanation ! Dearest, you will never let anybody but me call you Doremy, will you ? "

Oh, well, you know the way lovers talk ; young lovers, as we were—I, a child of eighteen, he not yet six-and-twenty. He insisted upon having my promise, insisted with an eagerness which such a promise was not worth. And I—I gave it. And so from that time forward I was never any more Dorothy to him excepting on our wedding-day, and he always called me by the quaint little name that he had coined out of his love and tenderness—just Doremy.

I did not tell him so, but I wrote to my father at once, and told him everything that there was to tell about my sweetheart. I daresay it was very incoherent, and probably Mrs Hamilton's letter, which went at the same time as mine, was much more explicit as to Captain Hamlyn's standing and personality Be that as it may, as soon as could possibly be, Captain Hamlyn received a reply from Muggrapore, in which my father said :—"I am coming up to Simla in a few days and shall be very glad to talk over the entire situation with you. From what I hear of you I do not see that there can be the slightest objection to your marrying Dorothy, more especially as my little girl seems to have set her heart upon you. It is no use my pretending," the letter went on, "that I am glad to lose my only child in this way. To be quite frank with you, I am glad in one way but exceedingly sorry in another. I shall be glad to feel that my little girl is happily settled in life with a man whom she can love and respect. I have not much to give her, but whatever I have will be hers eventually. Perhaps I ought not to say it, and yet I feel that I honestly can say that, in winning her, you have won a treasure. She is what her mother was before her, a good, true, loyal and unselfish little girl. If this marriage comes about I only hope and pray that you will treat her as she deserves to be treated."

I could not help crying a little over my dear father's letter. It was so simple, so honest, so full of love for me, and so unselfish. If I was unselfish, as he said, I had indeed learned to be so from knowing him, for surely a less selfish man than my father never lived upon this earth. As for Captain Hamlyn, or Eddy, as I had taken to calling him, that letter served to put him into the highest and wildest spirits.

"He may say 'no' in the end," I said warningly, when he was speaking quite as a certainty of our future life together, "and then where will you be?"

"My dearest child," he replied, "no man on earth could be such a brute as to say 'no' after writing me a letter like this. It seems to me, young woman," he went on severely, "that you are beginning very badly with me. Your main idea is to make your bear dance, to keep me on the grill and to take rises out of me. Don't you think you ought to be very much ashamed of yourself?"

"No," I replied, "I think it is far better for you to find out all my faults and all my shortcomings before we are married, so that if you wish to change your mind you can do so before it is too late."

"Change my mind!" he repeated. "Why, what next? I shall never change my mind, never as long as the world is round."

"Oh, don't say that," I said, half sighing, "don't say that! I have never been very sure myself that the world is round."

"But it is."

"But we do not know it. We only half believe the wise men who tell us it is. I believe that it is like a flat cheese, and I don't believe it is really round."

"Well, I will qualify my assertion," he exclaimed with a laugh, "and I will say that I will never change my mind about you as long as the world is a world. There, will that satisfy you?"

So we talked. Oh, how foolish it all was! And we meant it all, every word of it.

Well, it was less than a week after this that my father suddenly turned up in Simla. He came without warning, walking in upon us one morning at breakfast as coolly and unconcernedly as if he had come from the next bungalow. Of course, we were not breakfasting alone, and when he had kissed me and shaken hands half-a-dozen times with Mrs Hamilton, he turned round to Captain Hamlyn and held out his hand.

"I suppose I need not ask who you are?" he said, in his pleasant, cheery, friendly voice. "I am very pleased to see you. All the same, I think you are a pretty trio to be trusted out by yourselves. Think of this little miss here being a married woman! Why, it is preposterous!"

"My mother was a married woman before she was as old as I am," I returned stoutly, "and you never thought she was too young to be married."

"No, I never did," he admitted, "I never did. You are quite right, Dottikins, perfectly right. You generally are. You will find, Hamlyn," he remarked, turning with a laugh to my sweetheart, "you will find that the easiest way to live in married life is to straightway lay down one tenet—that the wife is always right!"

"And was that what you did, sir?" Captain Hamlyn asked.

"Well, as a matter of fact, she always was right," my father replied, with the first trace of a cloud which had passed over his face.

Later in the day the two men had a long talk together, and by-and-by, when my sweetheart had gone back to his hotel to dress for dinner, my father found his way into my bedroom. "You are going to dress, Dottikins?" he said. "Well, I won't keep you, child. I like that young man of yours. I wanted to tell you so."

"Oh, daddy, dear, how kind and sweet and good of you to like him."

"Is it such an impossible task?" he asked.

"Oh, no! But I did not quite expect you to look at him with my eyes."

"No, no, but I want to do so, and I am glad to be able to do so. He is a fine fellow, Dottikins. Not rich, but what is money when it is put against happiness? A mere trifle, a nothing, a thing not worth considering. You will have enough, as much as you have always been used to. You have done better than finding a gold mine. I like your young man he *is* a man, and a fine attractive fellow into the bargain. I like everything about him ; he wants to be married at once ; he would not be half as fine a fellow if he didn't. And I don't know that I see the good of waiting. I did not have to wait long my-self—it was too long, though the time seemed short to everybody excepting ourselves. I leave it to you two to settle when and where the knot shall be tied."

He had evidently said as much to Eddy himself, for, when I went into the drawing-room, dressed for dinner, I found him already there and completely full of the subject.

" Why, you must have dressed like a flash of lightning ! " I exclaimed.

" And you must have dressed like a slow coach," he retorted.

" No, I did not. But my father came into my room, and that hindered me for a little while."

" Yes ? And what did he say ? "

" Oh—different things."

" Did he tell you that he would leave the final details to us ? "

" The final details of what ? "

" Of our marriage."

" Well—something of the kind."

" That we might be married when and where we like ? "

" Well—something like that."

" Then we might say—"

" To-morrow morning," I suggested.

" No, miss, not to-morrow morning. But we might say, here in Simla, in a fortnight or three weeks at the outside."

"Oh, Eddy!   But that is rushing it."

"No, it is not rushing it.   As marriages go, out in this country, it is quite a respectable, veteran sort of an engagement.   You will have ample time to get a new frock made for the occasion, and we should get it over before there is a chance of your father having to go back to Muggrapore."

"Oh, but he has come up for long leave."

"Well, dearest, leave is very doubtful just now for any of us.   Things are not going too well in various quarters, and your father might be recalled at any moment."

"Did he say so?"

"Well, he mentioned it as a possibility."

"I don't think that they could be so inhuman as to recall him before he has had his leave out," I said disbelievingly.

"Oh, my dear child, if anything happens out of the common, nobody cares whether we have finished our leave or not.   Besides that, I might be recalled, and if I have to be recalled, I would rather take you with me."

He certainly gave me no peace during the next few days, and eventually our marriage was settled to take place in something less than three weeks' time.

And it did take place then, but my father was not present to give me away, for several days previous to the date which we had fixed he came home with a very grave face.

"Dottikins," he said, "I am afraid I have very bad news for you."

"Oh, Father, what is it?" I cried.

"Well, I have been recalled."

"Not to Muggrapore?"

"Yes, to Muggrapore."

"Is there no getting out of it?"

"No possible chance of getting out of it," he replied promptly.

"But my wedding!" I cried blankly.

"Oh, your wedding can come off without me. Everybody will understand I am wanted down at Muggrapore, my dear, and I must find some good friend who will take my place for the occasion. I shall wish you just the same happiness as if I were standing beside you."

"But it must be put off," I cried.

"No, no, put-off weddings are not lucky, everybody says the same thing. There is no reason why it should be put off; in fact, there is all the more reason why it should take place just the same. It is my wish; you will bear that in mind, Dottikins. It is my wish that under no circumstances should your wedding be postponed, even for a day."

Well, what could I say in the face of this, other than that he should have his way, and that my marriage should take place exactly as it had been originally arranged? My father looked out an old friend, who promised to escort me to the altar, and to give me away in his stead, and the following day he bade me good-bye more solemnly and with more gravity than he had ever done in his life before.

"I feel sure," I said to him, just at the last, "that you are keeping something back from me."

"No, no," he replied. "I am saying good-bye to my little girl, that is all. You know you will never be quite the same to me again."

"I shall never be any different to you," I cried.

"Oh, yes. You think not, but it is only right and natural that you should be. Dottikins," he added earnestly, "don't think that I am grudging you to Hamlyn. He is a good fellow, and you will always remember that I liked him, that I liked everything I saw of him, and everything that I have heard of him. You have chosen very wisely, my child. I am pleased and satisfied with you."

I kept up fairly well until my father was really gone, then I broke down and cried—well, as only the young do cry. It is in after life that one learns what terrible grief tearless grief is. I remember I cried that day until I was ill and exhausted, and not all my sweetheart's tenderness and love could help me to shake off the awful foreboding of coming trouble which overshadowed and oppressed me.

"Come, come," he said ; "you are making a very poor show for a soldier's daughter. What sort of a soldier's wife will you be, do you think, if you are upset like this by a mere matter of business ?"

"It isn't a mere matter of business !" I exclaimed. "They might have left him. He has only one child, and she doesn't get married every day. It is a special occasion. They might have left him for once. It wouldn't have been so hard if he could have stayed just to see us married. But to be married without him! I would rather have waited."

"But it was your father's wish that you should not wait. I am quite willing to do what you like," he said, suddenly dropping his bantering tone, and speaking very gravely. "You know that, Doremy, surely ?"

"Oh, yes, yes. I will go on. I will do just as Father told me, but you must admit it is hard. Why should he have been recalled, and recalled so soon when he has so much leave owing to him ?"

"Because he is wanted down at Muggrapore. And, after all you know dearest, a soldier's duty, whether he is of greater or lesser importance, is his duty, and should come first of anything with him. Of course, your father being in command makes all the difference in the world, and it would have a very bad effect upon the troops if commanding officers seemed willing to shirk what others of less importance have to face."

"But what is there to shirk?"

"Well, you know that the health of the troops down at Muggrapore is not good. Hamilton has never had a day's leave. I believe that your father was given his wholly and solely on your account."

"But did he tell you so?"

"He all but told me so."

"Do you mean that the cholera is worse at Muggrapore?"

"It is very bad, and your father's presence there tends to make the scare less general. It is one of the penalties which a man has to pay for being a popular commandant. Believe me, child, even in the face of your wishes, of your wedding, he would not have it otherwise. No real soldier would."

"I don't believe," I said, with what was almost a moan, "that I shall ever see my father again."

CHAPTER V

SORROW CLOUDS

EVERYBODY said that ours was the prettiest wedding that had taken place in Simla for years, and although I was so disappointed and so upset to think that my dear father was not able to be present at the ceremony, I was conscious during the whole time that in every other respect the affair was exceedingly well managed, and extremely gay and pleasant.

There were several of Captain Hamlyn's brother officers staying in Simla at the time, and one of these, a Mr Alaric St Leger, acted as his best man.

"Of course, in an ordinary way, I should have had my cousin," he told me, when the question of his best man was first mooted. "Old Bill and I have always been the greatest possible chums, and if it had been within the bounds of possibility to get him. I should as soon have thought of jumping over that railing," pointing to the rail protecting the edge of the chud, "as of asking any other fellow to perform that good office for me. But poor old Bill happened an accident just before we left England, and had to stay at home on sick leave, so that he has never been out with the regiment at all."

"And he is the Honourable Edward Hamlyn, who is in the 23rd?" I remarked, for I had noticed when glancing at an Army List one day that my sweetheart was not the only man of his name in the 23rd.

"Yes, he is the other one, but he has always been called Bill ever since I can remember anything. No, I don't mean that his own people call him Bill, but he was always called Bill at Harrow, and he was always called Bill at Sandhurst."

"And were you at Harrow and Sandhurst together?"

"No, we were not," he replied, "we were just of an age to miss being together. I was at Harrow, and I was at Sandhurst, but not at the same time as my cousin; in fact, he is five years younger than I am."

"And he is Lord Clovelly's son?"

"Yes, he is. Lord Clovelly, you know, is my uncle. Ah, Bill's a dear old chap; never was a better fellow going. Curious accident that was of his, just an unlucky hit with a cricket ball, but, by Jove, it laid him on his back for six months! And I hear that he is only just beginning to get about again. I fancy, unless he is quite fit, that he will stay with the depôt instead of coming out here next year. Naturally, his father is very anxious about him, because, you see, he is the only son."

"And you are the only son!" I exclaimed.

"Yes, but, of course, my life is not as precious as his."

"Perhaps not, to his father," I said, half reprovingly, "to other people more so."

"Ah, you think so, dearest, you think so, but, really, joking apart, he is the heir, and it is a precious life. I should not be surprised if my uncle stopped his coming out altogether. I know when I was last down at Clovelly he was not at all anxious that he should stay in the Service."

"And he has sisters?"

"Yes, he has several sisters."

"Married?"

"Some of them—that is, two of them. One is not married."

"And is she nice?"

"Oh, yes, a delightful girl."

"Pretty?"

"Ye-es, I suppose so," he replied, in the doubtful way in which a man frequently does speak of his sisters and his cousins. "One of them—the beauty of the family—married a man in the Guards, and the other married a big manufacturing chap. I never could understand why she did, but I suppose she had her reasons."

"I suppose she was in love with him," I exclaimed.

"Well, she might have been, of course. I never saw him except on the day of the wedding. I didn't think much of him, and Charlotte Hamlyn certainly did not look as if she was particularly devoted."

"But she would not have married him if she had not been in love with him," I persisted.

"She might not—no. But, as a matter of fact, I don't think that she was. Women don't always marry for love, you know, Doremy, even in England, and my delightful cousins are rather hard young women; I don't think the tender passion would enter very much into their calculations. Now, with Bill things are different. He is such a dear chap, such a good fellow, such a chum, but he is very different to the girls; everybody likes him. I don't think anybody is very enthusiastic about them."

So it came about that in the absence of his cousin Mr Alaric St Leger filled the place of best man at our wedding. I had four very pretty bridesmaids, and what with the uniforms, the gay dresses of the ladies, the wonderful liveries of the different servants and the profusion of flowers, our wedding was certainly as gay a festivity as it had ever been my lot to attend.

We had a strange quantity of presents, some of great beauty, and none that were not worth having. Everybody combined to wish us well, to help to make the thing go, and when at last we went off on our four days' honeymoon, which we spent at a little bungalow a few miles away, it seemed as if our way through life was likely to be one blaze of unbroken sunshine.

As we left the church a telegram was put into my hands. It was from my father, and read: " God bless you, my darling. I am thinking of you and wishing you all joy. With you in spirit always.—FATHER." I gave it to Eddy as we got into the carriage without a word. Precious as it was, I almost wished that I had not received it, for it seemed to accentuate the cloud which had hung so heavily over what should have been, and what in reality was, otherwise the happiest day of my life. But in the presence of an intense happiness, clouds, even when they are very dark and lowering, soon pass. I could not long be unhappy. I was blissfully contented in my new existence; with every moment I seemed to care more and more for the man to whom I had given my life's troth. He was so kind, so thoughtful, so considerate, so forgetful of himself; he always seemed as if he thought only of me, and after all, what was I to inspire a love so unselfish as over and over again he proved his for me to be? Mrs Hamilton had called me pretty, and not she alone, but other people. Well, my looking-glass told me quite otherwise. I was tall rather than short, a slender creature, with a certain grace and dignity in the carriage of head and throat which proclaimed itself even to my own unprejudiced eyes. I had a good skin and plenty of silky, dark hair which had never known the torture of the curling tongs. I had rather nice grey eyes and a nose that was straight and small—a nose that had nothing distinctive about it and was certainly not beautiful any more than the rest of my face was. And yet my dear Eddy worshipped me. If I had combined the beauties of every Venus that the world has known in my one person he could not have loved me with greater devotion or have lavished more adoration upon me. He even consented to take me down to Muggrapore that I might spend the remaining part of his leave with my father.

"I do it against my better judgment, Doremy," he said to me, "because I think it is foolish to run into danger when you can possibly keep yourself out of it, and, under any other circumstances, I should say absolutely no ; but when I realise what it must have been to your father to give you up to me, I feel that it is not in me to say anything but yes to so natural a desire. I will only ask you, dearest, while we are there, to be guided by me in taking every precaution for your safety. I love you for your pluck in being willing to go, but I will have you remember that pluck carried to excess becomes foolhardiness, and you, darling, are too sensible and too good to be foolhardy."

"There is nothing to show any particular pluck, Eddy," I exclaimed. "This cholera is in the native lines, not near our bungalow. I don't want to run in and out of the native hospital doing sick nurse, and that sort of thing. I want to go down and see my father, that is all."

"Yes, I understand, dearest, I quite understand, but it is only that I am so anxious, so uneasy at any danger which may chance to threaten you, which makes me take such extreme precaution for your safety. I don't know that your father will not blame me very severely for taking you at all. I think we ought to have let him know before we decided on going."

"Father would certainly say that I am not to go," I said promptly. "Father is the most unselfish person in the world, and he would put a stop to our going for a certainty. And I have set my heart upon seeing him, and spending a little time with him before we go to join the regiment."

But we never did go down to Muggrapore. After our honeymoon, which had extended into ten days instead of four, we went back to Simla and spent a few days there, intending to go from thence straight down to Muggrapore. I well remember that the day before our return to Simla I had my fortune told by an old woman who came up to our bungalow for the purpose. I had no belief in fortune-telling; indeed, I had had no experience of it. This particular old soothsayer was a hideous specimen of native humanity, and she told me a great deal of rubbish which my memory does not retain. Only one part of her sayings stayed in my mind—"There is a curious want of finality in your life," she told me, "there is no continuance; you keep nothing for long, not at least in the early part of your life, but your lord's heart will be yours for ever, come weal, come woe, come joy, triumph, sorrow, separation and parting, he will still be yours to the very end of time."

I repeated what she said to Eddy, whose knowledge of Hindustani was naturally exceedingly limited. "Give the old girl a good tip," he said, with careless good-nature; "after all, she has prophesied about the only thing that is really worth having."

The old hag took the silver, which he jingled in his hand towards her, and looked him searchingly up and down. "Tell the Burra-sahib that he makes too sure," she said to me; "that is his greatest fault, he makes too sure of getting what he wants. He will have a fall one day that will blast his dearest hopes. You stand both of you in a blaze of sunshine, a glory of light; but the sorrow clouds are hovering very near, and one day they will come down like a curtain and shut you away the one from the other."

"What does she say?" my husband asked.

I repeated the old soothsayer's words to him. "Oh, come along, dearest, it is all rubbish!" he remarked contemptuously. "We have each other, and we have our lives before us. Don't let us waste a minute of the time over such trash as this." And then he caught me by the arm and drew me away, leaving the old woman muttering darkly where she stood.

Without doubt she had told me a good deal that was mere clap-trap. She had made shots as to my past, some good, some indifferent, some totally wrong, but, however good or bad she might be at her trade, that one prophecy lingered in my mind, and before a week had gone by part of it had come true, for on the very eve of our departure from Simla to join my father at Muggrapore, Mrs Hamilton received a telegram from her husband bidding her break the news to me that our journey was useless.

To this day I have never realised how, between them, my husband and my friend contrived to break the horrible tidings to me. I was hours before my dazed brain could take in the fact that I had seen my father for the last time—that he, of all others, so cruelly recalled from his just leave of absence, had fallen a victim to the fatal scourge which was devastating the native troops.

"It is what that old woman said!" I cried despairingly to my husband. "'You are standing in a blaze of sunshine, a glory of light, but the sorrow clouds are hovering very near.' Oh, Eddy, Eddy! It has come true already! Why did we ever let that old woman come to me with her hideous prophecies? It will all come true. What else was it that she said? 'One day they will come down like a curtain and shut you away the one from the other.'"

It was in vain that he tried to console me, in vain that he swore all manner of vengeance upon the old soothsayer if he should ever come within reach of her again. I was young, I was well-nigh broken-hearted, and not even the coming of a letter in the dear handwriting, which I should never receive again, tended to comfort me. My dear, dear father—his last thought had been for me.

"I am feeling horribly ill to-night, Dottikins," he wrote to me, "and I doubt not that this diabolical cholera has got a good tight grip of me this time. I have weathered it before, but something tells me that it is all up with me at last. This is only a line to bid you happiness and God-speed for ever, and to express my gratitude that Almighty God has permitted me to see you happily and suitably married. I am leaving you with an easy mind, feeling assured that Hamlyn is a right good fellow, and will take care of you as well as even I could wish. Too ill to write more than to send my love and my last good wishes to Hamlyn—my last hope that he will take care of you."

There was a moment's silence. "And so help me, God, I will!" said my husband, in a very solemn voice.

CHAPTER VI

A JARRED NOTE IN A HARMONY

LOOKING back from my present standpoint to the time of my father's death, I can only think that the circumstances of my life at that period were designed by Providence in especial mercy to my youth and inexperience of the world. I have often since shuddered to think what would have happened to me if my father had died leaving me an unprotected girl in India. As it was, I was taken right away from every association of my early life, I was spared all the most harrowing details of my great loss, and in my new life there was nothing which served in any way to remind me of the old one.

The 23rd were then at a very good station in the Punjaub, and we were lucky enough to secure a charming little bungalow just vacated by an officer on the staff who had gone home for a couple of years' leave, so we had no trouble in settling down in our new home. We had, indeed, a home ready-made for us, for these people left us everything just as they used it themselves—plate, linen, knick-knacks, and even their domestic pets. It was very different for me to go thus to Muttrahabad, straight into a charming home, with well-trained servants, and everything comfortable and cosy to welcome me, than if I had had to do as most young wives in India must, scrape along anyhow until we had got some sort of a home put together.

It was surprising how it softened the blow of my father's death. I felt as if I had got into a haven of rest and peace from which I should never be ousted again as long as I lived. And still, the old native woman's gruesome prophecy stayed in my mind persistently. I do not mean to imply that it always stayed in my mind, but it came back from time to time with more or less painful vividness—"There is no finality in your life. You keep nothing long, at least, not in the early part of your life." At such times I had to remind myself of that other prophecy of hers—"Your lord's heart will be yours always."

It was to Muttrahabad that my father's belongings were all sent home, not the furniture of our bungalow at Muggrapore, but all his and my personal belongings. My own things had been packed up by my father's orders immediately that my marriage was a finally settled matter, and had been actually sent off by him the week previous to his death, but Captain Hamilton had gathered together everything that he believed I should most value, the pictures, a few choice books—as choice as anybody ever has in India, that is to say—a few skins and rugs and various personal odds and ends that my father had regularly used. All other things were sold, as is the custom at such times, and the money for these, together with the little money that my father had had to leave, was handed over to me in accordance with his last will, strangely enough made and signed on the very day of my wedding. He had not had very much to leave—something over a thousand pounds.

"You had better put it along with your money, Eddy," I said to my husband, when I received the

cheque for the amount from the lawyer who had
managed my father's affairs.

"Not at all," he said.

"But I don't want any separate money. I would
rather you would take care of it. I don't understand
money."

"The best thing that we can do," said my husband,
"is to put it in a bank by itself, and to keep it for
emergencies. For instance, at the end of a couple of
years we shall have to turn out of this place and
furnish for ourselves, and as my little all is well and
safely invested in England, it would be a pity to sell
out for furnishing purposes. Besides, it is always as
well to have a shot in the locker for absolute emergency use. One cannot tell in this beastly climate
what a single day may bring forth. By far the best
thing to do would be to put it into a bank in your
own name."

Eventually we agreed to do that. And so our life
went on, and I never gave my little patrimony so
much as another thought.

We were really very gay at this time. The 23rd
was a go-ahead regiment, and one and all seemed
determined to enjoy every scrap of gaiety that could
be squeezed out of a life in Muttrahabad. Not even
my mourning kept me in seclusion for more than a
few weeks. I was a bride, and as a bride I must be
fêted and petted. I was very young, and in spite of
my great grief I did not find it practicable to isolate
myself from the life that was going on around me.
At first, when I began to go about I felt that I was
wicked and unfeeling. Then I reminded myself that
after all it was hard to visit my sorrow upon my
husband, and I felt that if my father could look down
and see me from where he was, he would understand

I was not going about because I had in any sense
forgotten him, or ceased to regret him, but wholly
and solely out of a desire to do my duty to the
utmost to the husband who had been so good and
considerate and tender with me.

And with every day that went over my head I
seemed to love my Eddy better, and he, on his side,
grew more and more devoted to me. How different
it would all have been if I had been left unprotected,
without any relations whom I had known as relations,
with only my modest little patrimony and a wretched
little pension to live upon, a waif and a stray, who
would live in other people's houses with only two
courses open to her, either to marry for a home, or
to develop into that wretched travesty of womanhood, an Anglo-Indian "spin." I used sometimes to
look at my husband with a kind of wonder. I have
often caught myself asking was I really Mrs Edward
Hamlyn? Was I really this gallant young soldier's
wife? Or was it all a dream, and should I wake up
some day to find myself in bed at Muggrapore, or up in
the bungalow which I had shared with Mrs Hamilton
at Simla? In a certain sense, there was a grain of
unreality in my life, as if it was something to which
I was not and never could get quite accustomed.
But I was very happy. I had only one cause for
dissatisfaction. There was only one crumpled leaf
in our bed of roses; only one jarring note in the
harmony of our true affection. It was that while
most of Eddy's people wrote to him sending good
wishes and presents, his mother, who had been
everything in the world to him, stood aloof. Of
course, our marriage had been very hurriedly pushed
on, and perhaps to her, with her English notions—
for, as he explained to me, English people, as a rule,

have longer engagements than ours was—there may
have seemed something almost indecent in the haste
with which our marriage had been arranged. Once
or twice I asked whether he had heard from his
mother, and he replied no; but after our wedding
and my father's death, he one day received a letter
which he put into his pocket without showing me.
It did not occur to me at the time to ask to see
it; it would have seemed to me then like an in-
quisitive piece of impertinence, even though I was
his wife. But a mail or two later, when the kindest
and heartiest of letters arrived from Lord Clovelly
and from Eddy's cousin, Mr Hamlyn—one enclosing
a cheque for one hundred pounds, with a wish that
Eddy should buy me anything that I liked with it, the
other full of the kindest and most affectionate good
wishes, and sending me a beautiful bracelet—it then
struck me that there had come not one single word
from his mother, whom one would have expected to
be the very first to wish a son joy and happiness in
his new life.

"How is it that your mother has not written,
Eddy?" I asked him.

He looked a little uneasy.

"Well, my dearest, look here, it's no use our beginning by having secrets from each other," he said
confusedly; "you have none from me, and why should
I keep one from you."

"Why, Eddy, what do you mean?"

"Well, dearest, the fact is I have heard from my
mother; I heard two mails ago."

"You had a letter from your mother?"

"Well, of course, I wrote to her as soon as I knew
that we were going to be married, and told her all
about you, and explained how it was that the affair

was coming off so soon. She did not take it as well
as she might have done."

"How didn't take it?"

"Well, she would have liked me to marry somebody
in England."

"But then you did not want to marry anyone in
England!" I exclaimed.

"No, I wanted to marry you. I never wanted to
marry anybody but you in all my life, but, of course,
one's mother thinks that—well, at least, mine does—
that she has a right to be consulted and considered,
and she doesn't seem to be at all pleased about our
marriage."

"You had better show me her letter," I said
quietly.

"It is not a pleasant letter, Doremy."

"That does not matter. I would rather see it. I
shall know then what she has in her mind, and
whether I can do anything to make her like me
better. It seems rather unjust, though, to dislike a
person whom you have never seen. Let me see the
letter."

He did not, however, show it to me at once. I
had indeed to use all my powers of persuasion to
make him hand it over, but at last he opened his
despatch-box and gave it to me, slowly and with
visible reluctance.

He had been quite right in saying that it was not
a pleasant letter. It was the most unjust, and at the
same time the most ignorant, letter that I had ever
seen. I do not mean ignorant in the way of spelling
and such like, but so ignorant of the life which I had
lived up to the time of my marriage. It was
evidently written by a woman who had an idea that
nobody who had been born in India could possibly

be a lady, and gave me very much the impression
that nobody who had been living long in India could
even be good.   It spoke of her well-known desire
that he should have married earlier in life, though,
after all, he was but six-and-twenty, so that he could
not be said to have lost very much time or delayed
his marriage very late, but it expressed the utmost
disgust that he should have been caught—yes, she put
it in that way—caught, that was the very word she
used—by "an Anglo-Indian adventuress!"   I felt as
I read the opprobrious words, as if all the blood in my
body were rising to my face, and such anger in my
soul that I think if I had not been already married,
I could have found it in my heart to break my
engagement.

"The idea of your being married in this hole-and-
corner fashion, in such desperate and indecent hurry,"
the letter went on, "only shows me that these people
in their eagerness to secure you are afraid to delay
lest you should find out the truth about them.   I have
never been," it continued, "so disgusted in my life."

When I had read the last cruel words I laid the
letter down upon the table in chill and deadly silence.
Eddy looked at me doubtfully.   "Doremy," he said,
"I was not willing to show you that letter, and I
know that it has hurt you far more than it ought
to have done.   You must try to think of it as the
letter of a prejudiced woman, who is totally ignorant
of the real meaning of her words.   My mother has
never lived out of England in her life.   She has
heard all sorts of tales about people out here, and
she judges us and you, whom she has never seen,
by that foolish and unreliable standard—hearsay."

"Answer me one question," I said.   "What did you
say to her in reply?"

"My dear child," he said promptly, "I never replied to it at all. I felt that it was useless to argue; I had no intention of allowing her or any other human being in the world to come in between us. I had already written to her announcing our marriage as an accomplished fact when I received it. Unless my mother chooses to write to me in a proper manner, I shall not communicate with her again. It is no use arguing with a woman on the other side of the world. When I am able to take you home, and she sees you for herself, then she will see how utterly mistaken she has been, how misguided, how altogether wrong. Till that time you are my wife, and you come before everybody in the world to me, even my own mother."

"I shall never meet your mother," I said passionately. "My own was so sweet, so gentle, so true, so good, that I judged all mothers by her. Eddy, I was ready to open my whole heart to this mother of yours, because I assumed that she would be something like mine. Now, my only hope is, that I may never, under any circumstances, meet her; certainly I will never willingly do so. I don't know how she dare blacken a whole countryful of women because she doesn't happen to be one of them. She must have a bad, an evil mind—yes, I must speak, I will speak—she must have a thoroughly evil mind to think evil so readily of those whom she has never seen. Your father must have been nice," I blurted out. "You must have got all your good and lovable qualities from him."

"Well, in a certain sense, perhaps I did," he admitted "My mother is a woman of very good birth, and was a great beauty in her day. In a certain sense she is a hard woman, and given to jumping at conclusions. I can only say to you that I utterly regret that she should have taken our marriage in the way that she has done. It is not reasonable and it is not kindly, but, after all, dearest, I am not my mother, and so long as we are everything to each other, does anything outside, even one's mother, count for very much ? The very fact that she has so openly avowed herself your enemy, will only make me cling to you the more, and love you the better. And, after all, my Doremy, we are married ; nothing can undo that."

"And you are quite sure," I persisted, "that in time to come you won't feel that your mother has been right—that I am a mere adventuress who —caught you ? "

"Nay, nay ; it was I who caught you, not you me. God knows," he went on earnestly, "I was eager enough to satisfy any woman."

"But to think that your mother should—should have such an idea—should credit me with such an idea !" I continued indignantly.

"Well, what does it matter ? You know, and I know, and everybody who was near us at the time knew, that I was desperately in love with you. What does it matter what somebody thousands and thousands of miles away chooses to think in such a case ? You see my other relations do not take this tone. Nothing could be more kind or more generous than my uncle's letter, for instance. And old Bill, how nice of the dear old chap to go himself and choose a wedding present for you ; how nice of my Uncle Clovelly to send a big cheque that you might have something which would really please you. You see, they are reasonable people, and they take a reasonable and worldly view of the whole affair. It is no use upsetting yourself about what my mother chooses to think. She will come round in time."

"She need never come round for me!"

"Well, then, if it is a case of choosing between you, you may always rest assured that you will be the one of my choice. And, besides that," he went on, with infinite tenderness, "I would have you put all this worry and annoyance right out of your mind for the sake of the one whom some day, I hope, you will sympathise with more easily than my mother seems able to sympathise with me."

CHAPTER VII

THE INFLUENCE OF ONE PERSON

UNDOUBTEDLY my mother-in-law was a woman of very strong character and of dominant will, for although she did not write to my husband, nor did he further communicate with her, she yet contrived to exercise a very great influence over our lives. I saw all the letters which Eddy wrote to his own people on the subject of our marriage. In answering Lord Clovelly's congratulations and in thanking him for his extremely handsome present to us, or rather to me, for he had expressed a wish that Eddy should buy me a present with the hundred pounds which he had sent, my husband had taken the opportunity not exactly of singing my praises, but of putting a word in season which would tend to prepossess his uncle in my favour. I must confess that I blushed a little as I read his words. He spoke of my extreme youth, of my simplicity of mind, manners and habits, and wound up by a description of my father's utter sacrifice of self on the altar of duty. It was a letter of which any woman in the world must have been proud, and I felt after it had gone that Lord Clovelly at least would be proof against any insinuations as to my being an adventuress. Perhaps it was foolish of me, but that horrid word simply stuck in my throat. I could not forget it, it seemed to meet me at every turn. "But surely," I thought, when I had read Eddy's letter to the end, "his uncle will understand that no woman who is really an adventuress could inspire a man to write such a letter concerning her."

After many weeks had gone by, however, he heard again from Lord Clovelly, not a letter purposely concerning me, but one on general topics such as he was in the habit of occasionally writing to him. At the end it said, "I am very sorry to find that your mother is so bitterly opposed to your marriage and that she is making such a trouble of it. I hope that you will not allow yourself to quarrel with her, even for your wife. A good woman would not, of course, wish you to be out-at-elbows with your own mother. Perhaps it is a pity that you were married in such a hurry, but, as I told your mother, the deed is done, and we can only hope that it may turn out for the best. I repeated to her all that you had told me of your wife, but I am greatly afraid that with her it is a case of 'Can any good thing come out of Nazareth?' I would advise you to write her as much as possible as if no cloud had arisen between you. After all, you are everything that she has in the world. Hers is not a happy nature, and, if you can spare her a pang, I sincerely hope that you will see your way to do it. For my own part, my dear boy, I like young people who marry to be happy and to be in love with each other; it seems to me a greater consideration than any other that one can name or think of. I shall therefore try to picture your wife only through your eyes until I have the pleasure of seeing her, when I sincerely hope that I shall feel that you have not half done her justice."

"Eddy," I said, when I had read the letter to the end, "your uncle is very kind, and he is very just;

but although he does not mean to be, he is already influenced against me. What can I have done to your mother that she, who loves you, should hate me for doing the same thing? I feel as if I should never see any of your people; I feel as if I could never face any one of them. It is dreadful for a lady to realise that she is regarded by a whole family as an interloper and a mere outsider."

"Well, dearest, in a family sense you are an outsider to everybody but me; that is natural enough," he exclaimed.

"Oh, yes, but I do not mean in a family sense. I have never before been made to feel that I was an outsider socially. You know," I went on, "if I had known all this I would never have married you."

"Oh, don't say that!" he cried.

"Ah, but it is true."

"Do you mean to tell me that you would have let my people influence you so much as to ruin my life and break my heart?" he exclaimed, catching hold of me and drawing me near to him.

"Yes, I am afraid that I should."

"Then all I have to say is, thank God that we were married before my people had a chance of getting at you!"

I felt a great wave of remorse sweep over me, a great tide of compunction which seemed to tell me that he loved me better than I him. And yet, was that so? Oh, no, surely not. If ever a woman was bound up heart and soul in her husband, surely I was that woman. I felt myself blush under his direct gaze. "No, I do not quite mean that," I said hurriedly. "But honestly, I do not think, Eddy, that you half realise how eaten alive I am with pride. I daresay I should have been angry enough and foolish enough for anything if I had known all this before we were married; but at the same time I could not give you up now, and I cannot help being glad that we were married before I did know anything about it."

"My dear," he said, "you make too much of my people's opinion. After all, it is only the opinion of one person — a person whose judgment is biased, and, moreover, based upon actual ignorance of facts. You see my uncle says himself that he shall keep an open mind about you, he shall only picture you through my eyes, through my description."

"I hope," I cried, "that I shall never see any of your people."

"My dear child," he said very gently, "if my dear chum Bill comes out, he will he the greatest friend that you have in the world. He is the dearest chap alive; you will like him as much as I do, and he will like you—well, next best to me, perhaps. I wish," he said, with a gay laugh, "that I was as sure of ever being Commander-in-Chief as I am that you and old Bill will be the very best of friends."

I said no more. I let him think so; but in my heart I felt convinced that Lord Clovelly's son and I would never be anything but the merest acquaintances, family connections, people at arm's length from each other first and last. And yet, when, a few months later, he came out to join the regiment, (for he had persistently declined the idea of remaining with the depôt), and Eddy brought him into my pretty, cool, shaded drawing-room, saying, "Doremy, this is my cousin, Edward Hamlyn, the 'Bill' you have heard me speak of so often," I felt all my prejudices and all my long pent-up anger and distress melting away, for he was the counterpart of my Edward Hamlyn, my husband. It became plain to me that Eddy had inherited none of his mother's beauty looks. He had come into the world stamped with the personality of the old Devon family of which he had been born. Bill Hamlyn, as he was always called in the regiment, was five years younger than Eddy, but he did not look it. In all my life I have never seen brothers more ridiculously alike than these two were in outward appearance. He had the same charming voice, the same quick, alert glance, the same intense blueness of the eyes, and the same delightful, unaffected manners. He gave one glance at me, and held out both his hands. "You and I," he said, "have got to be tremendous chums, because, you know, they say that women-folk do not like their husbands to have any chums but themselves. Now, I have always been Eddy's chum ever since I can remember anything, and I cannot give him up, even to a wife—that is to say, not altogether. So, Mrs Eddy, you must just make up your mind to have me for a chum as well, and then you know we shall hit it off quite splendidly."

He was so fresh, so breezy, so hearty, that he fairly conquered me. He was delightfully impertinent too. Before an hour had gone by he had taken to calling me Mrs Doremy. "Where did you get such a wonderful name?" he exclaimed. "I never heard of it before. It sounds like a poem or a touch of music. Who first thought of it?"

"I did," said Eddy, promptly.

"You? Why, my dear old chap, we shall have you blooming out as poet-laureate before long. I never heard such a charming name in my life, even for a charming lady," with a little bow towards me.

I could not help liking him. Everything fell out as he predicted, and we became the greatest of friends; indeed, it was from him that I first gathered any really reliable information about that unpleasant lady who stood in the background of my life like a bogey ready to spring out upon me at any moment—my mother-in-law.

"Why does she hate me so?" I said to him one day, a week or two after his arrival.

"Aunt Cordelia? Oh, well, Aunt Cordelia is not exactly the kind of woman who tends to make things more pleasant under any circumstances," he admitted hesitatingly. "You see, when she married my uncle she was a great beauty, not so young as she had been, and she seemed to have satisfied herself that my governor never meant to marry anybody, and you see he did. My uncle was one of those happy-go-lucky, devil-may-care sort of men, very much like what Eddy is, and he was always quite devoted to the governor, and I don't know, but I think she was a bit disappointed."

"But he had a right to marry!" I exclaimed.

"Well, that is what the poor old governor himself thought, so he went and got married; but I believe Mrs Richard was not at all pleased about it. Really, I would not worry about her opinion if I were you."

"But she has set your father and all your people against me."

"No, not so bad as that; not quite so bad as that. She has not set me against you for one."

"But she has influenced your father against me."

"No, not my father."

"But your sisters?"

"Oh, well, my sisters are—well, they are not much

use to anybody. They are very nice and all that, but I don't think you would care about them very much. They are so taken up with fashion and society and all that sort of thing, that they have not got much time left for thinking about other people's affairs."

"Not one of them has written to Eddy since they first wrote."

"No. Well, the truth is, Mrs Doremy, they wouldn't. I don't think they write to each other much ; I don't think they go in much for what you may call family affection. Eddy and I keep up that sort of thing ; I don't think the girls ever do. As for my dear old governor, you must not think that he is your enemy."

"No, but he is prejudiced against me."

"No, scarcely that. He is biding his time until he sees you. I had a talk with him only the night before I left home on the very subject, and he said then, what was perfectly justifiable, that there was a great deal in what Eddy had to say, and a good deal in what Aunt Cordelia had to say, and that he should judge for himself when he saw you."

"Yes," I exclaimed, "judge for himself with a mind already prejudiced in the other direction ! He can't help it," I cried, as he was about to expostulate, " Eddy's mother called me an adventuress ; she said that I had caught him."

A quizzical look came over Mr Hamlyn's face. " What are you laughing at ? " I asked.

" I was thinking," he said, with the ingenuousness of youth, " that perhaps Aunt Cordelia judged you out of her own bushel. I would not upset myself if I were you ; Mrs Doremy, it is not good enough. And, after all, dear old Eddy is the best fellow in the world; you are satisfied with him, and he is satisfied with you. What more do you want?"

"Well, I want just a little recognition from his people," I replied; "then I should be perfectly happy."

"I am afraid," he said, "that, as long as you are in India, you will not have that recognition, however much you may desire it. When once you go home, and they see you for what you are, you will have as much recognition, both from Eddy's people and from Eddy's friends, as the most exacting lady in the world could consider her right. If I were you, Mrs Doremy, I would make up my mind to be contented with that certainty until the time comes. After all, what can it matter to you what a lot of people whom you have never seen, and who have never seen you, choose to think about you? Look at me, for instance. I came out here feeling— shall I confess it to you?—that it was a ghastly bore that my greatest chum had gone and got married, feeling that life would never be quite the same again, and in a kind of way as if I owed you one for having married him; but as soon as I saw you, why, you must have seen for yourself that I went down before you like a row of ninepins in a well-played game of skittles."

I put out my hand to him in an impulse of gratitude. "Mr Hamlyn," I said, "I did not think, some- how, that I should like you, but I cannot help myself. You are quite fit to be Eddy's cousin, and you cannot expect me to say more than that. I felt before I saw you that you would be stiff, and stuck-up, and super- cilious, and horrid—yes, I did, I admit it freely—and yet I liked you nearly as much as Eddy before you had been in the room five minutes."

"That is all right," he said heartily. "I told you that we should be the greatest of friends. But don't you think, Mrs Doremy, since you are Eddy's wife and we are cousins, that you might leave off calling me Mr Hamlyn? It must sound to outsiders as if our relations were not over and above cordial, and we want to create just a contrary impression to that, don't we? So, Mrs Doremy, what if I were to leave off your grand married title, and you were to call me Bill?"

And, from that moment, he and I were Doremy and Bill one to another.

CHAPTER VIII

A FIAT AND A CHOICE

AFTER Bill Hamlyn and I had made such a satisfactory compact of friendship—which, by-the-bye, we never broke—I ceased entirely to discuss the Hamlyn family with my husband. I had no wish to bore him on the subject, and I could not shut my eyes to the fact that whatever they chose to do and whatever line of conduct they chose to make their own, he was not in any way responsible for it, and could not, while living at so great a distance from them, make them see matters with his eyes. Besides, it distressed him, and any expression of my annoyance at the line which they had taken generally had the effect of giving him a racking headache. So I very soon, after Bill Hamlyn came to India, ceased to mention the family in any way.

Not very long after the arrival of Lord Clovelly's last letter, Eddy wrote to his mother. He wrote exactly as if he had received no unpleasant letter from her and in due course of time she answered him, and a more or less frigid correspondence was the result. He always wrote to her as if she was on the best of terms with him; she always wrote to him as if he were still unmarried; indeed, she never, after that first letter, which was written immediately on the receipt of the news of our engagement, mentioned me in any way, good, bad or indifferent. It was not

E

an easy situation for me to bear, but I could not help feeling that it was in reality more hard for Eddy than for me. He made a rule of bringing me his mother's letters to read and also of bringing me his to her, that I might read them before they were mailed. At first I demurred, not wishing to seem to be spying upon one whom I trusted so utterly and loved so intensely, but Eddy quickly disposed of my objections. "I should not dream of receiving or writing letters of which you knew nothing," he said quietly, "and I must ask you to read these as well as others. If there is anything at any time that you object to, dearest, you have only to tell me."

"It is not likely, Eddy, that I should object to anything!" I exclaimed indignantly.

"My dear child," he replied, "two heads are better than one, and I might chance, quite inadvertently, to say something which would be painful or annoying to you. You know that I have no desire in the world but to make you happy, and if by accident I chance to say the wrong thing, it will be better for both of us that you tell me of it before it is too late to amend it than afterwards."

I could not help seeing the reasonableness of his remark, so I made no further objection to reading the correspondence which passed between himself and his mother.

It was not so very long before our little child was born, though it proved to be not the much-hoped-for boy upon which Eddy had set his heart. I don't know why men do seem to set their hearts upon having boys when they start a family, because girls generally seem to be more to their fathers than boys are—to be nearer, closer, more one with them. I don't think that Eddy was very much disappointed, but he had always spoken of the child that was to be as "the little son," "the boy," "he," and we had quite decided between ourselves that it was to be called Richard Massingham Hamlyn, after his father and mine.

However, when the baby came, instead of the big beautiful boy, with the Hamlyn blue eyes and the Hamlyn crisp curling hair, the new arrival turned out to be a frail, golden-haired, grey-eyed girl, taking entirely after me. Not that I had golden hair, but tradition had always declared that I had been blessed in that way as a baby. We had so little expected a girl that we had actually no name ready for it, and I was so ill that some weeks went by before the little stranger had any sort of a name to call her own. In due course of time we christened her Frances Margaret. Margaret was my mother's name, and Frances was merely a fancy of my own. Eddy's cousin stood as her godfather, and Mrs Hamilton and another old friend of mine were her two godmothers. She was a dear wee thing, as good and healthy as she was pretty to look upon. I was fortunate in getting a most devoted ayah, so that to me baby was personally no trouble whatever. This was indeed just as well, for after her birth I was never quite the same, not as long as I was in India. I seemed to be just fading away; not from any actual complaint, yet never feeling quite well. I had no strength, no energy, no desire to do anything. They used to dress me and take me out for a morning drive, and then I would go in and look at breakfast and spend the rest of the day in a state more or less of collapse until the cool of the evening, when they would dress me and take me out for a drive again.

Then I was taken up to the hills. Eddy had

special leave of absence, and the doctors of Muttrahabad hustled us off full of assurances that it would be the making of me.   But it was not the making of me.   I got a shade or so better just at first, and then I settled down again into the same lethargy of ill-health, finding everything an exertion, everything a trouble, not un-happy, but living a life that was more or less of a blank.

"You know, my dearest," Eddy said to me one day, when I was just recovering from a dead faint which had lasted longer than usual, "you cannot go on like this.   You will die if something cannot be done."

I put out a feeble hand and took his.   "I am afraid, Eddy, that I am going the same way as my mother went.   Of course you know she died of cholera, just as dear Father did, but, all the same, I have her constitution exactly.   She never could shake off the effects of illness, and I am just the same."

"You ought to go home," he said.

"Oh, but I could not possibly go home.   I have nowhere to go to ; I have no interest in going home ; it would be quite absurd.   Besides, my constitution cannot need a climate which it has never known."

"My dear child," he said, "you were born in India, but you inherit an English constitution, and the fact that you have never been home has nothing to do with the equally indisputable fact that a good long stay in England would probably set you up for good and all. At all events, the best thing we can do is to see what the doctors have to say about it."

So the doctors came and "sat" upon me, as they phrase it out in India, and the verdict was that, at at all and any cost, I was to be sent home.   I raised every objection that my feeble mind could devise and suggest.   I might as well have talked to so many stone walls.   They had got it firmly implanted into their stupid heads that home I was to go, and nothing that I could say served in any way to shake them from that opinion.

"Then, of course, my husband will be able to go with me?" I exclaimed, when I found that they had made up their minds about me.

The senior doctor looked at me doubtfully. "Well, of course, Hamlyn has been out such a very short time; his leave is not due for ever so long yet," he said. "If he felt the climate more we could sit upon him and certify him sick, but I am afraid that would be a little too bare-faced even for officialism. You couldn't get up a little illness, could you, Hamlyn?" he asked, turning appealingly to my husband.

Eddy burst out laughing at the bare idea of such a thing. "Why, my dear fellow, I have never been ill in my life!" he answered. "It would be such a clear case of malingering. The very men in the ranks would laugh at the bare idea of such a thing. I am afraid, Doremy, I cannot manage that much, even for you."

"Well, then, I refuse to go," I said resolutely. "I have never been home, and I am very young to go alone. I have no relations, nobody to go to, and I really cannot face such a journey by myself. I would rather stay here and die."

"You will die unless you do go home," said Dr Harrison, positively.

"I would rather die here, then," I declared positively. "I am sure that I should die if I were sent to England by myself. It has never been home to me. I call it home as everybody else does, because it is the jargon to which I have been used all my life, but India is my real home. I should die for certain long before I set foot upon English shores."

The senior doctor was about to answer me when my husband stopped him. "I don't think we need finally settle it now, Harrison," he said, putting his hand upon the other's shoulder. "The wife and I will talk it over. It is as she says, that she is so young to contemplate such a journey by herself. We will talk it over, and see how it looks when she gets more accustomed to it. It is not necessary to decide it off-hand."

So, one by one, the doctors filed out of the room, each bidding me adieu with an air which told me plainly that they regarded me as a doomed woman. When the last one was gone—that is to say, when Dr Harrison had taken his leave, which he did at the door with a whisper to Eddy—a whisper which I heard quite plainly, or at least a part of it, Eddy came back into the room where I was, with a great assumption of cheerfulness in his manner.

I literally cast myself into his arms. "Oh, Eddy, Eddy!" I cried, "it is all over between us! You and I have not had a very long journey together, but we have got nearly to the end of it now."

"No, no, my dearest," he returned soothingly, "you mustn't take such a pessimistic view of things as all this. You are ill and unnerved, but it will be all right by-and-by. You are young, you have every chance of pulling yourself together again if you only do what we tell you."

"No," I said, "no, it is too late. Don't try to deceive me, I heard what he said—'No time to be lost.' What does that mean? That if I stay here I shall die. If I go over there, I shall die just the same. I would rather stay here with you and die here."

"I cannot let you say that, darling," he said in a desperately anxious voice.

I saw that he was trying not to frighten me, but his face was blanched under all its bronze, and his lips were trembling. "I wish to God," he said, in an exceedingly bitter voice, "that I had even the decent shadow of an excuse for getting myself certified sick that I might take you home. If you won't go without me I must chuck the Service; but you must remember if I do that, I am throwing away my whole career, and my people will be more set against you than ever. Not that it would matter in the least, only one has to think of the future when one is not well off. I do wish," he said, looking at me wistfully, "that you would consent to be guided by those who do know what they are talking of. You must know, darling, that it is utterly hateful to me to think of being parted from you even for a single day; but for your good, your welfare, your safety, I could not put my own inclinations first. After all, you would have the child, you would have your own ayah, you would go with people you know. Think what it would be to come back strong and well, as you used to be."

"Think what it would be to die over there alone," I said wretchedly. "No, no, Eddy, I would rather stay here; I would rather stay here, and face the certainty of death, because I should be with you to the end. I have never been alone in my life; I have never known what it was to depend upon myself. You cannot imagine the desolation that the very thought of such a journey has for me. Oh, don't ask me to do it. Don't ask me to do it."

"I can't help asking you to do it, Doremy," he said anxiously. "If I had no love for you, and the doctors advised that course, I should still ask you just the same as I am doing now—to do that which is the best for your health and safety. Besides that, dearest, there is not the slightest doubt that it would be the best thing in the world for the child."

" For the child ?"

" Yes. Of course, no child is as well in India as it would be in England. The chances are a hundred to one against a child's life in a climate like this."

" I never knew that," I said quickly.

" No, but at the same time the doctors say it, the doctors think it. Our little girl is all right now, but then she is such a mite, not yet six months old. But when she begins to get her teeth, when the summer heat comes on, why, in England, she would have twenty times, nay, a hundred times, the chance of thriving that she would have in India."

" Do you really think so ? "

"The whole experience of people who have had babies out here tells me that that is so, the whole experience of the doctors declares the same thing. Why should these men lie to us ? It is not to their interests to save a child's life, unless it happens to be their own. From them you get an unbiased opinion."

" But baby is so well," I exclaimed.

"Yes, she is well, and I pray to God she may always keep well, but she would be better if she were out of this climate for a time. However, we need not decide everything to-day—now—we will wait awhile, we will wait a few days, and see whether you pull up a little through staying here. Only don't tell me that you care for me so little that you would rather die here than save yourself by going home."

He said no more about it then, but during the next two or three days I thought of nothing else than of what the doctors had said. Should I really die if I remained in India ? Would the effect of the climate be such that my beautiful, flourishing baby-girl would

dwindle and pine away? I could see by the way
that he watched me that Eddy was desperately
anxious. Ought I to do what they wished, to yield
to older and wiser heads than my own, and turn my
back upon everything which hitherto had made my
life? And, on the other hand, if I consented to go,
what would become of me? Must I, a girl but just
nineteen years old, go all those thousands of miles to
the other side of the world, among a people whose
ways were not my ways, to a country I had never
seen—I, who had not the energy to let my servants
dress me, and my husband to lift me into my carriage?
Was I to go thousands of miles by land and sea, with
no one to lean on, no one to think for me, care for
me, protect me, and, on the other hand, only the
alternative of seeing the world gradually blotted out,
and all that I loved left standing on the shore from
which I was fast receding? What a choice! To
stay with my love and die, or to go out alone into
the unknown, on what was at best only a chance
of living!

CHAPTER IX

THE BEGINNING OF OUR JOURNEY

IT cannot be said that I gained at all in strength during the next two weeks. If anything, at the end of that time I was weaker, and by some strange fatality our little girl began to loose her healthy looks and to get cross, irritable and peevish. Her ayah had the patience of an angel, but all the patience in the world could not alter the fact that she was beginning to have trouble with her teeth, and that she was what is technically called "getting them hard."

Dr Harrison, whom we called in to attend to her, took me to task in the roundest terms. "Mrs Hamlyn," he said, "it is no use my coming here and pretending to you that a little prescription will set that baby all right. The child is suffering from the climate; she will not be well as long as she is out here. Take her home, and in all probability she will grow into a strong, healthy, flourishing child, with as good a chance of living as any other."

"But why should she suddenly fail as she has done?" I exclaimed.

"I don't know why—at least, I do know. Because it is what the majority of children do in this climate. That child ought to be taken home; you ought to go home. You must forgive me for speaking to you quite plainly, but I think you are exceedingly obstinate and exceedingly inconsiderate

towards your husband, who is almost beside himself
with anxiety and distress.   One would think," he
said vexedly, "that England was a land full of
bogies and hobgoblins.   My dear lady, you will find
nothing there to hurt you or make you unhappy,
except in the fact that you will be parted from
your husband for a little time.   If you could put
in a twelvemonth in Europe, Hamlyn would be able
to get a decent spell of leave; but it is perfectly
useless for you to think of holding out as long as
that before you or the child go.   If you do not
go this season I don't think either of you will have
the chance of going."

I have thought since that he took advantage of
my natural anxiety about the baby to press the
necessity of my own case more forcibly upon me.
Little Frances certainly was ailing, of that there
was no doubt; and equally there was no doubt that
if I remained in India I should very soon have a
change which would have been a final one; but I do
not now think that the child, brought up with care
and kept in the hills, would have been any the worse
for not going home to England.   As it was then, I
was more divided against myself than ever.   I could
make up my mind to die, that was simple enough,
but I could not make up my mind to let the child slip
through my fingers.   And yet it was so hard to utter
the words which would part me, even for a time, from
my husband.

At last, however, Eddy suddenly solved the difficulty.   "Doremy," he said suddenly, one day when I
was sitting under the punkah watching the child
lying feebly in her ayah's arms, "I have an idea."

"Yes.   And that is—what?"

"Well, it is a project which will cost money, a good

deal of money, but it will break the long journey to you, and make you more satisfied to go home than anything else that I can think of. I cannot get leave to go home and stop with you, that is utterly out of the question ; but I could get three months' leave to take you home, settle you there—that is, in some nice, suitable place—in a house of your own, and leave you. That would be a different thing to going home by yourself, wouldn't it ? "

"Oh, yes ! " I exclaimed eagerly. "That would be quite different! I think I could bear that."

"Then," he said, "I will take the necessary steps at once, put the case to the powers that be, and throw myself on their mercy."

I had not very much opinion of the mercy of the powers that happened to be at that time. I had always believed the authorities to be without bowels of compassion ; but Eddy, full of faith, sent in his application, and gave his reasons at length for preferring a request for prolonged leave, and not a little to my surprise, and greatly to his jubilation and the satisfaction of the doctors, he was granted a period of four months for the express purpose of taking me home to England.

"There ! You see ! " he said triumphantly, when he brought me the letter announcing the privilege which had been vouchsafed to him. "There is nothing like asking for what you want, and telling the exact truth about it! I said how young you were, how inexperienced, how utterly friendless, and what a desperate case of necessity it was. So we will pack up our things, and we will have a couple of months at home in fine style. The only thing is, my dearest, that the main cost will have to come out of your emergency money."

"That does not matter!" I exclaimed. "We put it aside for emergencies, and surely no emergency could be more necessitous or imperative than to save either my life or dear baby's!"

And then I caught the child from her ayah, and hugged her close to my breast, until she set up a feeble and wailing cry of very decided remonstrance.

It was wonderful how soon we managed to get our belongings put together and the arrangements made for our long journey. Personally, I did nothing towards helping matters on, for with every hour I seemed to get weaker, just as Frances seemed to become more blanched and feeble with every moment that passed over our heads. Still, I had given my consent, that was the great thing, and Eddy worked with a will, for he was determined that we should not remain one day longer than was absolutely necessary.

At first I had been anxious to go back to the bungalow at Muttrahabad, in order to gather together a few things from which I did not wish to be parted, even for a few months, but Eddy absolutely vetoed any such idea. "It is not at all necessary, dearest," he said promptly. "I will write immediately, and give instructions to have anything you want packed and sent down to Bombay to you. Your ordinary things you won't care for; but do you tell me exactly what you want, and let me make a list at once, that I need not lose a single post."

After all, there were not many things that I really was very much set upon having to take with me. My jewellery and personal treasures I had in my possession then, and all that I really wanted from Muttrahabad were some miniatures and various odds and ends that had belonged to my father and mother. These, together with the rest of my wardrobe, Eddy ordered to be sent down to meet us at Bombay, and in three days after this we began our journey down country together.

Of course, baby's ayah went with us, and also my own ayah, and Eddy's bearer went as far as Bombay. At that point he thought it would be better to send my own ayah back to her district, and to engage for me some English maid who might wish to be going back to Europe.

The journey down prostrated me most frightfully. I tried to complain as little as I could, but I fear that I succeeded very badly. Looking back, that journey lives in my brains more like a hideous nightmare than a reality through which I actually passed. I have a dim recollection of scorching heat, frightful thirst, misery and inconvenience of all kinds, of a little child who grew more lifeless with each hour, and of a patient, forbearing husband with all his anxious soul in his eyes. Still, we did arrive at Bombay in due time, and there I somewhat revived in the comparative luxury and comfort of the hotel, where we stayed during the two days which elapsed between our arrival and the departure of the P. and O. boat by which we were to go to England.

There was plenty for Eddy to do during that two days, for he had many arrangements to make for our journey which he had been compelled to leave to the last moment. For instance, he had to engage me an English maid, which was not a matter of such extreme case after all. However, he did at last find one who seemed suitable and at the same time capable. As a matter of fact, she was not a lady's maid, but was a professional nurse who had been out to attend upon a young English lady of rank at the birth of her first child.

Eddy was very jubilant at having secured her. "My dear," he said, "I feel quite easy in my mind about you now. This is the grandest chance! We might have come this journey a dozen times and not happened to meet with a trained nurse who would be able to look after you right until you get to England, and indeed for as long after as you choose to keep her. She will make all the difference to you, and it will be far better for you than having a native ayah, who would probably be sea-sick, and certainly helpless and frightened half the time."

I was not by any means so jubilant myself. You see, I had never been waited upon by a white person in my life, and there seemed to me to be something almost improper in expecting a dignified English-woman, who was wearing a very smart distinctive garb, to wait upon me in an everyday sort of way; in fact, she took me altogether under her protecting wing, and really patronised me to such an extent that I was afraid to call my soul my own.

"You know," she said, "I am not a lady's maid, neither am I an Indian ayah, so that I hope you won't expect me to know precisely your ways and what you wish doing. In three or four days I shall have shaken down into my place, and I hope you won't feel the loss of your own people at all. I am accustomed to fitting myself into any nook into which I chance to stray, and I hope that when there is any little thing you want that you will tell me of it. So many ladies in delicate health go on suffering because they are unwilling to speak, anxious not to give trouble and all that sort of thing; but pray, Mrs Hamlyn, do try to remember that I am only anxious to land you in England looking very different to what you are looking just now."

I assured her that I would really try to give her as much trouble as I possibly could, and I must say Nurse Mordaunt was extremely kind to me. She took me thoroughly in hand, as if I was a helpless baby— I was really but little better—and washed me and dressed me as good-humouredly and deftly as if I had been a little child.

"How is that baby going to be fed on the journey?" she inquired.

"Oh, Captain Hamlyn will buy goats to take with us."

"Oh! And she will be able to have her fresh milk twice a day at least?"

"Yes. There is no other way of managing it that I know of," I replied.

"How many goats will he take?"

"I should say four. Because, you see, I am taking a good deal of milk—the doctors ordered it for me— and, of course, we cannot have baby stinted in any way."

"No, no. That relieves my mind of a good deal of anxiety. I don't believe in artificial foods for children. I am quite sure that they are a mistake," she went on, speaking in keen professional tones. "Half the infant deaths that occur are solely due to that cause, I am convinced of it; and then, too, most of them are made so that fresh milk is a positive necessity in using them, in addition to the stuff that you buy in the tins."

"Ah, you see, I am quite ignorant of all that," I said a little blankly. "I did not even know that you could buy stuff in tins to feed babies on."

"More is the pity that one can," rejoined Nurse Mordaunt. "'Murder in tins' is what I generally call it!"

At last, the evening before the sailing of the *Poonah*, Eddy came in with the cheerful announcement that everything was absolutely ready for our journey. " I don't think, dearest," he said, " that things could possibly have fallen out and arranged themselves better. As far as I can see there will not be a hitch for the entire journey. I have got superb goats—splendid creatures—and, luckily enough, the very best saloon cabin in the whole ship. You will travel as comfortably as a princess ! We shall have a perfectly gorgeous voyage ! And I expect by the time of our arrival, that you will be so pulled together that you will make me spend the whole of my leave tearing round London seeing sights and gay life. Tell me, dearest, don't you feel better already for having made the effort, and for knowing that you are really going home at last ? "

I was very weak, very much in love, and very young, and I told him that I did feel marvellously better ; whereas, in truth, I was possessed by an awful foreboding of coming ill, by a feeling that I was going to a strange country from whence I should never return. I felt, somehow or other, as if I had got to an epoch in my life—one of those halting places on our mortal journey which we did not mark with a white stone—rather with a black cross !

It is no exaggeration to say that I never closed my eyes that night, the last that I passed upon Indian soil. Eddy, on the contrary, slept like a top, and woke betimes in the gayest and most brilliant spirits. " I feel," he cried, " like a schoolboy going home for the holidays ! Nay, I do not believe that ever, even in my school-days, I felt so happy and so jubilant on the first day of my holidays as I feel this morning. If I were not ashamed to do it, I would go out and stand in the middle of that square and chuck my hat into the air from sheer gaiety of heart. As for you, you little Anglo-Indian, you take everything so coolly that you are quite aggravating. I don't believe you are a bit glad that you are going home at last—even with me."

"Oh, yes, I am," I answered rather lamely. "Oh, yes, Eddy, indeed I am!"

"No. I believe that when you find yourself just on the point of starting again for India, you will feel exactly as I do to-day."

"I don't know. If you are there I certainly shall feel so," I answered. "I am not so much happier because I am going home, Eddy, because home is nothing to me; where you are is my home. You ought not to grumble because I feel like that."

"Grumble!" he cried. "When did I ever grumble at you? Why, my Doremy—Yes? What is it? Hullo! What is this?"

He had taken a missive from his bearer, who came in at that moment. He tore it open and read it, and I saw his hands begin to shake and his face blanch as I had never seen it blanch before.

"Eddy!" I cried. "What is it?"

"Oh, Doremy! Doremy!" he cried. "I don't know how to tell you!"

CHAPTER X

A RUDDERLESS SHIP ON AN UNKNOWN SEA

I GOT up from the long bamboo couch upon which I was lying, just under the punkah, and went unsteadily across the room towards him.

" What is it, Eddy ? " I asked.

He turned and looked at me. " Oh, my darling, my dearest, how am I to tell you ? How could I foresee that they would be such brutes as this ? What shall I do ? What am I to do ? "

" You have not told me what it is."

" My dear, I am recalled."

" To the regiment ? "

" Yes. Something is wrong. The colonel telegraphs to me—' All leave stopped. Return immediately. Trouble on the frontier. We may have received our orders, and marched out before you can rejoin us. Do not delay a single moment.' Doremy," he said, " if this had only come a few hours later I should have been beyond recall. What am I to do ? I cannot take you back to that cruel up-country journey, with every day growing hotter and hotter, when every arrangement is made for your journey. It may seem to you as if I had played you false ; tricked you. I swear to you that this is as great a blow to me as it can possibly be to you. Don't send me back heart-broken, feeling that you have cut off your last chance of salvation, don't take away the child's one hope of living. Nurse Mordaunt will stick to you until I can join you. I will make her promise me, whether you are ill or well; and you will have Ayah, you will have the child. You will pity me sufficiently not to refuse me this last shred of comfort?"

What could I do? I said yes. It was for my good, he had made every arrangement, we were on the very eve of starting—the eve, nay, we were on the very point of starting. I had no time to think, so I said yes. I had no time to grieve. It seems to me, looking back from now, that my dazed brain refused to take in the full meaning of what that telegram had conveyed. I had not sufficient will-power left to set my wishes in opposition to my husband's, to those round about me. I believe that I consented, I feel sure that I did, but it was a consent that was only wrung from me in the apathy of my intense despair.

I let them do with me as they would. I remember clinging desperately to him as if, since we had only a brief span of time left together—fewer hours than I could count upon the fingers of one hand—I would not waste so much as an instant of the time. "No, don't ask me to eat anything," was the only definite request that I made to anybody.

I uttered no parting injunctions, lavished no farewell kisses upon him I was leaving; I was too wretched to make any sign of my intense misery. So those two or three hours dragged their short length away and my most distinct remembrance is of going through the great cool hall of the hotel to the carriage which was to take us down to the ship. I remember distinctly hearing a tender woman's voice say in pitying accents—"How very ill that poor young lady looks! I suppose she is going home."

I turned and looked at her. She was fresh and strong and bright, evidently just out from England. She could never have known what a travesty her words sounded to my sad ears. Going home! What a mockery! Going home! Rather was I going like a rudderless ship on an unknown sea, with the length, breadth, depth and currents of which I was all unfamiliar. I was leaving behind me my hold-fast upon life, my commander, my navigating lieu-tenant, my rudder, my one stand-by.

I remember very little about my actual parting with Eddy. I have a distinct recollection that he kept fast hold of me as long as we were left to-gether, that he allowed nobody to touch me, but carried me himself on board the ship, and that he carried me again down to my cabin. I remember hearing him talking earnestly to Nurse Mordaunt— I mean that I was conscious that an earnest con-versation was passing between them, but of what he said to her, or what she replied to him, in solemn truth I grasped nothing. I believed that I was dying. Never before had such overpowering deadly faintness taken possession of me. I was conscious of a sharp, imperative rap upon the cabin door and of an exceeding bitter cry—"My Doremy! My Doremy!" And then I remember absolutely no-thing; all was utterly and entirely blank until I came to myself to find Ayah and Nurse Mordaunt bending over me, the one pouring something liquid and cold over my clenched hands, and the other hold-ing a scented handkerchief to my nostrils.

"Where am I? What has happened?" I exclaimed

Then memory came to my aid, and I realised my horrible situation. "Oh, let me go back! I cannot go, I never consented to go—not alone. . . . I would rather stay in India and die. It is not too late. Put me on shore. Let me go back. I don't mind dying, I don't really, nurse. Where is Captain Hamlyn?"

She looked at me with infinite pity. "My dear," she said, in a very kind and tender voice, "what you ask is impossible. We have already started on our journey."

"No, no, don't say that; don't say it."

"I must say it," she said; "it is true, dear lady. Try to accept it as your fate, and believe that it is all for the best. Your poor husband was so anxious, almost beside himself with anxiety. His only consolation in leaving you was that it was for your good and to save the child. See! If I lift you up you can come to the window and have a last look at him. I daresay he is still standing watching us go."

She lifted me in her strong arms as if I had been no more than a little child, and carried me to the porthole. I saw that the shore was fast receding, but could distinguish no one from the crowd of watching figures left behind. Small as the effort was, it was too much for me, and, after straining my eager eyes for a minute or so, I fell back again into Nurse Mordaunt's arms.

She was very good to me, very wise, very judicious. She spent a great deal of her vitality in trying to bolster me up into something like life again, and I am afraid that I was but a poor and ungrateful recipient of all her skill and care. I used to feel and sometimes to say that I should bless her if she would only let me lie still and die quietly. At which she would shake her head and reply, "Ah! but the husband—would he

bless me ? I don't quite think so. If you are tired of
him, Mrs Hamlyn, he is not tired of you, and I promised him that I would stay by you, and stick to you,
and do my best for you, and that is a promise which
I mean to keep. Come, come, you have got the
wrench of parting over. Try to count the days now
until you meet again."

"We shall never meet again," I said one day when
she was urging me in this strain. "I am entirely
convinced of that. How can I get well when I know
not what has happened to him ? How can I have the
heart to think of myself, when he is gone into danger
on the frontier ? "

"But it may be entirely a false alarm. For anything that you know, that danger may be over, and
your husband may follow you by the very next ship.
Keep a brave heart, my dear, and hope for the best.
'Hope on, hope ever,' that is a fine motto for us all.
Look at the improvement in that dear baby of yours.
Does it not make your mother's heart positively
dance to see her taking her food and noticing people,
and showing off all her pretty ways, instead of
being the lifeless little creature that she was a week
ago ? "

"I don't think, Nurse," I said drearily, "that my
heart will ever dance again ; there is no dance left in
it. I have left all my joy, all my hope behind me in
India. If I knew exactly what had happened to my
husband, I think I should feel different, but the un-
certainty, the suspense—oh, it is too horrible ! I don't
think you know what I am suffering."

"No, my dear, I don't, for I have never been
married," she said kindly. "But still, in any case,
you would like to please him, wouldn't you ? And
you cannot please him better than by taking care of

yourself, by doing everything you can to restore
yourself to your proper state of health. You ought
to think that if you are suffering, he is suffering just
as badly, if not worse. And if he has health and
strength on his side, he has all the pain of knowing
that you, poor little frail thing, have neither the
heart nor the strength to battle with your troubles.
If you had seen his poor face when he had to go,
leaving you looking like death, not knowing, indeed,
whether you would ever come out of that faint or not,
oh, you would have been so sorry for him, you would
set yourself, like a schoolboy to a task, to get strong
and well, so as to be able to send him a cable the first
time that we touch land. Come now, tell me, don't you
think such a husband is worth making an effort for?
Think what it would be to him if I could send him
a word saying, 'Both invalids decidedly improved.'
Why, it would make a new man of him, it would put
a new heart, new life into him. He would jump for
joy, and be ready and willing to bear anything that
might happen to come."

Somehow her brave words did serve to put new
life into me, and for Eddy's sake I tried—oh, I had
never tried so hard in my life to do anything—to
throw off the lethargy which threatened to overwhelm
me. I made great efforts to get up on deck, and
there I would lie for hours under the awning, trying
to take an interest in things that were going on
around me. I forced myself to eat and drink also,
though often it went sorely against the grain with
me. And with every fresh effort that I made did that
dear and good woman do her utmost to comfort and
to help me, praising me and petting me as if I were
doing something for her benefit rather than for my
own, sometimes treating me as you would treat a

spoiled child, and sometimes making believe that I
was a rational woman, with some hope in her heart,
instead of being merely a mass of broken nerves,
heart-sick with despair.

Under her strong, fostering care it was wonderful
how I did improve both in health and in spirits. I
was lonely, wretched, home-sick, heart-sick; but at
the same time I had already begun to look forward
to the blessed time when Eddy would join me or I
should rejoin him. I had begun, like a school-girl, to
count the hours to the holidays. I began to take an
eager interest in the welfare of the child, and certainly
little Frances grew and throve apace with every day
that went over our heads.

How that good woman did ply me with odds and
ends of food calculated to build up my strength again!
"How is it?" I said to her one day, "that you are
able to get all these things cooked at all sorts of odd
times?"

"A woman of my profession," she replied briskly,
"understands the use of the oiled feather. I never let
my patients go without proper things to eat when they
are to be had for the asking."

"But are they to be had for the asking?"

"Well, practically they are. I make a friend of
the steward. Well, first of all, I make a friend of the
captain. Then I make a friend of the steward, and I
tell him that I have a lady in my care who is delicate
(not ill, you know, oh, no, it doesn't do to tell him that
passengers at sea are ill; he would hate that; but
somebody who wants feeding up and little attentions),
and I get him to introduce me to one of the cooks,
and then I explain to the cook, what he knows perfectly well, that sick-cooking is a great trouble, that
every nurse ought to be able to sick-cook beautifully

because it takes time, and is too finicky for a *chef*—
it always pay to call a cook a *chef*—with a large
number of meals on his hands. And then I am soon
mistress of a little stove and a couple of little pans,
and I have a little store of arrowroot, and gelatine
and such-like things, which I manipulate without upsetting the valuable time of the *chef*, who has so much
responsibility on his hands. And then I throw out a
hint that there will be a sovereign for somebody at
the end of the journey. Oh, these people are very
easy to manage," she said knowingly, " but they have
to be managed in the right way."

" And then the poor patient has to be managed in
the right way," I suggested.

" Well, the nurse who wants to cram her patient
with food as you would cram a cow with medicine is
neither more than less than a fool, and ought to have
her badge ripped off. Some nurses, you know," she
went on, " seem as if they cannot go into a house, or
into any kind of an establishment, without trying
how much they can do to upset all the domestic
arrangements. I am not one of that sort. I like to
see people sorry when I go, and glad if I trouble to
show my face again afterwards. One hears long-
winded tales about nurses being badly treated. Pooh!
I never get badly treated."

" I am sure," I cried, " you would never deserve it."

" That is why I never get it. Now, that obliging
young '*chef*' below here, he has given me two nice
little pans, one for meaty things and one for milky
things, and never once since we started, though I
have been down at least four times every day, have
I given him his pans back burned or not set to
rinse."

" What do you mean by being set to rinse ? "

" Well, filling them up with water as soon as you
have done with them. It makes all the difference
when a pan is done with whether you pop a little
water into it or not, or whether you leave it to get
caked and hard."

She turned round and accosted a sailor who happened to be passing. " What is the fuss, John ? " she
asked, in her brisk, pleasant, capable voice.

He told her that we were just nearing Aden.

Nurse Mordaunt turned round and looked at me.

" Now, I wonder," she said, in her brisk way, " I
wonder whether we shall have a word from your
good husband ? At all events, whether or no, we
shall have the satisfaction of sending a reassuring
cable to him."

CHAPTER XI

MY FIRST IMPRESSIONS OF HOME

I DID receive a message by cable from my husband
that day, indeed, as soon as we touched at Aden.
It seemed very short, but really it was as long as I
could reasonably expect. It said—"Fixture here.
No frontier news. All anxiety."

Nurse Mordaunt sent off our message to Eddy
from this place. She merely said, "Invalids steadily
improving."

"It is no use wasting money," she said sensibly,
"because we have no more information than that
to give him, and, of course, he will have a letter
from you much earlier than you can have one from
him."

I felt more satisfied after I had received Eddy's
message, because, if things remained quiet on the
frontier, and the threatened disturbances were quelled,
there was more than a chance that he would be able
to follow us and spend at least some time with us
in England. I scarcely, now that the wrench of
parting was over, regretted that I had been as it
were forced into leaving India. It was plain to the
meanest observation that the doctors had been right
in saying that such a journey would be the making
of me. With every day I recovered strength, and
became less of an invalid. I do not mean to say that

I was radiantly well, or that I was in anything like a normal condition of health, but I was not so terribly shattered and nerve-broken as I had been during the last few weeks. I was able to take an interest in the child, and to talk a little to my fellow-passengers, and to read and write quite long letters to Eddy. I used to write lying in my deck chair, upon a blotting-pad propped half on my knee and half upon the arm of my chair though I was only strong enough to do but a few lines at a time.

So our long journey wore itself away. When we reached Malta, Nurse Mordaunt insisted upon my going on shore and taking a drive. She also coaxed me into several shops, and tried to arouse my interest in that way. Oh, I was very much better than I had been, and after we got out of the Mediterranean and into the cooler breezes, I picked up my strength in a most wonderful manner.

" Why ! " Nurse exclaimed to me one day, when I was walking on deck, " Captain Hamlyn would hardly know you ! To think that this brisk young lady is the death-like little creature he carried on board is almost incredible ! "

" I don't feel like a brisk young lady, Nurse," I said deprecatingly.

" No, no, but you feel very different to what you did, and you look a thousand pounds better, while that dear baby is already a perfect picture."

That was quite true, and by the time that we reached our destination I could not shut my eyes to the immense improvement which had taken place in my own appearance. I was more like dear Father's " Dottikins " than I had been at any time since my marriage.

How well I remember my first sight of English

shores, of home—the home for which I had longed
so eagerly all my life. What a strange fate it was
that I should have come to it alone. I had planned
so often in my childhood the home-coming with my
dear mother, I had longed to come home with my
father, and both were lying quietly asleep in their
Indian graves, and would never see their native land
again. Then I had been so resolute in saying that
I would never return without my husband. And
by what a strange accident I had been forced from
my resolution, and sent across all those weary miles
of land and sea to seek health and strength upon the
shores of my native land, quite alone except for a
little child, who understood as yet nothing of the
difference between one country and another.

We reached Southampton just at the end of
October, and after staying there for a single night,
went the following day to London. On the whole
I was disappointed—yes, intensely disappointed. I
had expected such a grand city, almost that it would
really be paved with gold. I had thought to see
great palaces and mansions lining the broad road-
ways, and to see crowds of radiantly happy, well-
dressed people promenading up and down as I had
been accustomed to see the smartest people promenading up and down the different malls in India.
And the reality was gloom, or the sharpest of
sunlight and shadow. Splendid mansions cheek by
jowl with sordid tumble-down dwellings, beautiful
horses and equipages side by side with fusty cabs
and donkey-carts, beggars and patricians elbowing
each other, and mingling with both strange, flaunting,
painted women with manners as brazen as their
singularly profuse hair.

"It is horrible," I said to Nurse. "What a dreadful city! What rush, what hurry, what bustle! Oh, I don't like this London."

"Ah, you will get used to that," she said quietly. "When you have settled down comfortably in your hotel and have had your dinner, you will feel more at home; and to-morrow morning, when you see Sir Fergus Tiffany, he will tell you whether you ought to remain here, or where you should go for the best."

"I don't like your London," I said vehemently. "Whatever Sir Fergus Tiffany says of my health, I would not stay in London, Nurse. The smoke, the gloom, the dinginess, they are all detestable."

"Ah, well, it is the end of October, it is the worst part of the year," she said with the indifference of one who is evidently quite used to the general atmosphere. "See," she said, looking out, "that is the National Gallery where all the pictures are. It is one of the finest squares in Europe."

"Yes, it is big, but very dreary, and all the people look like flies walking about," I answered disconsolately. I looked out of the cab window. "I think your London is horrid," I said.

"Don't judge too hastily," said nurse, with a laugh. "Nobody sees the best of London on the day of their arrival from anywhere. London is best the better you know it."

I felt but little better satisfied, all the same, when we reached the hotel to which she had recommended me to go. It was not a very imposing building, but she said that they knew her, and that I should be extremely comfortable there, also that it was very quiet and convenient for the West End. I suppose it was all these things, but I was not used to English ways. I felt cold and wretched, and Ayah made me feel still colder, for she shivered and shuddered, and her teeth chattered, and when at last we got to the hotel, instead of finding everything ready for us, as we should have done in India, we had to wait ever so long before we could be accommodated with a private sitting-room; and even then they seemed to think that it was a most wonderful thing that I should require a fire.

"You will not require fires in your bedrooms, madam?" said the smart chambermaid who came to attend to us.

"Indeed, yes," I said indignantly, "in each bedroom, and plenty of wood. You do not understand how cold this climate is to anybody just arrived from India."

"You shall have a good supply of coals, madam," said the chambermaid, with an amused look at poor Ayah's brown face and expressive eyes.

Ayah curled herself up to the fire as near as she could very well squeeze, and lay there like a dog, chafing baby's little blue hands and coaxing her to take her milk, talking to her in soft Hindustani and unmistakably wishing that she were back in her native sunshine again.

Oh, how I did feel the cold, the damp, the thickness of the atmosphere! And shall I ever forget my first experience of a London fog, which put in an appearance the very next day! Nurse said it was a slight fog, that it was not really very bad, and that such an atmosphere as this was quite common in London during the autumn and winter months. I called it horrible. I sneezed and choked and sat huddled over the fire, feeling almost as wretched as poor Ayah looked—my eyes smarted, and my nose was quite sore. "Is it like this all over England?" I cried at last impatiently.

"No, no; this is peculiar to London," Nurse answered cheerfully. "You will soon get used to it."

"I shall never get used to it," I exclaimed indignantly.

"Oh, yes, you will. Besides, it won't last. I daresay it will be quite gone by the afternoon; at all events, it is ten chances to one that to-morrow will be a beautiful day."

But it was not gone by the afternoon, and the next day was not in any sense beautiful. Indeed, it was not until the third day after my arrival that I was able to go in a cab to keep an appointment with the great physician, Sir Fergus Tiffany.

To anyone who has been accustomed to medical men in India, or to military doctors, an interview with a great London specialist is at once a surprise and a revelation. In one sense I was charmed with Sir Fergus Tiffany. He was so bland, so urbane, so kind, so fatherly; but he told me nothing, or I should say he told me nothing definite.

He examined the child thoroughly, and then bade Ayah take her to the fire in the next room and keep her warm. "I do not think," he said, as the door closed behind her, "that you need have any anxiety now about the child. The voyage from India has evidently done great things for her, as your nurse here says. She is getting of an age when she must have care in feeding, and I will write you out a suitable dietary for a child of her age and of her tendency to trouble with her teeth, which I would have you follow as closely as is reasonable. What I mean is this—is Nurse Mordaunt remaining with you?"

"For the present, yes."

"Ah! Then I need hardly explain to you. You

G

understand, Nurse, follow the dietary as closely as is possible under existing circumstances."

"Very good, Sir Fergus," said Nurse, quietly.

He then made a thorough examination of my lungs and heart, tapped me and sounded me in every direction, until I began to feel as if I must have every disease of the chest known to the medical profession.

"Nothing radically wrong," I heard him murmur to Nurse. "Certain delicacy, heart not very strong, lungs should have care. How long are you staying in London, my dear lady?"

I told him that I was staying only until I could gain a definite opinion from him as to where I had better go for the winter. "I don't like London," I said decidedly.

"I would not keep you in London—no, not in London. I would like you to stay a fortnight, and I would like to put you on a course of tonic medicine and of equally tonic baths. Then I think it would be best to strike a mean between this climate and the one to which you have been used."

"Do you mean that I am to go to Egypt?" I said blankly.

"Scarcely so far as that," with a smile, "no, scarcely so far. I do not often prescribe Egypt for my patients. I have never known very much good result from a winter in Egypt; I much prefer several places on the Mediterranean."

"You mean the south of France?"

"Yes, the south of France or northern Italy. I do not believe in a very enervating climate. Now there is San Remo, but San Remo is for people in consumption, and I don't know that that would be particularly cheerful for you. You are not in consumption, nor at

all likely to be. There is a little place not very far
from Nice that I think will suit you to perfection.
It is bright without being glaring, quiet without
being dull. There is a nice colony of English resi-
dents and a very good English doctor. I know him
intimately. He would look after you and see that
you had everything comfortable, and that you were
taken care of. The place is called Florestella."

At this point Nurse Mordaunt gave vent to a
murmur of satisfaction. "I was hoping that you
would say Florestella, Sir Fergus," she said, in her
bright and capable way.

"Ah, it is not the first patient of mine that you
have taken to Florestella, Nurse, not the first by a good
many. I think Florestella would suit Mrs Hamlyn as
well as any place I know, and would be good for the
baby. Then, too, it would enable that dusky lady in
the next room to winter in Europe. I suppose you
have no wish to get rid of your ayah?"

"Oh, dear, no! I should be lost indeed without
her," I cried, with quite a rush of energy.

He asked me a good many questions—questions
about my husband, about my life, my father and
mother. It was as if he were trying to diagnose,
not my present state of health, but my constitution
—what one might call my hereditary tendencies.

"Well, if Captain Hamlyn comes home it will be
quite easy for him to join you at Florestella, and
would indeed give him a little more time with you
than if he had to come all the way to England. And
it would be very good for him, too. It is a very good
climate, a restorative climate."

"I don't think that my husband needs anything of
that kind," I said, with a laugh. "He has never had
a day's illness in his life; in fact, I do not think he

knows what ill-health is. One place is very much
the same to him as another."

"Except," put in Nurse, smiling, "except that he
has a preference for the place where madam is."

"Ah, yes!" I returned with a quick sigh. "But
then that is natural."

"Very natural," said Sir Fergus, holding out a kind,
white hand. "Well, now, do you stay in London a
fortnight, let me see the effect of my treatment upon
you, and then do you get away to Florestella, and
settle yourself there in a nice comfortable little hotel
which I will recommend to you, the hotel where I
send all my patients. We shall soon see if you are
not as strong and well as if you had never been in
India, or had an illness in your life."

As we drove away down Harley Street, Nurse Mordaunt turned and put a question to me.

"Now, Mrs Hamlyn," she said, "what do you think
of Sir Fergus?"

"Oh, I think he is quite delightful, Nurse; almost
too charming."

"He is nice," she said, half proudly. "Indeed, I
always feel when I take a patient to Sir Fergus
Tiffany for the first time that I am not only taking
them to a great doctor, I am introducing them to a
great pleasure. There is nobody quite like him. You
may be a duchess or you may be a charity patient,
Sir Fergus Tiffany's manner is always just the same.
He takes no more trouble with a duchess than he does
with the poor soul who cannot pay even a single fee.
His kindness is endless, his charity unlimited, his good
heart—Oh, what a heart it is! I don't know," she
went on, "that I ever knew any human being for
whom I have such a boundless respect as I have for
Sir Fergus Tiffany. And I was so hoping that he

would send you to Florestella. It is a dear little place, all among orange groves and myrtle trees, and set on the side of a hill which slopes down to the blue waters of the Mediterranean. The air is bright and crisp, and the life delightfully free and simple. Indeed, I think there is not such another place in all the wide world."

"You have been there more than once?" I asked.

"Several times. Many people go there year after year, and those who once get bitten with the love of it always seem to pine for it again. It is a little gem, half village, half town, and quite unspoiled by what makes most of the big places on the Riviera so unbearable. It is quite simple and primitive, quite unfashionable, and yet," she said, with a smile, "Florestella has a fashion of its own."

CHAPTER XII

FLORESTELLA

A WHOLE week had gone by since my first interview with Sir Fergus Tiffany. I was already greatly improved in health, and my first dislike of London was beginning to wear away. Nurse Mordaunt and I used to leave Ayah and baby in the hotel, to keep as warm as they could by the blazing fire, and go off on various errands of business or of pleasure. I liked hansom cabs, and when I had been to a good fur shop, and had bought myself a warm sealskin coat, I felt quite ready for any kind of climate in which I might happen to find myself.

I had instructions to go to Sir Fergus Tiffany every third day; and every day I had a very special kind of bath, which took two hours of the morning, while in the afternoons I did my shopping, for, naturally, I did not see being in London without taking the chance of buying myself some new and pretty clothing. I got through a good deal of money, but I enjoyed myself amazingly, as much as it was possible for me to enjoy anything which was not shared by my husband. I had a letter from him during that visit to London, written, poor dear, very soon after our departure, and full of regret and anxiety. I felt rather like a fraud, to think that he was worrying and anxious about me, and here was I gallivanting about London in hansom cabs, buying new dresses!

It did seem hard upon him, but I sent him a cable on our arrival, and, whether extravagant or not, I sent him another before I had been in London a week, just to say that I was better. I wrote to him, of course, but I did not see the good of his remaining for several weeks in an agony of anxiety when, by spending a few shillings, I could set his mind absolutely at rest without any delay whatever.

When I went to Sir Fergus Tiffany for the third time, he told me that I should be quite able to go to Florestella at the end of another week, and that I might safely make my arrangements in accordance with that opinion. I certainly liked London better than I had done at first, but I was delighted at his verdict, partly because I was so glad that he really thought me improved in health, and partly because I was well pleased at the prospect of getting out of the London atmosphere, which tried me terribly.

"I will write to the hotel at once, this very day, and arrange about our rooms," I said to Nurse, as we drove through Cavendish Square. "You know I like London much better than I did, but I shall be delighted to find myself in sunshine again. I cannot think how English people look so well, and yet have no sunshine."

"But they do have sunshine," said Nurse, smiling. "They do have sunshine, only not just at this time of the year. In spring and in summer London is lovely, and people grumble then because they have too much sunlight."

"Ah, well, I like sunshine all the year round. I shall be delighted to find myself at Florestella," I cried.

She was silent for a minute or two, then she looked at me half hesitatingly. "Mrs Hamlyn," she said, "you have relations in England?"

" Yes, I have some relations, cousins and such like, but I have never seen them, and I have never had any communication with them whatever. They are the same as nothing to me."

" But your husband, he has relations ?   He told me at the last moment, just as we left Bombay, that if I was in urgent need of consultation—that is to say, meaning if you should be dying or anything of that kind, that I was to write or telegraph to his mother or to his uncle, Lord Clovelly.   Are you going abroad without seeing either of them ? "

I felt myself stiffen all over.   "I have no desire to see either my mother-in-law or Lord Clovelly. Nurse," I said quietly, "if I had been at any time in a dying condition, it would, of course, have been best for you to carry out my husband's instructions, which were, however, meant only to be followed in case of dire emergency.   Of my own free will I shall never meet Mrs Hamlyn, my mother-in-law.   She has not been nice to me, she has not been nice to her son in the matter of his marriage ; she is not a nice woman. I have no desire to see her, and I don't think that she has the smallest desire to see me.   Besides that, she does not live in London, or near London ; she lives in Devonshire.   I believe it is a very long journey."

" Yes, it is a long journey, but Lord Clovelly—possibly he may be in London," she suggested.

" I have no wish to see Lord Clovelly.   I want to see nobody.   I am quite a stranger and alone, pray do not say anything more about it.   Nothing would induce me to go near any of these people."

" I see," she murmured comprehensively.   " Excuse me for speaking of it, pray.   I had no wish to pry into your private affairs ; it was only that I wanted to remind you that, if we are going to Florestella

in a week's time, you have but little chance before
you of paying or receiving visits."

"Oh, that is all right, Nurse. You are most kind
to me," I cried. I put my hand upon hers because
she had been so good, so anxious about me, so more
than careful of my interests, that I would not have
hurt her feelings or have appeared wishful to snub
her for the whole world. "Captain Hamlyn will not
expect me to go near his people," I went on. "You
see they have not been quite as nice to me—at least,
his mother has not been quite as nice to me as she
might have been—as for his sake she might have
been," I added; "and it will be time enough for me
to meet them when he returns home. By myself I
shall never go near any of them."

Nurse said no more on the subject, neither did I.
The week went by, Sir Fergus Tiffany expressed himself completely satisfied with my progress, and, on
the day that we had originally appointed, we turned
our backs upon London and set our faces towards
the blue waters of the Mediterranean.

I found Florestella all, and indeed more, than Nurse
Mordaunt had claimed for it. It was, as she had said,
a gem of a place, set like a nest on the side of a hill,
with quaint little streets, quaint, picturesque houses
snugly hidden in groves of orange and myrtle trees,
bathed in sunshine, and the most cheerful little place
that I had ever been in. The blue waters of the
Mediterranean were an everlasting charm to me, and
Ayah used to sit sunning herself and baby, with every
expression of satisfaction on her lips and in her dark
eyes.

I found the little hotel to which Sir Fergus Tiffany
had recommended us extremely homelike and comfortable — something more than comfortable. He

had called it a little hotel, but it was not in reality
a very small place, but was, indeed, a long, low, ram-
bling building, standing in a beautiful, well-kept
garden, and having various villas and *dépendances*
attached to it. It was in one of these villas, which
communicated with the garden, that we had our
suite of apartments, which consisted of a charming
sitting-room and three fine and airy bedrooms. It
was not cheap—oh, dear, no! But then, as I said
to Eddy when writing to him and describing the
exact details of our every-day life, where would have
been the advantage of saving a few pounds at the
expense of my health, which we were so anxious to
completely restore? And apart from the actual cost
of living, our expenses were very small and our life
quite simple.

I spent a good deal of time idling about the gardens
and the quaint little streets of Florestella. I made
friends at the hotel, just friends in passing without
any great intimacy on either side, and Nurse and
I used to share their drives and their little excursions
in the immediate neighbourhood.

"If Captain Hamlyn does get leave," said Nurse
to me one morning, when I had received a letter from
Eddy, in which he spoke of matters on the frontier
having simmered down a good deal, and that there was
more than a chance he might be able to join me after
all, "he will scarcely believe that it is really you that
he will find here. You know, Mrs Hamlyn, it is a
great extravagance keeping me any longer, because
I am really of no use to you now."

"Oh, don't leave me!" I cried. "I am getting
better, but I should run down again to a certainty
if you were not here. You act as a check upon me,
you are the last link with my husband, and I feel

more safe about baby whilst you are here. Don't even speak of going away—you can't want to go away," I answered almost fretfully.

"No, no. I don't want to go away, but I am thinking of the expense to you."

"Oh, well, I am better, and I don't mind the little expense if my health is quite restored. I am getting on fast, Nurse, but I shall not get on fast if you go away. I prefer you to stop."

"Then, of course, I will stop," she said promptly. "I don't generally like an idle life, or to remain longer with a patient than there is actual need of my services, but I am very happy here with you, and I am quite content to remain as long as you think I can do you the smallest good. By-the-bye," she remarked, in a different tone, "you know that there are some new people come this morning?"

"No, I did not know it. Who are they?"

"It is an Austrian princess—a sweet-looking elderly lady, with an invalid daughter. Such a string of people they have brought with them, such a string of people! They have taken the royal suite on the first floor, but if the young lady finds the noise too much, they are going into the Villa Florestella as soon as it is vacant."

"And what is the matter with the daughter?" I asked.

"A kind of fading away, from what I could gather," nurse replied. "I saw her helped out of the carriage. She looks very ill."

"Is she young?"

"Oh, yes, quite young—not thirty I should say, though you never can tell with invalids; perhaps not more than seven or eight-and-twenty."

"Poor thing!" I said, with a sigh. "Ah, well, she

could not come to a sweeter place than this, and I
don't know if it would not be easier dying in such a
sweet spot than in some great gloomy city."

"I don't think the place makes much difference
when you get to that," said Nurse. "Most people
when they come to die care very little about it one
way or the other. In all my experience of nursing,"
she went on, "I have never in my life once seen any
fear of death. With those who go sharply after quick
illnesses, they know very little about the end, and
those who go slowly get so physically worn out that
they do not care much which way it goes with them."

"Yes, that was how I felt when I left India,"
I replied. "I would much rather have stayed there
quietly and died comfortably, than have come over
here alone and got well, as I have done."

"But you are glad now?" she said, in her bright,
decided way.

"Oh, yes, I am glad now for my husband's sake,
because he will be so happy to have me strong and
well again. And, of course, there is baby to think
of; for her sake as well as for his I am more than
glad that I made the effort, or rather," I added, with
a smile, "that you and Captain Hamlyn made it for
me."

"Yes, yes. I knew you would feel like that," she
said, in a tone of much satisfaction.

I did not see the Austrian princess or her invalid
daughter for more than a week after their arrival
at the Hôtel des Anglais. I heard, through Nurse,
that the invalid Princess Elisabeth, as they called her,
was suffering from the effects of her journey. Then
she told me that the princess herself had been for
a walk in the gardens, and that Princess Elisabeth
was going out in a bath-chair later on. A few days

after this I saw the two ladies, the younger one being
wheeled in an invalid chair by a very tall man-servant,
while her mother walked beside her. It was only a
passing glimpse that I caught of them. The invalid
struck me as being very sweet-looking, but very
fragile and ailing; the mother was tall and of a distinguished appearance, with an imperious carriage of
head and throat, with that sweet yet proud expression
of eyes and face which somehow one learns to
associate with the *grande noblesse*, and very seldom
finds in that class when one is brought into contact
with it. I was conscious from the mere glance I had
in passing, that both were elegantly dressed, that the
servant wore a very elaborate livery, that they were
unmistakably people of great wealth as well as of
position.

From time to time I met them about the gardens,
but they did not in any way associate with the other
inmates of the hotel. They were quite the richest
and the most important people among the guests, and
as they were extremely exclusive and made no ad-
vances towards a single soul, naturally nobody among
the guests was able to make their acquaintance.

I used to hear the latest news of Princess Elisabeth
through Nurse Mordaunt, who quickly made the
acquaintance of the English-trained nurse in attendance upon her. "The young princess is a little better
to-day," she used to say to me, when she came to my
room in the morning. "I saw her nurse just now.
She has had a better night, and feels very much
refreshed. I don't believe that they will pull her
through; and yet, if any place in the world will
restore her to health and strength, Florestella is that
place. Ah, here is Ayah. Well, Ayah, how is your
charge this morning?"

It happened that Ayah's English was exceedingly limited in quantity, so instead of answering Nurse Mordaunt other than by a smile, she addressed herself to me. "Missy Baba is not very well this morning," she informed me. "Would the mem sahib order nurse to come in and see her?"

"Nurse," I said, turning to her, "Ayah is anxious about baby; do go in and see what is the matter."

CHAPTER XIII

STRICKEN FLORESTELLA

WHEN Nurse Mordaunt came back to my room after visiting baby, she was inclined to make light of her indisposition. "Oh, there is nothing the matter with the child," she said; "that ayah worships her so much that she is over anxious. She has had a fretful night, but what child that is teething does not sometimes have that? It would be just as well if the doctor sees her when he comes to you this morning. But you must not be surprised at her age if she does ail from time to time, and Ayah is absurdly anxious."

Nurse's words proved to be true. The doctor pronounced that little Frances was slightly upset over a tooth that was in process of making its way through her gums, but beyond prescribing a simple, cooling powder, he did nothing, and he bade us not have any anxiety about her. For several weeks this kind of health remained the child's portion. She got each tooth with a certain amount of trouble, and with a good deal of fretfulness, but she did not lose weight, and she certainly throve generally.

I had grown thoroughly accustomed to my life at Florestella before I had any definite news of my husband. I do not mean that I did not hear from him—that I did every mail—but until this letter he sent me no definite news of his plans. The trouble on the frontier had not simmered down so effectually as to allow him to have leave to join me in Europe; on the contrary, I eventually received the news that he had got his orders for " the Bhozàr Expedition," and was to start immediately. " Before you receive this I shall be actually at the front," he wrote. " I have not cabled the news to you because I shall be in no more danger than if I were still at Muttrahabad. You will understand, my dearest," he added, " that in all active service no news is good news. If any harm should happen to me you will hear it soon enough, so if you do not have my letters quite regularly, you are not to fret yourself to fiddlestrings, and think that I am dead and done for. If anything happens to me you will know it within a few hours. Write to me as often as you can, tell me all the news that you have, and I shall expect your assurance in each letter that you are not fretting and moping, and wearing yourself to a shadow with anxiety. Keep all your energies for getting well, and thinking of the blessed time when we shall be together again."

It was all very well to say that, to bid me neither mope nor worry, but what woman, who loved her husband as I loved my Eddy, could know that he had gone to the front on a dangerous expedition, and yet go on enjoying herself as if nothing out of the common had happened? Not I, for one. The receipt of his letter was a terrible shock to me, and my health fell away with alarming rapidity.

" It was just as well," said Nurse Mordaunt, a few days after I had received the news of Eddy's whereabouts, " that you did so resolutely keep me here. I am afraid that you are not as thoroughly established in health as you might be, since this news has so com-

pletely unnerved you and thrown you back again.
But you must be brave; you must make an effort;
you must think of the husband who is always thinking of you, and of the child who may one day need
you far more than she does now. Now I have got a
nice little cup of strong bouillon; it is something
quite superior to the ordinary wash they give you in
this part of the world, and I want you to dispose of
it at once."

I was like a child in her hands. I had to do what
she told me, and I drank the strong broth—which
I disliked intensely—as I would have taken some
nauseous draught of medicine at her hands. But I
did not recover my strength quite as well as she
desired me to do, and my anxiety about my husband
was increased by my inquietude as to little Frances,
who seemed by this time to be losing strength with
every hour and to be relapsing once more into the
pitiable state in which we had brought her from
India.

About this time, too, the neighbourhood of Florestella was greatly disturbed by rumours of an insidious
kind of low fever which seemed to be permeating the
entire district. At that time of day influenza had
not set its seal upon the world, but I have often
thought since that surely influenza did not in truth
come from Russia but from that particular neighbourhood of which Florestella was the centre.

"I think we ought to move on, Mrs Hamlyn,"
Nurse said to me one day, when I was sitting out
under the orange trees watching the child lying still
and inert in Ayah's arms.

"Yes, but where shall we go?" I asked.

"I will make inquiries. I feel suspicious about
this place. I see so many children playing about

the village who look as this baby looks, not so much
definitely ill as bleached and transparent. In two
or three cases I have stopped and asked the mothers
what ailed the child, always to receive the same
answer, an indefinite allusion to 'the fever,' as if
feverishness was quite a common complaint among
them. I fancy there is something wrong with the
drainage and the general health of the place. I
should like to move on."

"The question is where?" I said anxiously.

"I will make inquiries," said Nurse, in her definite
and decided tones.

The result of her inquiries was to assure us that
the only healthy spot for miles around was Florestella. She appealed to the doctor, and the doctor
told her that many invalids had been hustled off to
Florestella from the other towns, and that they had
brought with them a certain amount of an indefinite
kind of epidemic which was troubling the entire
Riviera.

"Do you think," I said to him, when he had given
us this piece of information, "that I should be wiser
if I took baby to England, or quite away from the
Riviera? Because I am now well enough to live
anywhere, for a time at all events, and she is the
most important patient of the two."

For a moment or so he did not reply. I saw Nurse
look at him anxiously, and with an indescribable
manner, which told me somehow that his reply was a
foregone conclusion.

"Mrs Hamlyn," he said, in a low voice, "I don't
want to frighten you; I don't believe in breaking
down people's hopes, particularly a mother who has,
as you have at present, the sole care of a child, an
only child, and other anxious troubles besides; but

indeed I cannot recommend you to take that child a long journey in her present state of health. It is a very bad time of the year for travelling, the child is exceedingly delicate, and her system has been a good deal undermined by this continued fever. I don't think you would succeed in getting her to England alive, and, believe me, to leave this place you would have to travel through districts which are far more seriously infected than Florestella. I cannot advise you to take her away just at present. I mean this," he said, hastily, before I had time to speak, "and if it were my own wife whom I were advising about our own child, I would give to her the same advice that I am now giving to you—you are safer here, the child has a better chance here than she would or could have by being moved just at this juncture."

"Then," I said, looking at nurse, "that settles the question. Here we will remain."

I thought she was a little disappointed. "There is no place higher up, no place within easy reach?" she said, looking at the doctor.

"Florestella has the cleanest bill of health for at least fifty miles around," he made reply. "Mrs Hamlyn, I will not hide from you the great danger that besets you. I am your countryman, you know —you must feel that I would not deceive you or lie to you for any consideration in the world; but, believe me, you are safer here than you would be in leaving, and the child has a better chance."

What could I do in the face of such advice as this? It would have seemed like flying in the face of Providence if I had done as Nurse Mordaunt plainly and unmistakably wished me to do—that is, pack up my belongings and leave Florestella immediately. I do not think, although I was so much better in health, that I had ever felt so helpless as I did that day. I felt as if I had no will power of my own; I felt as if I was caught like a bird in a trap, like a fly in a spider's web; I could only lean on these two strong natures—and they were opposed to each other.

"I wish," said Nurse, vexedly, when the doctor had taken his leave of me, "I wish that he had said differently. I should like to get you away from this place. I feel nervous and uneasy both about you and the child."

"But the doctor gave chapter and verse," I said to her. "He gave us good reasons. I could not take upon myself to carry a sick child on such a long journey at this time of the year, when the doctor had warned me that it would probably be her death. And he did, Nurse, he was quite positive about it. Think what it would be in England now, with the east winds blowing, and Ayah cringing and shuddering, and the poor child with inflammation of the lungs, or something of that kind. Why, she would not have a chance, even if she got there alive."

"No, I would not take her to England, but there are other places besides England to which we might have gone. We might have gone over the border into Italy, and found some healthy spot where we should have been free of this pestilence—this insidious epidemic, which nobody seems to understand."

"Yes, that is true enough," I said, "if we had gone in the first instance; but, as Dr Knowles said, we have to get through a large district that is much more full of infection than Florestella. You know, Nurse, Florestella does stand high."

"Yes, yes, it stands high, but I wish we stood somewhere else," she said anxiously.

For a few days after this, my baby rallied wonderfully, and became quite bright again. A mother's heart catches eagerly at any sign of improvement in a sick child, and I felt, oh, so gay, so glad, to think I had done the right thing in following the doctor's wishes, so thankful, so joyous, I almost forgot that my husband had gone off on an expedition of the gravest danger, and that we were by no means out of the wood yet.

"You see, Nurse," I said triumphantly, "the doctor was right. She is pulling up beautifully. Why, look at her, she looks quite herself again."

"Yes, yes, I was only anxious for your sake and hers, and thankful am I to see the smallest sign of improvement in her, Mrs Hamlyn," said Nurse, promptly.

There was nothing mean, petty, or small about Nurse Mordaunt's character. She frankly owned herself wrong, and admitted the fact with cheerfulness and thanksgiving.

I had no letter from Eddy by that mail. In the English papers I saw some small and meagre accounts that a certain expedition had been sent to Bhozàr. It gave no details, spoke of it as one of those petty wars which are of no account, and only laid stress upon the necessity of teaching the hill tribes of the Bhozàr district a sharp lesson which they would not forget in a hurry. Ay, but those sharp lessons often cost very dear to those who teach them. I am afraid, soldier's daughter and wife as I was, that at that moment I would cheerfully and gladly have left the hill tribes of the Bhozàr district to do what they would, so long as my nearest and dearest were out of their reach. I had often heard it said that women have no true imperialism, that they have but a small

love of duty, that they can never dissociate the detail
of personal feeling from a general idea of honour and
glory, and assuredly I had none of these feelings, and
never could feel in sympathy with those wives of
olden time who had urged their men-folk on to doing
great deeds against desperate odds. I felt no pride
that my husband had gone to the front on an exceedingly dangerous expedition, and that he might come
back covered with glory and medals, and even with a
title—oh, dear, no! I would have foregone all earthly
honours and all the imperishable laurels of history to
have had him safe and sound even in fever-stricken
little Florestella.

It was not many days after this that my new-born
hopes about baby and the safety of Florestella all died
out. "Nurse," I said to her one day, "you are getting fidgety and uneasy about something. What is
it? Don't keep me in the dark if you have any
news."

My mind had gone instinctively out to the husband
from whom I had not heard by the last mail. "Tell
me," I went on, "have you had news from India?
Don't keep anything back from me. It would be mistaken kindness to do so."

"Oh, no, Mrs Hamlyn," she replied, "I have had no
news from India; I should not keep it a moment if I
had, even if it was the very worst that could happen.
I am uneasy and nervous—it is no use pretending
otherwise since you have observed it. They tell me
that the epidemic—fever—whatever it is—is very
much worse, and that Florestella itself is getting more
unsafe with every hour. That poor young Princess
Elisabeth is very ill; they don't think that she will
leave this place alive, and one of her English nurses
died yesterday."

"What!" I exclaimed.

"Yes. It has been hushed up, they don't want the people to know, but she died of the fever. It is like a plague; I have never seen anything like it, in all my experience. It seems to steal upon people unobserved, to sap their strength, and then they are gone like a snap of the fingers. I cannot make it out. I have never seen anything like it. The only thing to do with baby is to keep her in the hotel and the gardens. Don't let Ayah set foot outside the gates. We know that the hotel drainage is better than the drainage in the village—at least, it is likely to be better in the usual course of things, and we must watch the child and you day and night. After all," she added, "it is a great thing that she is keeping as well as she seems to be."

"What are the people in the hotel saying?" I asked.

"Oh, the landlord is pitiable about it, quite abject. I met him this morning, and I spoke to him of the dreadful state of affairs all round, and, poor soul! the tears came into his eyes, and he said it was a judgment upon Florestella, but he could not tell what Florestella had done. These southern people are so superstitious," she ended, with a half contemptuous smile.

But alas, alas! With all our care, with all our precautions, our hopes, our watchings, we did not succeed in keeping the dread enemy at bay. Another week went by, a week in which my little Frances seemed to pale and blanch and dwindle like a plant that is denied light and water. Then there was a few hours' increase of fever, and we three, so widely different— Nurse, Ayah and I—but all alike in our love and our anxiety, stood gazing down upon a little form

from which the spark of life had fled for ever.
It was all over—I had no child now. I had done my
best. I had struggled through the bad time, more for
Eddy's sake and for the child's than for my own, and
this was the end of it. I was a childless mother,
broken, sick, and practically alone upon a foreign
shore, with a husband who hourly carried his life in
his hand, and that upon the other side of the world.
And I was not yet twenty years old !

CHAPTER XIV

THE PRINCESS ELISABETH

I was very ill for many days after my baby was taken away. All the arrangements for her little funeral were of necessity left to Nurse Mordaunt, who came and sat by my couch, and told me in her kind and tender voice, which I had not previously in my admiration for her decisiveness of character thought it would be possible to modulate to such gentle and subdued accents, all the arrangements which she had made on my behalf. She had chosen my little darling's last sleeping-place on a sunny slope of the graveyard high up the hillside, so that she would lie for ever in the golden sunlight which had mostly been her portion during her short sojourn on this earth.

"The lovely scented petals of the rose trees which bloom all over the graveyard will shower down upon her," Nurse said, holding my hand in hers. "No little child could have a more fitting place in which to lie," she ended gently.

I heard all that she had to tell. I had no tears. I did not weep, and wail, and fret and cry as some young mothers would have done—my grief was beyond that.

"I met the princess this morning," Nurse continued. 'She had come out into the garden to get a breath of

air before going to lie down. She had been up most
of the night with her daughter."

"And her daughter, how is she ?" I asked.

"Very, very ill. The princess stopped, and asked
after you; she bade me say that she was sorry for
your loss, and that she sympathised so much with
you. She told me that she had sent for some flowers
for you."

Late that evening Nurse Mordaunt brought me a
great, loosely-tied bunch of pure white blossoms, all
sweet-scented and fresh as the day, with a visiting
card attached to the end of one of the broad white
streamers with which the bouquet was tied. It bore
the name and coronet of the Princess Barzadiev, and
at the very top was written in a delicate pointed
hand, "With heart-felt sympathy from an anxious
mother." Nothing so far had touched me so much
as this message from one who was watching her only
daughter quietly fading away, one who had everything
that wealth, skill and love could do at her command,
and who was yet as powerless to stay the dread blow
so fast approaching as I had been in the case of my
little child with only her babe's feeble hold upon
life.

I think every lady in the hotel must have sent me
flowers that evening. When they carried my little
Frances away, the tiny bier upon which her little
white coffin lay was so heaped up with pure white
blossoms that the silken covering which shrouded it
was in reality not needed.

"Put the princess's flowers with my own," was the
only instruction that I gave.

So I let them take her away—the child I had come
so far to save—the child who was lost to me, so far
as this world goes, for ever.

Some days went by before I was able to leave my
sofa and get out into the air again. Even then I
was good for so little and had so little reserve of
strength that I was obliged to avail myself of an
invalid chair.

Poor, heart-broken Ayah was pushing it along a
secluded pathway one day, and Nurse was walking
beside me, when we came suddenly upon the Princess
Barzadiev, who was walking alone, having evidently
just come out of her apartments for a breath of the
cool morning air. She stopped on seeing us and held
out her hand to me—such a slim, white, refined hand,
just a match for her delicate, high-bred face. She
addressed me in very good English, and though she
said little about my loss, yet contrived to make me
feel that she had real sympathy with me. "I have
thought of you so often during these past few days,"
she said, "because, you know, my heart is aching
with the same sorrow which has torn yours so cruelly.
I cannot hope ever to take my only daughter away
alive from this spot where we have hoped such great
things might be done for her. If we could have got
away a month ago there might have been a chance—
a poor chance, and yet one at which we would have
caught so eagerly. As it is, this terrible fever has
her in its clutches, and it has become a question of
how long her strength will hold out against it, nothing
more than that."

I knew not what to say; I was very young, and I
was broken down by my own troubles. I think I just
held her hand and listened while the tears ran down
my face in mute sympathy, which perhaps needed no
words. I tried, when I found my voice, to thank her
for the exquisite flowers that she had sent me, and for
the sympathy which she had expressed for me. Then

Nurse asked, in her direct, simple, and frank way, whether she had succeeded in replacing the nurse whom they had lost. The princess told her no, that the remaining nurse was almost worn out, and that her own maids were doing their best to take her place. " But," she said, in her sweet, sad voice, " they are French women ; their cleverness consists in making one's toilet, not in sick nursing, and Nurse and I have to do the best we can between us."

I looked at Nurse Mordaunt and Nurse looked at me, a question in both our eyes, and hovering upon both our lips. Then I nodded to her, and she said, " Oh, madame, if I could be of any use to you, Mrs Hamlyn would not miss me very much. She has the ayah at her disposal."

" Oh, I could not take your one comfort away from you," cried the princess, instantly.

" Pray, don't speak of it like that. Nurse Mordaunt is a comfort," I cried. " I don't deny it, but it will be a greater comfort to me to feel that she is with you in this sore strait. And besides, I can see her sometimes, and I have Ayah, who has been with me ever since my little child was born. She understands me, she can do everything that I require. I am not ill, madame, only troubled in heart and mind. Pray, if Nurse Mordaunt will be of the very smallest comfort to you, take her as freely and ungrudgingly as I give her to you, as I know and I feel from your message and your kindness to me, you would have given her to me."

For a moment I think that the princess was tempted to refuse our offer, then she suddenly bent down and, taking both my hands, kissed me upon either cheek. " I can never repay you," she said. " No words, no actions of mine could ever make you feel how grate-

ful, how intensely grateful I am to you, but your
mother's heart will tell you more than my lips could
possibly do."

She kissed me again, then turned and clasped
nurse's hand in hers. "Come round to my rooms,"
she said, in a choking voice, and then, drawing the
fine laces with which her head and shoulders were en-
veloped still more closely round her, she turned
abruptly and left us.

"You don't mind? You quite understood me?"
Nurse Mordaunt exclaimed, turning towards me
when we had watched the straight, slim, black-
robed figure disappear along the alley of myrtle
trees.

"Oh, yes, Nurse, I quite understood. My need of
you is over, Ayah can do everything that I require,
and, after all, I am not ill, I am not like that poor girl,
who is actually at death's door. I am afraid, Nurse,"
I said presently, "that you have another sad experience before you. You cannot hope to be more than
an alleviation to her."

"That is a great deal when you come to the end,"
she rejoined.

So she left me, and took up her new charge, spending all her time with the Austrian princess and her
sick daughter. Of course, she was still my nurse;
I had only lent her for the moment to these strangers,
who were in trouble as I was. She slept in her own
room, the room next to mine, and she came in and out
when she was off duty, always full of the sweetness
and kindliness of the Austrian lady's character, always full of the unspeakable resignation and patience
of the Princess Elisabeth. "I have always heard,"
she said, "that the Austrian nobility were so eaten
alive with pride. They may be so, but it is a different

kind of pride to what we call such. These ladies may be proud ; they may be too proud to know people who have made their money in byways and highways, who have soiled their fingers by all sorts of illegitimate bargainings and transactions, but in everyday life they are delightful ; so simple, so charming, so homely, and yet of such dignity. It is a pleasure to be with them, to associate with them. Those two French maids," she added in a different tone, "are not up to very much. They may be good in their own line, they may be able to dress their ladies well and take care of complexions, but in an emergency—pooh! they are not worth their salt.

"I thought they had done their best?" I said, in surprise.

"Yes, so they say, and a very poor best it is. There is a creature called Stephanie, Princess Elisabeth's own maid, who has been three years with her ; she has no more idea how to dress an invalid's hair than she would have as to how one should groom a horse ! She has no more idea how to make her comfortable, how to settle her and refresh her than a child. She is not very young, but her only idea of making the poor thing's toilet is to bring her a lot of scents and face-washes, and such like, and then to get curling-tongs and curl her fringe up ! Idiot ! Forgive me, Mrs Hamlyn, for unburdening my mind of all this out to you, but I cannot say anything there. Princess Elisabeth is filled with an idea that Stephanie is the most devoted creature on the face of the earth. I call Stephanie a fool, but all the same, Stephanie is a perfect marvel of wisdom in comparison with the other idiot who waits upon madame herself. Talk about French women being natty and domestic and homely, this precious pair

are fit for Bedlam! I asked Victoire, yesterday,
if she would fetch a little wrap for madame, who
was sitting on the balcony, and who had just gone
out from her daughter's room with every probability of getting a chill and a severe attack of fever.
She went and fetched her a thing that would have
done to go to the opera in, a thing all point lace and
glittering spangles that rattled, and feathers and
satin and such like. I looked at Victoire," Nurse
Mordaunt went on, "and Victoire slunk out of the
room abashed. Oh, I think she was ashamed of
herself—yes. Of course, it is something to make
a flighty Frenchwoman feel that she has shown
an appalling want of sense. I went to the door, and
I said, 'If you will bring your lady something soft
and woolly, which will keep her warm without
making a noise, you can put that thing away.
She brought a very nice Shetland shawl, and I
wrapped the poor lady carefully in it to her extreme
gratification."

"And Princess Elisabeth, how is she to-day?" I
asked.

"Very ill. I don't think the end can be very
far off now. She is so thin, so transparent, so
bloodless, so lifeless; and, Mrs Hamlyn, she is very
anxious to see you."

"To see me!" I ejaculated.

"She says you have saved her mother so much
anxiety, and added so much to her comfort by giving
me up to her. It is no use to tell her that I was
really unnecessary to you, she won't believe that.
She asked me if I would say to you with her compliments that it would give her the greatest pleasure
if you would pay her a visit if only for a few
minutes. She said, 'Say to the English lady that

I am not very strong and I cannot talk for long, but I would like to have half-a-dozen words with her. 1 am too weak to write, but I can express myself with a look.' I told her, poor thing, that I knew you would come. I have talked to her a good deal about you and your anxiety about your husband, of your pluck, and I have told her over and over again of how he came down to Bombay with you, how ill you were, how unwilling to leave him, how distressed he was when he received his message of recall. I have told her over and over again, for she never seems to be tired of hearing it, what a brave, gallant, upright, handsome soldier he is, of how he loves you, and of how you love him. It is her favourite subject of conversation. She never seems to be tired of talking about you or of hearing me talk, so if you will come you will add one more kindness to what you have done for them already."

I almost laughed. It seemed so preposterous that I, a little unknown nobody from far-off India, who had come alone, ill, friendless, to this great continent of Europe, should find it in my power to do kindnesses to these rich and powerful women who were as the salt of the earth. Truly it was a case of the mouse and the lion. "Why, of course, Nurse, you knew that you could answer for me. I wil come with pleasure, and do you give me a nod if I tire her or if my visit seems to be too much for her. I will try to be very quiet, I will try not to upset her in any way, but you might give her a hint that I am not well, that I am in trouble, too, and not to say much about my anxieties, and my troubles, because I am easily upset and unnerved. When shall I come ? "

"If you come round in a quarter of an hour I think that would satisfy her, and I will tell you when she has had as much as she can bear."

It was then just hard upon sundown. I let Nurse go back, and when a few minutes had gone by, I wrapped a black lace shawl about my head and shoulders, and went across the garden from our villa to that part of the hotel in which the princesses' suite of apartments was.

The princess herself received me. "Mrs Hamlyn, this is so kind of you," she said. "My daughter had such an intense desire to see you, and I confess that I hesitated to trespass further upon your goodness."

I made haste to assure her that I was but too pleased to come if my coming would give the very smallest pleasure to her dear invalid. And then she bade me accompany her to her daughter's room.

So I was taken immediately into the chamber where the young Princess Elisabeth lay a-dying.

CHAPTER XV

I ONLY stayed a few minutes by the bedside of the young princess on that my first visit to her. Of course, I saw at the first glance that her days were numbered; the most unprofessional eye could not have mistaken the signs of approaching dissolution so painfully manifest in that sweet face. It was a sweet face, not very much like madame, her mother, and yet bearing something of the same impress.

"It is so kind of you to come and see me," she said, holding out a thin and fragile hand which lay burning in my own like a red-hot coal, " because I am such an invalid at present, and cannot talk much or in any way entertain you. I wanted to see you—I had a great desire to see you—to thank you with all my heart for having given up your charming nurse to me. It was unfortunate that my second English nurse was taken ill, and had to go back to England, and that my mother was not able to replace her as easily as she imagined she would be able to do."

So they had not told her of the nurse's death, and probably she knew nothing of the fever with which Florestella was stricken. I hastened to assure her that in truth it had been no great sacrifice on my part to give up Nurse Mordaunt to her. " You see, I have my ayah," I said, " and she understands my ways and is able to do everything that I require. I was indeed very glad that Nurse was able to come to you."

"Ah, that is your kind way of putting it," she said, lying back on her pillows and looking at me with her large hazel eyes; "that is your way of putting it, Mrs Hamlyn, but because you do not allow that your kindness is worth mention, my mother and I are not obliged to agree with you. You will never know the difference that it has made to us to have such a nurse as this suddenly placed at our disposal. Some day, perhaps, we may be able to repay your self-sacrifice, but only in a measure, never as it deserves."

The effort of talking seemed to exhaust her terribly, and Nurse looked at me warningly, as if it would be best if I took myself away.

"I think you are tired to-night, princess," I said to the invalid. "Don't you think it would be better if I came in again to see you? At any time, if you send Nurse for me, I will come to see you with pleasure."

She just touched my hand again and smiled. "You are very good," she said, under her breath, as I rose from my chair, "you are very good. Come and see me again."

Nurse Mordaunt went out of the room with me. As she closed the door behind her, I turned and asked her a question. "Will she live through the night, do you think?"

"Oh, yes," Nurse replied, "she may live for weeks; she has a wonderful store of strength behind all that exhaustion. She will rally presently; she does that every day, that is the worst part of her complaint. She might have lived for months, or dragged on even for years, if it had not been for this fever. Poor girl, it is that which is sapping her life out at the veryroot."

As I passed down the corridor, I saw the princess,

who was in her sitting-room and on the look-out for me. "I was afraid to stay in the room with my daughter," she said, drawing me to the window, "because every extra person who is breathing the air tends to exhaust her. That is why I slipped away when I had taken you in. Tell me what you think of her."

"I think she looks terribly ill, madame," I replied.

"Yes, yes, more than ill. I shall not have my child with me long. I am quite prepared for it. I have expected it, feared it, dreaded it for months past, but it has been very near during these past few days. It comes nearer with every moment. She was pleased to see you?" she continued, with a great effort at cheerfulness.

"She seemed to be so; she begged me to go and see her again. You will send for me, madame, at any time that I can be of the smallest pleasure or distraction to her."

"You are remaining in Florestella?" she said.

"I am remaining for the present because I dread leaving, and the doctor fears for my taking a journey while my health is so bad as it is just now. I don't think that I shall get the fever. I don't feel like it."

"Ah, one never knows. It would be better to get away. I cannot go, of course. . . . I could not move my daughter in her present condition, that is out of the question. But you—your tie here is broken; you have yourself and your husband to think of. My dear friend," she went on, laying her slim hand upon my shoulder with a gesture of affection, such as only the shadow of grief ever begets in those who have but just learned to know each other, "for his sake, you ought to get away."

"Not for a few days," I said, drawing a deep breath.

"I am not fit to take a journey, and Ayah is not fit to do so either. I have to think of her a little. Some Anglo-Indians do think of the natives, you know, though the majority do not. Some treat the natives as if they were dirt under their feet, and as if their lives were worth nothing; but this poor soul clung to my little child with a devotion which has outshone any devotion which I have ever seen, and I cannot drag her off on a journey until she has somewhat recovered from her exhaustion and grief. I shall remain here for the present," I ended. "People who have been used to living in India do not run away like scared rabbits from the mere chance of infection."

So I remained on, and every day, sometimes twice, Nurse Mordaunt would come round and fetch me to pay a visit to the young princess. Sometimes I would stay half-an-hour beside her, not talking much, but just sitting there; at others she would be tired in ten minutes, and one day she said to me, "Mrs Hamlyn, do you sing?"

As a matter of fact, I did sing; not very much, not to pride myself upon it—for I had never had the advantage or chance of receiving really good training —but I had a pleasant little mezzo-soprano pipe, and I sang, or I had been used to sing, to please myself, and those who loved me. Having found out so much, she insisted on my singing to her. She was passionately fond of music, and the landlord of the Hotel des Anglais, who would, I think, have given his head to make the Austrian ladies happy or comfortable, brought in a little piano from his wife's sitting-room, and put it in the large and airy apartment into which Princess Elisabeth's bed was moved every morning through the folding doors from her sleeping chamber.

After the coming of the piano, I used to spend hours
there during the course of the day, going over all the
songs that I had ever known, not attempting to sing
grandly, but just crooning over the airs which were
her favourites and mine; and sometimes the princess
herself would come and sit listening, and once or
twice she came into the corridor with me, and told
me, with tear-laden eyes, that never, never should she
be able to make me any adequate return for what I
had been able to do for her. "But I cannot help
being anxious and uneasy about you," she ended.
"You ought to be away from this place. It is not
right of you to stay here. The risk is too great."

"I shall not go away just at present," I replied
quietly. "The doctor thinks that I am better where
I am, and I have written to my physician in London,
Sir Fergus Tiffany, who confirms his opinion. I am
taking great care of myself. I carry a perfect phar-
macopæia of drugs and preventatives here," touching
the bosom of my dress, "and I am taking quinine and
all sorts of strengthening medicines and tonics. I don't
think you need worry about me, Princess, I don't indeed; and while I can make such a difference to
Princess Elisabeth I would rather stay where I am
than go out into the world among strangers again.
You forget," I went on, "I am not like someone who
has a home to go to; my home is thousands and
thousands of miles away. If I went back to it, I
should be alone just the same. I could not go to
join my husband. No woman could get to the Bhozàr
district where he is, and if she could get there she
would not be permitted to do so, as affairs are at
present, so that I am better here than I should be
anywhere else. Don't trouble yourself about me; I
am happier here, and therefore I think that I am safer.

"Ah!" she said, with a sigh, "I would that I could take you both away back to our home in Styria. It is bleak there in the winter—that was why we left it —but we have no fever."

I thought as the words fell from her lips that, if they did not have fever they had other things quite as deadly; but it was of no use saying it, so I held my peace.

"If it would be any service to you to go there now, to take your ayah, and make it your home," she said eagerly, "indeed, my dear Mrs Hamlyn, the castle is absolutely at your disposal. Only you would be alone, for my son has been away for many months now upon a long hunting expedition — truly, I hardly know where. He knows nothing so far of the trouble we are in, I mean of the grave danger that besets his sister. Of course, he knew that we were to spend the winter in Florestella, that was arranged at the same time as his long journey was planned out."

I thanked her very gratefully for her kind thought, but said that I preferred to stay in Florestella rather than face the loneliness of a place where I should know nobody, and could not even speak the language of the people about me.

So I remained on in Florestella, spending the greater part of my day in helping to put the time on—the time that was so weary and so distressing for the dying young princess.

I heard twice from Eddy whilst I was thus occupied, both letters written in ignorance of our little child's death, both very full of the every-day events around him, speaking of the difficulty of making war against these guerilla-like hardy tribes, who had incomparably the advantage over the British and even the native troops, inasmuch as they were at home in the district.

Both letters spoke of the extreme privation that they were undergoing, and of the poor arrangements which the authorities had made for their safety and their well-being. " If it were not for our doctors," Eddy wrote in his second letter, " I really do not know how the poor devils of invalids would come off. Their devotion is beyond all praise, and their pluck something astounding. What do you think of Stewart— the gay lady-killer, who was always loafing around Muttrahabad, a regular squire of dames—making beef tea and mutton broth with his own hands for his patients? And yet I see him do it day after day. I never thought Stewart had it in him. He is a regular brick, and no mistake about it."

The letter went on to tell how rejoiced he was to think that we, his two precious invalids, were actually in Europe safe and well, and recovered from all immediate danger. " When I remember," he ended, " how resolute you were in refusing to go away, and how wonderfully it all came about that you should go in spite of yourself—for you know, dearest, I could never have forced you to do anything against your will—I can only think that a merciful Providence intervened to help us both at that juncture. You don't know how often I have thought of your resolute determination not to leave me; you will never understand how intensely I loved you for being unwilling to do so, and I don't think you will ever realise how utterly grateful I am to think that you were made to go in spite of yourself. I feel that the same Providence which has watched over you and brought you and the dear child to renewed health and safety, will watch over the fate of your always loving and devoted husband; at the same time, I do nothing foolhardy. I take care of myself, I run no unnecessary risks — only cowards do that. Every time that I safeguard myself I say in my own heart, ' It is for Doremy. Doremy loves me. Doremy would miss me. I must watch over myself for her sake.' "

Somehow that letter comforted me more than any letter that I had received from Eddy since our parting; it seemed to bring him nearer to me. True, he did not know as yet that we were childless, but I was comforted to know that he was always thinking about us, as I was always thinking about him.

Princess Elisabeth put the same question to me every day—" Have you news of your husband ? " And when I told her that I had received that last letter of his, that I had just heard from him, that he was well, in good health and taking care of himself, her sweet face was radiated by a smile which told me as nothing else would have done that I had indeed won my way deep into her heart. Poor thing! she was so ill that day—oh, so ill—so full of fever, and yet so thoroughly exhausted. My heart ached for her more than ever.

As the season advanced the severity of the prevalent epidemic slowly and surely increased. Those who were able to leave had flown from the district, but those who were unable to face a long journey, or unable to leave from other reasons, found themselves caged like rats in a trap. Florestella was not the worst of the fever-stricken towns in the infected district, but it was more than bad enough. Every day familiar faces disappeared. Sisters of Mercy went trudging to and fro throughout the town, and we who were in fair health were conscious, without knowing the actual facts, that an unusual disturbance was abroad. Strange and disquieting rumours came to us hourly of those who had slipped away to other and less dangerous places, who had been refused admittance lest they should carry the fever in their train; others who had fled elsewhere for safety had found themselves literally out of the frying-pan into the fire, had found themselves from a town with a comparatively clean bill of health in one which was a seething mass of insidious corruption and disease.

"Best to stay where you are," was the fiat of the doctor, when I asked him as to the truth of these rumours. "I give you the same advice to-day that I gave you when you asked me about the poor little child. She had a ghost of a chance here—not a great one—but still a chance—taken away she would have had none. I say the same to you now. Take the tonics that I give you and the precautions that I recommend to you, and you may be tolerably safe; make an effort to escape, and you will almost certainly be caught as you fly."

But I had not the smallest intention of flying. I felt that his advice was sound and good, and as long as Princess Elisabeth wished for me, just so long would I remain within reach of her.

"I would like," I said to him, "just one thing."

"And that is, Mrs Hamlyn—?"

"I would have liked to have got my poor ayah back to India, but I suppose that is out of the question. I could not arrange for such a journey here, and at this time. I suppose I shall have to keep her until I am well enough to go back myself."

"You will not go back to India at present?"

"Not if my husband has any chance of coming over; but, failing that, I shall certainly go back before the hot weather sets in, that would be in

May or April, possibly. I could not stay over here indefinitely if I were well enough to make the journey back again. I suppose there is no help for me but to keep ayah where she is. After all, this climate is not like the English one for her, and she has little or nothing to do in attending to me. Still, I would have sent her back if it had been fairly easy to arrange, For myself, I shall remain here as long as Princess Elisabeth has any need of me. She likes me to go and see her, and she is wearing away so fast. She cannot keep me very long."

"Not more than a few days," the doctor replied gravely. "I do not say it to them, although her poor mother knows what my every look means—but a few days will see the Princess Elisabeth Barzadiev over her earthly troubles."

CHAPTER XVI

ON BOARD THE "KAISERIN ELISABETH"

DR KNOWLES'S prophecy concerning the Princess Elisabeth Barzadiev proved to be absolutely correct. Only a few days after his conversation with me on the subject, she passed quietly and painlessly away in the presence of her mother, the two nurses and myself. The princess was wonderfully calm. She showed no inclination to give way, or, indeed, to give vent to her feelings at all.

"I have been prepared for this for a long time," she said, as we sat together at the window of her sitting-room, which overlooked such a fair and smiling scene that it seemed difficult to realise that there could be in so bright a world anything so sad as parting and death. "I have done everything that a mother could do. She could not have weathered the storm; she had suffered enough. I am satisfied that she is at rest with the Holy Mother, who did not see fit to listen to my prayers that my child might be spared. When she is laid away to rest, I shall leave Florestella immediately."

"But where will you go, Princess?" I asked.

"I shall go home. It will be quite simple. My son's yacht is at Nice, and I have already ordered it to be brought here without delay, so we shall avoid going through the badly-infected districts, and will go from here straight to the Adriatic. Had you

wished to leave I should have offered it to you, but it
only arrived from England a week ago, and at that
time you had definitely declined all idea of leaving as
long as Elisabeth wanted you. Now I want you to
resign yourself into my hands; the sooner you are out
of this place the better. Do you go with me to Styria
and remain with me until your husband joins you, or
until you have definite news of him. That will be
better for you than going to strangers, and it will be
the greatest mercy and kindness that you could possibly
show me. You don't know," she said, "you cannot
think, how I dread going home among my own people,
to whom my one girl was the joy of life and the light
of their eyes. She was worshipped at Ischelstein. If
I take you there and tell them how you, at the risk
of your very life, helped to soothe her last hours,
gratified her smallest wishes, did for her as no sister
could have done better, you don't know how they will
worship you, how they will try to repay you for your
goodness to me and mine. Come, you will not refuse
me this last great kindness."

"Oh, no!" I said. "But I think it is that the
kindness is all on your side. When you consider how
friendless I am, how unhappy and how desolate until
I meet my husband again, why, to be with you, with
such a bond between us, will not be like going into
a strange house. It will not be like going among
strangers; it will be like going home. Some day,
perhaps, my husband will be able to thank you; I can
never do so properly."

"Nay," she cried, "it is I who have to thank you,
not you me. Pray never again let me hear you say
one word of thanks. You don't understand, my
child, quite all that you have done for me."

We had a painful but very quiet time to get through

before we could leave Florestella. In those days the
last sad offices for the dead were very quickly carried
out; there was no time for sentiment. As soon as they
could be decently shovelled out of sight and out of
harm's way, the poor worn-out remains of those who
had died of the deadly epidemic, which was fast ruin-
ing the entire neighbourhood, were carried up to the
graveyard on the hillside; so on the second evening
after the Princess Elisabeth's death, she was carried
out of the hotel which had been her last home on
earth and laid close beside my little child under the
rose trees and the myrtle blossoms in the sunny graveyard. There was not the same profusion of flowers
lying upon her bier as had been sent for my baby girl.
Those who were left at Florestella were much too
nervous, too full of fear, to trouble about those who
had been taken. I remembered that when they had
carried my little child out of the villa in which she
had died, the landlord himself had been waiting at
the door, and that I had seen him salute the little
coffin and that he had stood bareheaded until it was
out of sight. When I held the princess's hand as we
paced behind the daughter's bier there was no landlord
to be seen.

"Where was the landlord, Nurse?" I said to Nurse
Mordaunt afterwards.

She looked at me with a very mournful expression.
"Poor fellow," she said, "he died this morning."

"Oh! You don't say so. And his poor wife?"

"She knows nothing about it. His wife has been
unconscious for some hours. I don't think she will
get over it."

"Who is nursing them?"

"Well, Mrs Hamlyn," she said, "we nurses are
accustomed to carrying our lives in our hands. As

soon as we had rested, after the princess's death, we
agreed with the princess herself that we should take
charge of the sick in the hotel. We are doing so at
her expense. I don't think that Nurse Rogers is quite
fitted to take up any more cases, but she is very
courageous and determined not to give in. For myself, I never felt better in my life, and I shall remain
here until there are no more sick to nurse, or until I
go with the others."

"But you are going with us to Styria?"

"No, I am not. I am coming after you to Styria,
when my work here is finished. No, don't say anything, Mrs Hamlyn," she went on, laying her hands on
my wrists, and looking at me with her wonderful,
direct, steadfast gaze, "don't say anything. I never
turned my back on my duty in my life."

"But it is not your duty, your duty is to me."

"No, you are not ill, and you have Ayah, who can
do anything that you want. You will be safe enough
once you are on board the yacht. I will come to you
as soon as I have got through my work here."

It was no use arguing with her; my arguments
had never prevailed with Nurse Mordaunt, and I
knew that they never would. She had made up her
mind to remain in Florestella, fever-stricken as it
was; she had promised to come out to Styria as soon
as she was free to do so—that is to say, as soon as
her conscience had declared her free to do so, and
with that promise I was fain to be content.

So she left me, and took up her brave way by herself. I never saw Nurse Mordaunt again. I shall
never forget her as she stood at the gate of the hotel
garden watching us go. She looked so brave and
strong and fresh, so self-reliant and so placid, the
most like to the Minerva of any human being that I

had ever seen. "I shall write to you when I have time," was her last farewell. "I shall turn up again in your life like the proverbial bad shilling. 'Naught,' you know, ' was never in danger.'"

"And you will send on any letters that come for me, Nurse, ?" I said.

"Oh, yes, most assuredly; it shall be my first care. Do you think I would let you be disappointed of a letter from him by so much as a single post? No, no, Mrs Hamlyn, I sympathise with you, and I admire you and love you too much for that. You shall have your letters all right. You have written to tell the husband of your plans?"

"Oh, yes, of course, I have done that," I cried, half indignantly. "I have done everything I could think of during this morning. I have left as little to trouble you as I possibly could. By-the-bye, Nurse, you never told me how it had fared with Madame Antoine?"

"Poor soul," said Nurse, her face falling, "poor soul! They have not been parted very long. I don't know who will carry on the hotel, or what will become of the children, but I shall do my best for them."

"You mean that she is gone?"

"Yes, she has gone. And, Mrs Hamlyn"—she drew me on one side—"if you have the chance of shipping that ayah of yours back to her own country again you had better do it. She looks to me very pinched and strange. If I were you I would get the princess to stop at Brindisi, and I would just put that lady on board the first P. and O. boat whether you find her a billet or not. I would send her back again without the delay of a single steamer."

"You don't think that Ayah is— ?"

"I don't think Ayah looks well, Mrs Hamlyn. If I

were you, I would send her home again. You will
quite readily find a European maid to suit you, and
she, poor soul, will not be really well until she is back
in India again. I think that is everything I have to
say to you. No, don't kiss me; it is kind of you, and
I love you for it. I have loved you very dearly since
I have been looking after you—very dearly; but I
will kiss you when I meet you in Styria; I will kiss
you twenty times then if you will let me. To-day I
don't think you would be any the better for it, so I
will ask you to say good-bye to me without it."

She came to the side of the carriage, talking hope-
fully and cheerfully all the time, and with a last promise that, when her work was done, she would come
straight to Ischelstein, she bade us her last farewell.

As I said, I never saw Nurse Mordaunt again; I
never saw the brave, grey eyes, the firm, smiling
mouth, or felt again the touch of the cool, capable
hands of that noble woman whom we left behind in
fever-stricken Florestella. Nurse Mordaunt never
finished her work there; on the contrary, the work
finished her—but here I am running on a little too
fast.

To go on with my story as it all happened, the
princess and I, within a hour and a-half of leaving
the Hotel des Anglais, found ourselves on board the
yacht *Kaiserin Elisabeth*, which was lying a mile or
so from shore in Florestella harbour. When I first
set foot upon her clean, white decks, I felt as if a
new life had opened out before me; a strange sense
of safety came rushing over me, and yet my eyes
turned instinctively back to the graveyard on the
hillside where the princess and I had left behind
us the dearest and sweetest tokens of our earthly
pilgrimage.

Well, it was no use looking back, no use repining. There were those on earth to think of, to live for, to consider. I turned away to see Ayah, poor wretch, leaning over the side of the vessel, her black eyes fixed upon little Frances's grave, her slight frame shaken by sobs, her dusky face contorted with grief. I was about to go across and speak to her when a touch from the hand of the princess stopped me. "Better leave her alone," she murmured. "Happier are those who can weep. You and I have no tears. How much better we should be if we had."

By-and-by, when she was more calm, I sounded her as to the advisability of our asking the princess to call at Brindisi that she might be transferred to the first P. and O. boat, and conveyed back to her own country. To my intense surprise, she implored me not to send her away; declared that she did not feel the European climate in the least; that she was practically friendless, and that she had no desire to go back to the very few relations that she possessed. "It will be time for me to go back to India when you go," she entreated me, with the tears streaming down her face. "Don't send me away; by-and-by there may be another Missy Baba, and then you will be glad of poor ayah, who loved Missy Baba with all her heart. Don't send me away," she cried. "It is bad enough as it is."

"What could I do? It made no difference to the princess whether I took with me an ayah, an English maid, or a French one. There was no difficulty about our passports, for the princess's was made out for her entire *entourage*, and she did not trouble to explain to those who had viséd the important-looking missive that I was not the Princess Elisabeth or that Ayah was not the English nurse whom she had brought into Florestella with her. The number of people was the same, and in those days of almost universal scare, that was more than sufficient.

So we went on towards the Adriatic, not hurrying on our way, hoping that we might have a clean bill of health—that is to say, that we might have passed the prescribed number of days without any outbreak of sickness which were necessary ere we could touch at any port without having to undergo a long quarantine. We had arranged before leaving Florestella that we should call for letters at Leghorn, but without attempting to land, which was just as well, for we should not have been permitted to do so; but we did contrive to get our letters and a batch of English papers sent out to us. Among the letters was one for me from Eddy, complaining bitterly that he had not heard from me for several mails. " I know, of course, darling," he wrote, " that all the postal arrangements out here are just beastly; still, when I miss hearing from you, I am always desperately anxious and uneasy. If anything goes wrong, I would rather that you sent me a cable. I should have a better chance, perhaps, of getting it than of receiving a mere letter."

So he did not yet know of the child's death. Something had gone wrong, and I, at sea in a yacht that was not permitted to touch at any port, excepting to receive letters thrown to us in a bag at the end of a rope, had no chance of telegraphing the news that I had to tell. And what would have been the good ? I made up my mind that I would send him a message from Venice, where we were to stop, and where we should be comparatively free if our bill of health was clean. Yes, I would do that.

But when we got to Venice, I had no longer any idea of carrying that plan into execution. I received two terrible pieces of news. One came in a letter written by a French Sister of Mercy, telling me that Nurse Mordaunt had suddenly been stricken down with the fever, and was dead; the other was contained in the English newspapers, and told me, with plain, uncompromising distinctness, that I was a widow.

CHAPTER XVII

A CHILDLESS WIDOW

THE news of my great loss came to me and was in
a measure broken by the way in which I read the
newspapers which contained it. Naturally we received a complete batch of English papers, those of
more than a week past, and by the merest chance I
happened to open the one which was of the oldest date.
As I spread the sheet the first words that caught my
eye were, standing out in bold, black letters at the
head of a column,—"THE BHOZÀR EXPEDITION.
SHARP BRUSH WITH THE ENEMY."

For a minute or two I was so stunned that I was
afraid to look down the column. It was just one
of the usual callous announcements in which such
incidents are told. It described how the Bhozàris
had attempted to take the English camp by surprise,
how our men had been prepared and had sallied forth
in the most brilliant style, completely routing the
attacking party, and dealing out death and destruction in superb and masterly style. "Our casualties,"
it ended, "are very small. Captain the Honourable Edward Hamlyn and four men of the 23rd
Dragoons killed; seventeen wounded, including two
officers; Captain Hamlyn severely wounded, and
Lieutenant Curzon, of the same regiment, slightly
wounded. Casualties among the native troops,

twenty-three.   None of a serious character reported."

I never thought of looking at the other papers.   I
sat there holding the one which had brought the fatal
news in my hand, and so the princess found me some
little time later.

"My dear—my child—what has happened?" she
asked.

I turned my face towards her. She must have
guessed my news from the pitiful cry which broke
from her lips. She dropped down beside me, and
putting her arm about me, drew the paper from my
nerveless grasp, while she eagerly scanned the column.
"My poor child! Oh, my poor child! It is hard upon
you," she exclaimed in tender and pitiful accents.
"What shall we do? Shall we go straight back to
Brindisi and take the first Indian steamer from there?
My poor child, what can I say to comfort you?"

What could she say? Simply nothing. I tried to
picture what my poor boy was suffering and bearing
alone, without a woman's hand near him, dangerously
wounded in that hateful mountain district. I tried
to calculate how long a time must pass before, by the
greatest good luck, I could possibly reach him, but my
brain was whirling, and refused to act. I could only
realise in a dazed and hopeless fashion that the blow
which I had been dreading had fallen, that I was face
to face, for the first time in my life, with the horrors
of the career which had hitherto been my pride.

The princess, still keeping her arm about my
shoulders, began to turn over the other papers. "My
dear," she said, "you may have further news. This
is an old paper. Here are some of a week's later
date." She released me that she might the more
quickly turn the crackling sheets over. "No news

in that," she said, laying it down, "nor in that," putting down the next one. Then she uttered an exclamation short and sharp—"Ah!"

I looked up eagerly. She turned and looked at me. "My poor girl! My dear child!" she said pitifully.

I put my hands before my eyes trying to shut out the hideous news which I saw written on her kind and tender face. "Don't tell me," I said. And yet, what was the good of keeping it? I knew.

She was very kind and very wise with me. She sat there beside me holding me fast in her arms, rocking me slowly to and fro, and murmuring over me as a mother might murmur over a wounded child. My own mother could not have been more tender or more sympathetic. And at last, after a long time, I whispered, "When was it?"

Little by little she told me all the sad details. Details, did I say? Well, such details as are given in a telegraphic war despatch. "Captain Hamlyn died of his wounds at daybreak yesterday." It was hours before I could bring myself to read the words with my own eyes, the fatal words which conveyed to me that I was indeed alone in the world, a childless widow, a woman scarce yet a woman grown, the light of whose life had gone out, whose sun of hope had been suddenly drowned, drowned in tears of despair. And yet I had no tears. I never shed one single drop of comfort for the best and dearest husband that ever woman was blessed with. I don't think that I quite knew what I was doing. I have a recollection that the princess asked me again whether I would like the yacht to retrace its course and to go out to India by the next steamer? "Because if you would," she said, "I will go with you. I can send messages home by the yacht. I am absolutely at your disposal."

But what would have been the good of my going out to India? I could not go out to the Bhozàr district, and even if we had been able to do so, we should probably have found the whole expedition over and the country abandoned, or at most, in care of a British Resident. What was the good of my going back all those thousands of miles over land and sea, only to find an empty and desolate home at Muttrahabad? Nay, it was not our home; it had been but a furnished bungalow, and Eddy had written to me that he had given it up definitely as soon as he knew for certain that he had orders for the Bhozàr expedition.

"On the other hand," the princess continued, holding my hand fast within her own, "here am I, a desolate woman, clinging to you with a bleeding heart full of affection, dreading that you should be taken away from me. I entreat and implore you to give the rest of your life to me."

" You have a son," I said to her.

"Oh, my dear, yes, I have a son—a dear, dear, good kind and only son—but when you come to be my age when you come to be bereaved of the everyday companion of eight-and-twenty years, it is not your son who fills up the whole of the gaping wound. Men do not feel things as women do, excepting for their wives. I know that when Louis hears the news of our great loss, he will be cruelly, bitterly wounded ; but he is a man, he is young, he has the world and his life before him, his deepest interest in life is yet to come. It will not, cannot be to him what it is, and must always be to me. He travels, he hunts, he has interests in a dozen pursuits from which I am entirely cut off. His grief will be for a time, mine for eternity. It is only human. I do not blame him—better son and brother never lived—but he is a man; it is women who grieve always. I am perhaps thinking most of myself when I ask you to cast in your lot with mine, and to take my lost Elisabeth's place, to let me in some measure take the place of that dear, gallant, brave soldier for whom your heart is broken to-day. If mine were a gay, bright, sunshiny house, full of young people, full of life and stir, I might have hesitated to ask you to share it; as it is, I feel that the bond between us two is out of our tribulation and our great bereavements. What do you say?"

What could I say? I had no money, I had come almost to the end of my small store by the time that we left Florestella. I had drawn out of the bank the last of what Eddy called our emergency money, just over three hundred pounds, at the time of my little Frances's death, thinking that I might have need of it to go back suddenly to India, and that I should feel more safe if I had it in my own keeping than if I had in that plague-stricken village to wait for funds. Even of that I had used some. "Madame," I said to her, "do you realise how poor and how friendless I am? I have no money—oh, well, something under three hundred pounds, which is so little that it hardly counts. I have no friends, no relations that I know of. I am quite alone. Do you realise what it is you are asking me to do?"

"I am asking you," she said, in her softest voice, "to come to me as you are, to be my dear adopted daughter; to try and forget with me the cruel and bitter time through which you have passed and are now passing. I know that it will be long before that blessed state arrives for you, but where do you think you will find anyone who will understand so well as I do, all those cruel pangs which are tearing your heart

at this moment? Come, say yes. Give me something
to live for, give me something to let my broken
mother's heart twine itself around, and let me find my
most blessed occupation in trying to bring the comparative happiness of forgetfulness to one who did
for me what perhaps nobody else in all the world
could have done."

In my desolation, my loneliness, my overwhelming
grief, I consented, and gave myself and my life into
the hands of one who seemed to be more like a saint
than anything in human form, than any woman I had
ever known during my whole life.

What happened afterwards is, speaking quite truthfully, more or less of a dream to me. I have said that
I had no tears. When I had once consented to become
the princess's adopted daughter, I seemed to surrender
all my will-power into her hands: indeed, I had no
longer any will of my own. I wished to have none.
She did with me as she would, and as her instinct
and her wish was to get back to Ischelstein, we continued our journey without any further interruption
or without breaking it in any way. I asked no
questions. I felt no impatience at the length of the
time we had to spend in railway carriages, I had no
preference as to food, and was, I think, only saved
from mental destruction by my extreme youth, and
by the fact that I was able to sleep as soon as my
head touched the pillow.

In due course of time we arrived at the Castle of
Ischelstein. I had known, of course, from the style
in which they lived at Florestella, and from the size
and beauty of the *Kaiserin Elisabeth*, that the
Barzadievs must be a rich and powerful family, but
until we drove in to the great courtyard of the castle
I had not in any way realised the princely splendour

of the princess's home and surroundings. What a place it was! A castle? Why, it was a palace and a castle in one.

We arrived just at nightfall, and it seemed to me from the rows and rows of twinkling lights which flashed on all sides that we had come to a town. "Is this the village?" I said to the princess.

"No, my dear child, this is the castle," she replied.

"This great place?" I exclaimed. "But surely these rows of lights are not all your own?"

"Yes, certainly. These are the castle lights, of course." She spoke in quite an ordinary tone, somewhat tinged with surprise, and evidently the spectacle was an everyday one with her. "I thought you realised, dear child," she said, "that Ischelstein was a rather large place."

"I do not think that I realised anything," I replied. "I have never seen any such place in my life. Who are all these people?"

"Those are some of the servants," she answered.

Some of the servants! They came out with torches and in shoals, and greeted the home-coming of the Chatelaine not with loud "Hochs" of welcome, but with rippling murmurs of sympathy. The princess was very pale, and was visibly moved. She spoke to one or two of the seniors, white-headed, stately personages, and passed at once, holding my hand, under the great entrance. There I found myself in an enormous hall, brilliantly lighted, a great echoing chamber with a groined stone roof, whose white walls were hung with great antlers and trophies of the chase.

There were more servants and retainers there, more murmurs of welcome and subdued sympathy. The princess walked almost to the great hearth, and there

she stopped before an elderly man who, by his appearance and dress, was apparently the head of the
household. To him she spoke in German. I did not
know very much of the language, but I had enough
knowledge of it to be able to follow her.

"Hermann," she said, "I wrote to you telling you
of Mrs Hamlyn, the English lady who was so very
kind to our dear Princess Elisabeth, whom you and I
and all of us loved so dearly. Mrs Hamlyn has had
a great loss since my saint was taken away. Her
husband, a gallant English soldier, has fallen in an
engagement with some hill tribes, far away on
the frontier of India. She is quite alone in the
world, and I have persuaded her to come to me
and be my dear adopted daughter. Will you
make known to my people that Mrs Hamlyn will
remain here, that she will live with me, and, as
far as possible, will take the place of Princess Elisabeth? I shall expect the same attention and courtesy to her as was always freely and willingly given
to my daughter. I can never repay her for her
past kindness, but I shall regard any attention and
any kindness that my people show in the future to
Mrs Hamlyn as an act of kindness and attention
given personally to me."

To my surprise, the major-domo, for such I imagined
was his position, dropped upon one knee and raised the
hand of the princess to his lips, then he stood up,
moved a step towards me, knelt to me also, and paid
me the same act of homage. I had never felt so
strange in my whole life. My English instinct was
to say, "Oh! get up! Please don't do that again,"
but when I saw that one by one all the principal
servants came forward, and repeated the graceful act,
I perceived that it was but the usual custom of the

house, and realised that if I meant to live amicably and peaceably with these people I must try to introduce no innovations, but must take my cue entirely from the manners and customs of the stately and dignified chatelaine of Ischelstein.

The little ceremony of home-coming over, the princess took me herself to the suite of apartments which she had ordered to be prepared for my reception. " I have put you in a suite of rooms quite near to mine," she said to me. " Not her rooms—those I could not give up even to you, but they are quite near both to hers and to mine. See, this is your boudoir—your own private room, into which nobody will come without your express invitation."

" Excepting yourself, dear Princess," I broke out.

" Ah, my dear, I shall hope to come here very often, but, at the same time, you must remember that I have my sanctuary in my child's favourite apartment. This shall be your sanctuary, and the more you ask me to come to it, the more assured I shall be that I have been able to bring some measure of happiness and comfort into your young life. This," she said, opening a door, " is your dressing-room, and this your bed-chamber, and that room beyond it is a chamber for your ayah."

As she spoke, she led the way into the cosy little room. " She will be very warm here. See, she has only to turn that stove on or off to make the room as warm or as cool as she likes. Do you think, Dorothy," she went on, as if she were anxious to say as little about my surroundings as possible, " that your ayah will prefer to remain with you for the present ? "

" I think so," I answered. " She is like her mistress, a lonely soul. She has no near relations, and of her distant kinsfolk she knows little, and

cares to know less. I think that all the affection
of her life was lavished upon my little Frances. If
she wanted to go back to India I would send her
back at once, but until she expresses a desire, or
until you plainly ask me to send her away, I would
like to keep her. She is the last link with my past.
She understands my Indian ways, she understands
me. I have nobody in all the world except poor
Ayah who can talk to me of the happy days that
will never come back again. I have nobody else in
all the world excepting you, Princess, from whom I
can hope to receive any joy and comfort in the time
to come. You are very wide apart, you two—the
poor, ignorant, superstitious native woman, and the
high-born, powerful, rich, noble lady."

"And yet," said the princess, putting her arms
round me, and holding me very close to her, "and
yet, Dorothy, in spite of the difference between us,
we have one great bond in common—we are three
desolate women."

CHAPTER XVIII

IN A GILDED CAGE

AFTER this there seemed to be nothing for me to do but to sit down and try to get used to my new life. As circumstances had fallen out, it was of course more merciful for me that I was taken away from all connection with my past and set down in a totally new existence. Everything was so strange and so new —the routine of every-day life and food, the hours, the atmosphere, the religion were all alike unfamiliar. Somehow, I never felt as if it were really I, Dorothy Hamlyn, who occupied that stately suite of apartments overlooking some of the most wonderful scenery in one of the most picturesque districts in Europe. I never felt as if I were myself. Looking back, I do not think that I grieved very much. I have an idea that I was too much deadened, too benumbed by my losses and by the extraordinary lifting of myself out of the life that had been mine, to really feel the grief which most loving wives feel for the loss of true and devoted husbands. I used to walk and move and eat and sleep as if I were in some strange dream from which, by-and-by, I should wake and say, "Oh, Eddy, I have had the most curious dream I ever had in my life! I have been in a strange world, a new life, and you were not there!"

Then again, at times the fancy would come over

159

me that there had never been that Indian past, that
it was but a dream-time conjured up out of my own
imagination.   A curious sensation that I had always
lived at Ischelstein, that I had always been the
Princess Barzadiev's daughter, used to possess me ;
and yet I had never seen her son, and I was called
Dorothy Hamlyn.   I do not think that I was mad
at that time, but I do think and believe that my
brain was so dazed and so bewildered, so benumbed
with what I had gone through, by the losses I had
sustained, that it had lost the power of working in
an ordinary manner.   And yet, from time to time,
there came upon me a full realisation of all my sad
and yet my happy past.   There was a sheaf of English papers locked away in the drawer of a wonderful
oaken bureau, to which I sometimes turned that I
might satisfy myself beyond all shadow of doubt
that there had been a husband, that there had been
a little child, that there had been a past, that the
past was over, and the husband and the child were
gone, and then I seemed to realise that there was
no doubt about it.   There, in plain English, in the
curt and cruel language of an official and telegraphic
despatch, was to be read the indisputable news of
my husband's death.   It came under the heading
of "The Bhozàr Expedition," and said : "Captain
Hamlyn died of his wounds at daybreak yesterday."

In the last paper of all I had found, some days
after I had reached Ischelstein, an announcement
which the princess and I had overlooked on first
receiving the sheaf of newspapers.   "We regret to
say," the paragraph ran, "that Lord Clovelly, whose
son, the Honourable Edward Hamlyn, was in the
Bhozàr expedition, was seized with a stroke of

paralysis on receiving the news, and expired last evening, aged sixty-three years."

So my last link with my husband's people was broken. Lord Clovelly had been the only one of all Eddy's family who had in any way maintained a clear and open mind about me, with the exception, of course, of the dear boy—Eddy's namesake and great chum. I had had it in my mind that I would write to Lord Clovelly and tell him of my grief and of my sorrow at his great loss, to speak of my affection for his son, and ask for details of his death, so far as he might know them. That paragraph, of course, put an end to that intention. There was no other member of Eddy's family to whom I cared to write; indeed, my strongest desire in my bitter hour of sorrow was to sever myself absolutely and completely both from them and from every other reminder of the past—especially from them. With the exception of the late lord, all Eddy's people had practically ignored me as a wife; as a widow, I would henceforth ignore them. Apart from this resentful motive, I had an almost morbid wish to keep my grief to myself, to share it with no one, and nothing but the most urgent reasons would have induced me to write about my loss to anyone—least of all to Eddy's mother or sisters.

As soon as we had settled down at Ischelstein, the princess had ordered for my benefit a full supply of English newspapers and periodicals. For myself, I would almost rather not have had them, for they were but so much more pain and grief to me, and personally they gave me no pleasure, for there was no news in them which had any interest for me. With Indian papers it would have been different. Still, it seemed so ungracious to want anything different to

what she provided that I said nothing, and used to
scan them over when she happened to be in the room
which we most frequently used, just that she might
see that I was apparently interested and pleased by
the attention which she had shown me in having
ordered them.

I suppose that a couple of months had gone by
since our return to Ischelstein when, on looking over
the *Times* one day, I caught sight of the name of
Hamlyn. It was but one of the ordinary announcements from the *Gazette*. This particular paragraph
ran: "23rd Dragoons. Sub-Lieutenant Alaric St
Leger to be Lieutenant *vice* the Honourable Edward
Hamlyn, deceased." The news did not specially
interest me; it was but an additional pain to come
across any mention of the familiar name, and only
served to remind me again of the cruel loss I had
suffered. I wondered in a vague kind of manner
who had succeeded my husband in the regiment,
and who had come in for the title; probably some
distant cousin whom I had never seen or heard
of, and should never meet in this world. Well, well,
I had thought once that I was a Hamlyn, too.
I was a Hamlyn now in nothing but my legal
name, and those whom I had known and those
with whom I had had communication were all dead
and gone.

I never told the princess of that last discovery.
She fancied, dear, sweet, angel woman that she was,
that I was getting over my great sorrow; she fancied
that I was in a measure forgetting my sorrows, or if
not forgetting them, that I was at least contented in
my new life. How was she to know that I was wont,
night after night, night after night, to sit in my
beautiful spacious rooms going back over the past,

wandering round and round like a bird in a cage, crying like Sterne's starling, "I can't get out! I can't get out!" and yet knowing in my own mind that I had nowhere to go, nobody to whom I could fly, that if I broke away from the bond of her kindness, I had no refuge, no plans, no hope. Was ever any poor girl so utterly desolate before? I think not.

Somehow, in spite of all the love and care which the princess lavished upon me, the stately magnificence and serenity of the life at Ischelstein seemed to suffocate me. I had been used to plenty of servants, like all other Anglo-Indians of position, but the troops of retainers and servitors at Ischelstein oppressed me. There was so much pomp, so much ceremony about everything that we did. If we went for a drive our way led us among peasantry who seemed to exist only for the purpose of giving homage to their lady. It was wonderful to me that the princess was, as her daughter had been, so remarkably simple in her personal tastes and manners, for she seemed, and indeed was, a veritable autocrat, not by her own will, but according to the manners and customs of the people over whom she ruled.

Owing to the princess's very deep mourning and my own, we were naturally extremely quiet in our life; indeed, we lived, so far as society was concerned, in almost total seclusion. To me it was a life of unendurable dulness. Heaven knows I had no desire for gaiety, but there were times when I would have liked to have seen people who did not cringe, when I would have rejoiced in stiff knees and straight backs. It was the princess's natural atmosphere, this atmosphere of homage; to me it was purgatory. And yet, what could I do? She clung to me with desperate affection and eagerness. "Dorothy," she said to me one day, "you are tired of this place. You don't like Ischelstein."

"Oh, yes," I replied, not speaking quite truthfully, out of sheer pity for the hunger in her sweet eyes, "but it is a life that I am not quite used to, princess; it is a life to which I have not yet grown accustomed. I think if I might have a saddle-horse, and ride every day, that I should feel more like myself. I have ridden all my life. I wonder would it be possible for me to get a riding-habit anywhere near here?"

"My dear child, we will send to Vienna for a tailor at once."

"Oh, but that would be such a trouble. Pray don't think of it," I said, choking down the but half-formed wish with a self-reproachful sense of my own base ingratitude.

But the hint had been good enough for her. Within a week a tailor arrived from Vienna, and I was measured and fitted for several riding-habits, such as would be suitable for almost any temperature.

"You should have spoken before," said the princess, when I half-reproached her with humouring me too much. "The horses are there doing nothing. What is one horse more or less, or a riding-habit or two, if they will make you happier? It is a very simple matter. I have spoken to them in the stables, and I find that there are two English horses broken to carry a lady. They are at your disposal from this moment."

So I found a new distraction in my life, and for a few weeks I was vastly benefited thereby; but even horse exercise did not fill the awful want and gap in my life. No, I rode here and there through the lovely scenery, over the great estate, into the neighbouring

towns, sometimes followed by a groom, and sometimes
I even ventured to go by myself. But I was not
much the better for it. I was pining for my old
life, pining for those I had lost, yearning for my
freedom, the freedom that would have been no use
to me.

"You will be more happy when Louis comes home,"
said the princess one day to me. I had not grumbled ;
I suppose that I was looking a little dismal, or shall
I say a little more dismal than usual. I know that I
was feeling more dejected and more lonely and for-
saken than I had ever felt in all my life before.
"You will be better when Louis comes. He will not
be long now," the princess went on. "I heard from
him this morning while you were out. He sails from
Cape Town to-day."

Yet I had no especial interest in this Louis of whom
she spoke so often, and of whom she had such great
hopes. You see, I had never known anything of
foreign races ; all the men that I had known in India
had been Englishmen of the same class, soldiers and
high officials, and the men whom I had seen in and
around Ischelstein did not commend themselves to me
by comparison with those to whom I had been used
aforetime. I had an idea that Prince Barzadiev would
be like all the others that I had seen, with his hair
standing up on end like a blacking brush, with a fierce
moustache trained to a hideous spike standing out
three or four inches on either side of his face, with
square toes and high heels and a wide black silk scarf
tied in a bunch at his throat. They were so different
to the class of men whom I had known before; they
seemed to do everything less well. They were very
polite, polite indeed to a servile degree, but I missed
the frank look, the pleasant, free intercourse, the

curious air of distinction, which characterise the voice
and manners of your real English gentleman.   In
truth, I did not look forward with any anticipation
of pleasure to the home-coming of Prince Barzadiev.
Indeed, I scarcely felt pleased when the princess told
me that the ways of the house would of necessity be
much changed with his arrival.

"It is six months now," she said, "since our great
loss, and although we shall not go in for entertaining—
not as we are in the habit of doing when my son is
at home—he will have many guests here for the hunting
and shooting.   It will certainly make life more varied
for you—less dull, less monotonous.   Oh, yes, it will
be very different when Louis comes."

Of course, I had no idea of what she was accustomed to think as ordinary entertaining, but it seemed
to me that the preparations for the prince's home-
coming were of the most troublesome and lavish description.   The whole place assumed an atmosphere
of bustle and expectation ; and that, in itself, was to
a certain extent exhilarating to one who was as
thoroughly bored and depressed by her surroundings
as I was.

Not a little to my surprise I found that the
princess's wish and her orders were chiefly that there
should be as little of sadness as possible in her son's
home-coming.   "They were always such friends,
Louis and my angel," she said to me, when I gave
some hint of my surprise.   "It is bad enough for
him to come home and find her absent, to find her
gone.   He has had his grief ; it is useless to try to
re-open a wound which must be a wound always to
both of us.   I wish everything to be as bright as
possible, that he may feel joy in his return rather
than a sadness which can do no good to anyone.

That is why I am making such festive preparations. You noticed when we came home in the first flush of our grief that the people uttered no shouts of welcome. You do not understand yet, my dear, the difference between a welcome and a reception. When I heard all our people murmur as they first saw me, I felt as if my heart would break. I do not want Louis to feel that. I want him to feel that he is coming home only—that is, coming to a home, not to an open grave."

CHAPTER XIX

LOUIS BARZADIEV

WHAT struck me the most of anything in connection with the home-coming of Prince Barzadiev was the extraordinary self-control which the princess put upon herself. As the day and hour of his arrival drew near her excitement became intense, painfully so. She was not like the busy house-mother who has to make sure, of her own knowledge, that every preparation is complete for the welcome home of a dear child; she had but to issue her orders that such and such things should be done, and she might have been as positive that they would be carried out as if she had merely ordered a pound of tea at a shop. Yet she was not satisfied to leave everything to her people. All that day she wandered in and out, restlessly and with apparent aimlessness. At least twenty times did she go into her son's rooms to make quite sure that nothing was wanting that he was likely to require.

"You have seen Louis's rooms?" she said to me, at last.

"No, I have not seen them," I answered.

"Come, then, with me; perhaps there may be something that you will be able to suggest," she said eagerly.

I knew quite well that I could make no suggestions, that she knew her son's tastes better than
anybody in all that great establishment, that I, a
total stranger, could not be of the slightest service
to her in this especial way; but I went willingly,
for it was plain to see how painfully anxious and
excited she had become.

The prince's rooms were just like any other suite
of apartments in the castle—large, airy chambers,
furnished with the same attention as all the others.
They were decked with flowers, and all the casements
were set open to the lovely August air. I was most
of anything struck by the fact that the view from
the windows was perhaps the least beautiful of any
that I had as yet seen from the castle. "These are
not the nicest rooms in the house, princess," I said
to her.

"No, you are quite right, Dorothy, they are not;
but Louis chose them when he was twelve years old.
He used to have your rooms. He took a fancy to
this suite, I could never tell why, and he would
never change them. They have remained almost
unaltered."

"Is your son like Princess Elisabeth?" I asked,
standing in the middle of the sitting-room and
looking about me with some curiosity.

"Oh, no, not the least like Elisabeth. He is like
his father; Elisabeth resembled my people. You
will think it strange that I have no portrait of my
son, but he has never been taken in his life; that is
one of his little fads. He has promised to be taken,
that is to say, he has promised to have his portrait
painted as soon as he is home again, just to add to
the portrait gallery—for no other reason. He has
never been photographed. We could never induce

him to be taken. Since quite a little boy he has had the greatest repugnance to any suggestion of the kind. I think," she went on, "if there were not so long a line of Barzadievs behind him that he would not consent to have his portrait painted, even for his family picture gallery. His is a singularly unassuming character; nobody would ever think he was the head of such an important house as the family of Barzadiev."

I do not know that the princess's words gave me any real reason to think so, but in a moment my mind conceived the picture of a man of extraordinary ugliness. I went out of his apartments with an idea firmly fixed in my mind that the prince was probably one of the ugliest men in the world, and therefore I was prepared to find him such when the actual hour of his arrival drew near.

In one sense his home-coming was less picturesque than ours had been. We had arrived late in the evening, to be received with torches and blazing lights on every hand; he came in the soft, mellow light of a waning August afternoon. We had come in closed carriages, while he came driving an English coach and four.

"They are come. Let us go out to meet them, Dorothy," the princess cried, holding out her hand to me. I would have drawn back so as to leave the mother and son to meet alone, but there was evidently no such idea in her mind, and I had, of course, no choice but to go with her as she wished.

We reached the great courtyard as the coach swept in under the huge archway leading to the quadrangle. A moment later the four coal-black horses had drawn up with a great clatter and dash, and the prince had swung himself down to the ground.

"My boy!" the princess exclaimed. "My dear Louis!"

I liked him the first moment I saw him. There was nothing stiff or stately about him ; he was quite different to his mother. He caught her in his arms exactly as an Englishman would have done, and kissed her at least a dozen times, held her away the better to see her, then caught her to him and kissed her again. Then he seemed to remember that there was a face near which he had not seen before.

"And this, I suppose, is Mrs Hamlyn!" he said, turning to me and speaking in extremely good English.

"Yes, this is Mrs Hamlyn—my dear Dorothy," said the princess, taking my hand again.

The prince uncovered his head. "Mrs Hamlyn," he said, taking my hand and then raising it to his lips, "I am indeed delighted to meet you. I have heard something of the great debt which my mother owes to you ; it shall be my endeavour to return your kindness so far as it is possible for me to do so."

"Nay," I said, choking down a great lump which rose in my throat, "the princess owes me nothing. The debt is all upon my side. You do not understand, prince, all that your mother has done for me."

He lifted my hand to his lips again. "We will agree to differ, Mrs Hamlyn," he said, with a very fine air of courtesy.

He turned with a singularly polite gesture and drew us both together, as it were, into the house. And then there followed one of those stately, half-ceremonious scenes such as had greeted us on our arrival. To him it was evidently, as to his mother, the habit of their everyday life that their servants should treat them in this semi-royal fashion, but

to me, accustomed even as I was to the courtesies of
Indian existence, it seemed curious to watch all the
bowing and scraping, which was evidently nothing
out of the common with them.

I had the opportunity while this was going on of
seeing what my hostess's son was like. He was not
at all like what my fancy had painted. I had pre-
judged him by the pattern of the men that I had
seen since my sojourn at Ischelstein ; but, in truth, he
was very different to any of these. In height he was
tall, and in figure he was as English-looking as any of
the men to whom I had been accustomed. His hair,
certainly, was cut quite close to his head ; but it grew
in a peak, and was of a rich, ruddy brown. His eyes
matched it in colour and were brilliant, his nose was
straight and inclined to haughtiness, his mouth a
genuine Hapsburg, with the moustache small and
carefully trained away from the lips. It was a face,
head and figure of great power—I mean of great
physical power. In years I thought he might be
two-and-thirty; indeed, I found afterwards that
that was exactly his age. He was dressed quite
in the English country gentleman's fashion, and
beyond the cropped head, had nothing whatever
of the foreigner in his appearance. He wore one
or two heavy rings, and a little pearl pin in his
tie—a single pearl, such as you frequently see
Englishmen wear. Instinctively I contrasted him
with the man who had been my *beau ideal* of
manly perfection. I did not wonder that the
princess was proud of him and devoted to him.
He attracted me and he repelled me ; he had
the manners of a prince and a something which
told me that he might, under some circumstances,
be a brute. He struck me as having inordinate

pride and extreme simplicity in an equally large
degree. It seemed to me that he was a man
capable of enormous depth of feeling, with a
something of cruelty where his wishes were
directly thwarted. He was the first man of
quality that I had seen since I had parted from
my dear love in far-away India, and by comparison with his memory he suffered in every degree.
I was almost sorry that he had come home, and
yet my dear princess looked at least a dozen
years younger from the mere fact that he had
come.

That evening we passed alone, just we three.
We dined together precisely in the same style
to which she and I had been accustomed since
our first coming to Ischelstein. There might have
been one or two more servants waiting; but that
was all the difference that was made. Then we
adjourned from the great dining-hall to the
princess's favourite room, and passed the evening quietly together.

"You sing, Mrs Hamlyn?" the prince inquired.

I shook my head half-deprecatingly, but the
princess made answer for me.

"Oh, yes, Louis, she sings delightfully. She
sang untiringly to Elisabeth during those last
days. It was the greatest joy and comfort to
her. Do sing to us, Dorothy?"

I could not very well refuse. I told him that
I had never had the opportunity of learning to
sing very well; that I had been all my life in
India, and that I was by no means proud of
myself in respect of that accomplishment. "I
do many things much better than I sing," I said
to him.

He laughed good - naturedly. "Mrs Hamlyn," he said, "supposing that you let me hear this poor singing of yours and leave me to judge for myself. I am sure that anything you do you must do well. I have heard already what a wonderful horse-woman you are."

"And who told you that?" asked the princess.

"Ah, I heard it. It was the first news that greeted me — that the English lady rode every day, and—well, my informant did not say like a centaur, but something as nearly equivalent to that as you would expect from a person who does not know the meaning of the word."

"I suppose Sigismund told you?" said the princess.

"Yes, it was Sigismund. He has a great admiration for you, Mrs Hamlyn."

"I am sure I ought to feel very much flattered," I remarked smilingly. "I have thought sometimes that Sigismund had a very poor opinion of my powers."

"You are quite mistaken there, of that I can assure you. But we will not let Sigismund's opinion for or against your powers of horseman-ship interfere with your singing."

I saw that there was no getting out of it, so I went to the piano and sang several songs, and although I know I did not sing them really well, they had the effect of drawing him across the room, and of keeping him chained beside me until I declared that I could not possibly sing any more.

"There! Was I not right? Does she not sing delightfully?" the princess exclaimed.

"More than delightfully," said he, with a bow to me.

When we parted later on for the night, he took my hand and raised it to his lips. "Mrs Hamlyn," he said, "I offer you my homage."

I bade him good-night almost curtly and went hurriedly to my own apartments. I can hardly say or express what I felt. I did not think that he admired me particularly; he had done nothing, said nothing, looked nothing but what was in strict accordance with the usual florid politeness of his race, and yet I had a feeling for the first time that my widowhood had been assailed, my loneliness intruded on. I had for the first time a feeling that I was no longer a thing apart from other men, sanctified by grief from all approach to those familiarities and tendernesses which are the forerunners of affairs of the heart.

I did not seek my bed for hours, but sat up thinking of my dear lost love, weeping and longing and yearning for what no time could ever restore, and in the morning I made my toilet with such a white face, and with eyes set in great purple circles, so that the moment the princess saw me, she uttered an exclamation of surprise and dismay. "Dorothy, my dear!" she exclaimed, "you are ill?"

"I am not very well to-day, dear Princess," I replied.

"But why? What has happened? Yesterday you were looking so charming, so unlike this."

"Yes. I—I did not sleep. I do not always sleep," I said to her. "Don't say anything about it. I shall be better by-and-by."

What else could I say? Could I tell this fond mother, so rejoiced in the return home of her only child, that the very sight of another man had brought back my own loss to me with ten-fold force? No, I could only toy with my breakfast, pretend to eat and drink, pretend to talk and take a deep interest in the every-day life around me, and feel that I had gone back a step, not so much that I had been foolish, but that I was in reality less grown accustomed to my great loss than I had had any idea of.

"You ought to go for a ride," said the princess. "You know, Dorothy, that a ride always takes away your headaches when they come."

"I do not care to ride to-day, Princess," I replied.

The prince broke in eagerly. "Mrs Hamlyn," he said, " I was on the point of asking you if you would honour me by letting me ride with you this morning?   I think you told me, Mother," he said, turning to the princess, "that you wished me to drive with you this afternoon.   We have a little pilgrimage to make," he added, turning again to me. "You will go with us, of course?"

"No," I said, realising that they meant to go together to hear a Mass for the repose of the Princess Elisabeth's soul, "I would rather not."

"I think, Dorothy," said she "that if anybody has the right to make such a pilgrimage in our company, it is you."

"I would rather waive that right," I replied.   "I am not feeling very well.   I do not think that I could bear it.   I should be happier knowing that you and your son were alone at such a time.   Please, do not ask me to go with you."   I saw that the prince was about to speak, to speak with some eagerness. I turned from the princess to him.   "You know, Prince," I said, "it is not quite an unselfish wish of mine.   I, like you and the princess, have had my troubles since she and I first met.   I have not yet, in any sense, got over them, or ceased to feel them. It would be most painful for me to go to the chapel with you this afternoon. I must beg you to excuse me, and to let me stay here by myself. If I were of your religion," I went on, " I would go as one of my dearest duties to pray with you for the soul of her whom you mourn."

He looked at his mother. "It must be as Mrs Hamlyn says, as she feels most inclined," he said in a gentle undertone.

"Yes. But do you take her out this morning with you, Louis. It would be good for her. I have seen her look like this before, and it always distresses me terribly. My dear, I know that you will enjoy a ride; you have ridden so often quite alone, when I have felt, oh, so sad, to see you start out by yourself, or with only a groom. It will be a pleasure to Louis to accompany you, and a pleasure to me to know that you are gone with a suitable companion. So, say that you will go."

Of course I had to go, in that I had practically no choice, and Prince Barzadiev and I, less than an hour afterwards, rode away out of the quadrangle together.

CHAPTER XX

A CASUAL QUESTION

AFTER the return of Prince Barzadiev, life at Ischelstein became quite different to the monotonous and stately existence which the princess and I had passed together since our return from Florestella. In one way it was very different to what the princess had led me to expect. I had gathered from her that her son was entirely devoted to every description of sport; I found him a regular stay-at-home. She had told me that they would not be entertaining largely, on account of their still deep mourning, and therein her prognostication was justified by the events which followed it; but she had also led me to understand that her son would have many men visitors for the hunting and shooting. I found them conspicuous by their absence. I think during the whole of that autumn that only three of the prince's intimate friends came to stay at the castle, nor did they come for very long visits. The prince himself both hunted and shot with tolerable regularity; but when his mother from time to time sounded him as to his intention of including his friends in his expeditions, he always put her off with a carelessness which, while it completely deceived her, revealed to me much of what was passing in his mind.

"Is Loris de Malkoff coming to you this autumn, Louis?" the princess asked of him one day.

"I don't think so. I have not asked him."

"But he always comes at some time during the autumn."

"Well, I have not seen him; I have not heard of him or from him since I came home," the prince replied.

"But don't you intend to ask him?"

"No, I don't think so."

"Don't you intend to have anybody here for the shooting?" she asked, in a tone of much astonishment.

"I don't think so; at least, not more than one or two," he said. "Colonel Wyndham is coming for a few days."

"Colonel Wyndham? He is English?"

I listened intently. I, too, had caught the sound of the familiar English name, and my heart came into my mouth, and my blood began to dance from sheer excitement at the prospect of once more seeing one of my own countrymen.

"Yes. He is one of the military attachés at the British Embassy," the prince replied. "I met him at the Archduke's last year. A very fine shot, a very handsome man, quite the best type of Englishman that I have ever met with."

It would have seemed curious, no doubt, to this mother and son, but a spasm of resentment shot through me. Why, they spoke of Englishmen as if to find a good specimen of the race were an unusual and rare occurrence! I forgot for a moment that it was more than probable that they regarded our men very much as I regarded theirs, on the whole unfavourably.

"And who else is coming, Louis?" the princess went on, dear soul, knowing nothing of the tumult raging in my breast.

"A man I met out in Swaziland," he replied, "a man called De Windt."

"And who is he?" the princess asked.

"He was out there on very much the same errand as myself. We chummed up, rather."

"Chummed up?" said the princess. "Does that mean— What does that mean, Louis?"

I could not help laughing, and the laugh perhaps saved me from any further feeling of resentment.

"Mrs Hamlyn can tell you," said the prince, smiling.

"It means," I said to the princess, "that they became comrades quickly and perhaps on little grounds, that they became intimate in quite a short time."

"Oh! I see. I never heard the term before, it is very curious. 'Chummed up.' Can we be said to have chummed up, Dorothy?"

"We could," I replied; "but I don't think anybody would be likely to use that term for us. It is almost exclusively a man's term, or for very young girls inclining to what we call slanginess."

"Oh, I see. Yes. Then we chummed up, but we do not call it chumming up, eh?"

"Precisely so, Princess," I replied.

"And we," said the prince, in an undertone, as his mother rose from the table; "we have never in any sense chummed up, Mrs Hamlyn."

"No, Prince," I replied; "somehow, I don't think that we have ever quite done that."

Little incidents like these were always happening.

I don't know how it was that the prince and I failed somehow to hit it off with each other. We went about a great deal together, because the princess would have it so. She would have me ride with her son, and many and many a time did I bitterly regret that I had ever mentioned riding as a favourite exercise of mine, but we never became intimate. For one thing, I had always in my mind the sense of belonging to somebody else, the sense of my widowhood, the feeling that although my husband was dead, gone quite beyond recall, yet that I belonged to him still. I had also always the sense that although I was living under Prince Barzadiev's roof, in a measure sharing his life, eating his bread—or his mother's, for, after all, what difference was there between the two ?—yet that he was not satisfied with things as they were, that left to himself he would have placed our intercourse upon a totally different footing to the plane upon which his mother and I had first placed it.

I don't quite know how the knowledge first came to me that this man loved me, yet before the season of Christmas had come I did know it ; and I knew it with a certainty which left my mind in no possible manner of doubt. I knew that I could have married him at any time, and, indeed, that he was only kept from proposing to me by my attitude towards him. It was an exceedingly difficult situation for me, because I had no possible reason, having once permitted myself to take the position of the princess's adopted daughter, for being on other than intimate terms with her son. I was not prepared to go out into the world, to renounce my good friend, for I had nowhere to go, nobody to whom to turn, and I

would not have wounded the princess's feelings for
any consideration; so that I could only trust to a
certain reserve and frigidity of manner, both wholly
unnatural to me, for staving off a crisis which
seemed to be inevitable. And yet I was most
anxious not in any sense to wound the feelings
of my good friend and protector by seeming
to slight her son when we three were together.
So there grew somehow to be two Dorothy Hamlyns, one who talked, and laughed, and sang, and
played, and tried to put off all the pain and the
sadness of life—the Dorothy Hamlyn that might be
called the home-bird—and there was another one
who rode and walked and lived an out-door life
with a chill air of stiffness and reserve which was
wholly at variance with the manner and appearance
of that other one. The princess never knew the
outdoors Dorothy Hamlyn, and, except in his mother's
presence, the prince never knew the domestic
creature of the same name.

Once, indeed, he spoke to me about it. "Why," he
asked, " are you so different indoors and out-of-doors?"

" I do not know that I am," I replied, which was
absolutely untrue.

"Oh, but you are,' he declared. "When you are
out with me nobody would know you for the same
bright and winsome companion whom I find in my
mother's boudoir. Why should you be so different to
her and to me?"

"Because," I said quickly, "I feel very differently
towards you."

"But why do you feel differently? Have I ever,
since I returned home, done anything to offend you,
Mrs Hamlyn?"

"Oh, no, prince, not the least in the world; but,"

I said, with a sigh, "I make an effort for your
mother's sake to put aside all my own griefs and my
own sorrows; I do not make the same effort for you."

"I wish that you would," he said wistfully.

I felt that only by the greatest caution and care on
my part should I avoid a declaration there and then.
"Prince," I said, "I feel that I am going to say something which you may think ungracious. I live in the
past; I cannot alter myself in that way; what you
ask is quite impossible."

"Were you then so fond of him?" he said, scarcely
above a whisper.

"Yes," I replied, "I was something more than fond
of him. I adored my husband. I cannot be gay
except to make an effort for one who has been through
terrible trouble, and who has always been most good
to me."

For some little time he rode on in absolute silence.
Then he suddenly leaned over and put his hand upon
my horse's neck. "Mrs Hamlyn," he said, "you are
my mother's dear friend and guest—something more
than that, her adopted daughter. Forgive me if I
have said anything that has pained you; you know I
would not do so for the world. I wish for your own
sake that you felt your loss less bitterly; I wish, for
mine, that you did not feel it at all. As things are
I must be content. We won't speak of this again."

I had never liked Prince Barzadiev so well as at
that moment. His words struck me as so full of
delicacy, of real chivalrous courtesy, that I looked up
at him and instinctively held out my hand towards
him. "Prince," I said, "we cannot help our hearts,
we women."

"Which is why we men love you so," was his
rejoinder.

We got on much more happily after that. I think
he expected less, and perhaps I gave more; at all
events, our intercourse when we were alone together
was less constrained, more—to use that slang phrase
which had sounded so odd upon the princess's lips—
more chummy; in fact, even the princess noticed
it.

"You are good friends with my son, Dorothy ?"
she said to me one day, with a curious wistful expression upon her delicate face.

"Oh, yes, Princess."

"You like him ?"

"Oh, yes, certainly, very much indeed."

"He likes you."

"I hope so," was my cautious rejoinder. "I should
not like to think that your son disliked me."

"That was not what I meant," she said simply.

And then she turned the subject, and began to
speak of other things.

It was Christmas time before the promised visit of
Colonel Wyndham brought him to Ischelstein. Several
times the princess had asked news of his coming. Mr
de Windt had actually come and gone, and one other
gentleman, an Austrain nobleman, whom I liked as
little as I should say he liked me.

Prince Barzadiev told his mother that Colonel
Wyndham had gone home to England for his long
leave, and that he would come to Ischelstein the first
week that he was free to do so.

The visit eventually resolved itself into a two days'
affair, Colonel Wyndham giving the very reasonable
excuse that he could not possibly get away for a
longer time. I was rather surprised that they invited no other guests to meet him, and I expressed as
much to Prince Barzadiev.

" Well, we should have had other people here," he answered, " but Wyndham particularly asked me to let him come to us as we are in ordinary. He knows, of course, that we are not actually entertaining or visiting much, and he is like all other good shots, he has no great love of a big shoot. And small blame to him, I say, for I think a big shoot is the most terrible bore in the whole world."

Evidently, then, this Colonel Wyndham wished to have the entire glory of the Ischelstein shooting to himself, and I don't know that I thought any less of him for that.

He arrived during the afternoon, just as the twilight was deepening into night. What was he like? Oh, well, the kind of man to whom I had been most used in my early days—a man in the very prime of life, four or five-and-thirty, a soldier all over, a gentleman to the tips of his fingers, polite, good to look upon, not over and above blessed with intellect, perhaps, and yet endowed with no small store of worldly wisdom. I had seen so many of the same pattern. The first sight of his good-tempered, steady face and grave contemplative blue eyes served to send me back—back from this oppressively stately castle, this exotic kind of existence, to the days when I was Dorothy Massingham and could flirt and dance and sing with the best of them. Ah, dear, dear, his presence was pleasure and pain to me, but mostly pain of the two sensations.

I saw but little of him during the first of the two evenings that he passed with us. Their quarry was brown bear, and their talk was of little else. I excused myself from singing for them, and for once, Prince Barzadiev was not keen on my complying with his request for music. We all went to bed very early, and when the princess and I appeared in the morning, the two men had been gone for hours, nor did we see them again until we met at dinner.

They had been fairly successful in their bag, and Colonel Wyndham was highly elated over the fact that to his gun had fallen the only bear which they had come across. "I feel, you know, Barzadiev," he said, "that you gave me that splendid fellow. By right he really belonged to you."

"Ah, that does not matter," said the prince. "I wanted you to have the chance of him. When you come back again to finish your visit, I will exercise my full rights. As you had only the one day's sport, I wanted you to have everything that there was to have."

"And you will come back again?" said the princess, hospitably.

"I should greatly like to do so, Princess," Colonel Wyndham replied. "You see, I could not hope to get more than the two days' leave just at this time, and after I have been home for a long spell to England, but, later on, if I have the chance, and your charming invitation is renewed, I shall come with the greatest of pleasure to try my luck again."

"I am sure that we shall all be delighed," said the princess, kindly, "and perhaps we shall have a larger party to meet you."

"That has been the charm of the whole thing," said Colonel Wyndham. "There are so many big shoots where one is only one of a crowd, and not the most important one at that," he added, with a laugh. "There is nothing like being the one guest for absolute enjoyment."

"I am delighted that you think so," she said, "for

I fancied that you would find us extremely dull;
but, of course, Louis knew your taste."

I did not get off quite so easily that evening as
I had done the evening before. Colonel Wyndham
was to leave on the return journey at midday, and
therefore was not especially anxious to go to bed in
good time, as he had been the previous evening.

"Mrs Hamlyn," said the prince, "you will sing
something for us to-night?"

"Oh, no, don't ask me to sing. I cannot sing," I
replied, speaking quite under my breath.

"Dear Dorothy, do sing something," said the
princess. "Mrs Hamyln sings delightfully, only she
is so foolishly retiring about it. She will have it
that she is not worth listening to, and really, she
sings delightfully."

"Oh, Mrs Hamlyn," said Colonel Wyndham, "do
let us hear you."

I protested that I did not sing as a general rule,
that I had never had the opportunity of learning to
sing well, and that I much preferred not exhibiting
my want of proficiency in public.

"But this is not public," he said, "and I really do
not think the princess would ask you if it did not
give her pleasure. I am devoted to music. Oh, no,
I don't understand it the least in the world, but I
love to hear it. Do gratify us."

I had to do it, of course. You cannot make a fuss
and refuse when people will persist in asking you to
do some particular thing. So I went to the piano
and did my best.

"I do not think," said Colonel Wyndham, when I
had declared myself quite unable to sing any more
for that evening, "that you ought to tell people that
you cannot sing, because you sing very charmingly

and delightfully, and you give your hearers much pleasure."

"If I had ever been taught singing—I mean if I had ever been taught properly," I said carelessly, "I should feel more assured perhaps ; but I have lived all my life in India, and really have not had the chance of studying music or anything else as I would have wished. That is my only reason for being so extremely modest about myself."

"Well, I should not tell anybody that you have lived in India. And now that you are in the way of really good teaching, why don't you take it up and work at it for a year or so? That would give you confidence as nothing else would do. Your talent is much too good to be wasted. Believe me, it is so."

"Ah, that is very kind of you, Colonel Wyndham," I said. "I have not felt much like studying anything since I came to Europe, but your suggestion is good. I will think it over. Princess Barzadiev loves music, and it would please me if I could give her more pleasure."

"I think that you would please everybody," he said. And then he suddenly asked me a question which served to make my very heart stand still. "I suppose," he said "from your name, that you belong to the Clovelly family ? "

CHAPTER XXI

TIME GOES ON

WHEN Colonel Wyndham asked me whether I belonged to the Clovelly family, he and I were sitting quite apart from the princess and her son. The prince, indeed, had just left the room, and the princess was at the further end of the spacious apartment, busily occupied with some fine and delicate embroidery such as her soul loved. I felt that my face had blanched to the very lips, but I contrived to answer him as steadily and as rationally as if his words had not awakened within me a rush of thrilling memories.

"My husband was Lord Clovelly's nephew," I said simply.

"Oh, really! I thought, of course, it must be the same family. I never heard of any other Hamlyns."

"Did you know Lord Clovelly?" I asked.

"No, I never met him. I knew young Bill Hamlyn, of the 23rd. An awfully nice chap he was. He was killed, as of course you know, out in one of those Indian expeditions—let me see—the Bhozàr district, was it not?"

"Yes," I replied. "And my husband fell at the same time. He was in the same regiment."

"You don't say so! Dear, dear, how very sad! I

189

had no idea that Bill Hamlyn had a cousin, not in
the 23rd, that is to say. Of course I only knew him
casually, I mean I only knew him in London, not as
a soldier. He was a nice young fellow. He had not
been out very long, had he ? "

"Oh, no, quite a short time. Do you know the
present Lord Clovelly ? "

"No," he said, "I don't know him at all. I have
been so very little in England since I have been
attached to our Embassy here. I fancy that it was
quite a distant relative who came into the title; but
when one does not know a family intimately, it
is surprising how ignorant one is of its various
branches."

"And I, too," I said. " You may think it very
strange that I know so little of my husband's family,
but I was married out in India, and I never saw any
of them excepting his cousin, who would have been
Lord Clovelly if he had lived. I had to come home
alone, for my health and that of my little child,
whom I lost at Florestella just before the death of
the Princess Elisabeth Barzadiev. My husband was
coming home with me, but he was recalled for the
Bhozàr expedition at the very moment of starting
from Bombay. I never saw him again, so you can
understand that, losing him and losing my child as
I did, I never cared to seek out any of the Hamlyn
family. After all, they knew nothing of me. I was
a perfect stranger to them, and I do not want to see
any of them. It would be too painful, too dreadful.
Pray, if you meet this Lord Clovelly at any time,
don't tell him that you came across me; don't tell any
of poor Bill Hamlyn's sisters that you have seen me.
They take no interest in me, and the knowledge of
their very existence is a pain to me. If my husband

had lived, or if even Bill Hamlyn had lived, it would have been different. He was my good friend, my husband's dearest chum. They are both gone, and all the happiness of my life went with them. You understand me?"

"Oh, yes, Mrs Hamlyn, I understand you perfectly."

"Don't talk about them to the Barzadievs. They do not understand—at least, they have troubles of their own. The princess has been an angel to me. If I were to live for a thousand years, I could never repay all the kindness and care and love that she has lavished upon me. There is nothing, or rather, hardly anything in my power that I would not do for the princess, but I have never talked much to her of my husband; it would seem to her if I did that I was ungrateful for all that she has tried to do to keep me from pining for my old life. So please do not speak of the Clovelly family or of my past to them, either now, or if you chance to be here again."

"I will do exactly as you wish," he said. "I quite understand you. You are intending to remain here, Mrs Hamlyn?"

"Oh, yes, I suppose so. The princess chooses to look upon me as her adopted daughter."

"You may become her daughter in reality," he said, half hesitatingly.

"I think not—I think not. Please don't suggest such a thing; don't keep such an idea in your mind. My loss is so recent, my grief so new, that even the sight of an Englishman, such an Englishman as those to whom I have been all my life accustomed, the very knowledge that an English soldier has been under the same roof with me for a few hours, has brought all the past back with a pain that is absolute agony. Of course, it is natural that you should think certain events might happen, but if you knew how the bare idea of it hurts me you would never think of it again. There, please don't say any more, the prince is coming back."

As the prince crossed the room towards us, Colonel Wyndham changed the conversation with an ease and dexterity which served to put my mind quite at rest, and then we three went and joined the princess at the other end of the room.

Between that time and the moment of Colonel Wyndham's departure at noon the following day, not one word of a private or personal nature passed between us two, and yet, when he bade me farewell, there was something in the clasp of his hand which said to me as unmistakably as if he had spoken it in plain words: "Don't trouble about what we were speaking of last night. I quite understand you, and will carry out your wishes to the letter."

I was alone in the boudoir when Prince Barzadiev returned from seeing his guest off at the nearest station. He came in chafing his hands together, and complaining bitterly of the cold. "I am afraid that Wyndham will have a terribly cold journey," he said, drawing a chair to the open fire and spreading his fingers to the warmth of the fierce blaze from the great logs of wood piled upon the hearth.

"Yes, it does seem very cold," I replied. "I saw that the dogs refused to go with you."

"Oh, they are sensible fellows. I would have refused turning out for any other reason. Tell me, Mrs Hamyln," he said, leaning back in his chair, while two of the great hounds who had followed him

into the room laid a wistful head upon either knee
" how do you like my friend Wyndham."

" Oh, I liked him," I said indifferently.

" I thought you would like him. He is a typical
Englishman of the upper class."

" Yes, he looks very English," I admitted.

" You know," he said, in a shame-faced kind of
way, " I was half afraid of his coming here."

" But why ? " I exclaimed.

" Well, you will perhaps think me very silly, Mrs
Hamlyn, but I thought it was just a chance that he
might make you feel dissatisfied with your surroundings."

" With my surroundings ! " I said, looking round
the room. " How could that be ? "

" Well, he is your countryman ; he is English ;
he might have given you a sudden yearning to go
home, to go back to England, to be among English
people again. You know, we sometimes forget that
we are foreigners to you ; at least, we are apt not
always to remember it."

" I don't want you to remember it," I said. " No
compatriot on earth could have been more kind and
good than your mother has been to me, or, indeed,
than you have always been. You ought not to say
these things, prince ; you make me feel that I am
wanting in appreciation ; you hurt me."

" And that I would not do, God knows, for the
whole world ! " he rejoined earnestly. " It is, as I
say, perhaps foolish of me to feel as I did about
Wyndham's coming here, but when one wants a
thing very much one is apt to think the whole world
wants it likewise."

" I wish that you would not say these things to
me."

N

"I know you do. I never meant to say it; I never meant to speak again; but somehow the very sight of your countryman, such a match for you in every way, was too much for me."

"Oh, prince," I said, "don't talk nonsense. Do you think we Englishwomen fancy every man we meet is in love with us—fancy that every man with whom we chance to stay under the same roof for a couple of days is a probable or possible husband? Oh, indeed, you wrong us. If I were a silly, romantic young girl, I might have such ideas in my head."

"You are a young girl," he persisted.

"Yes, I am young in years—only twenty years old —but so old in feeling. Some people, you know, live an existence, not a life; some people go from beginning to end of their time and they never love, they never love at all; they never know great sorrows or great joys, they might almost as well never have been born. But all are not like that; and I, although I am still young, have lived both in joy and sorrow till I feel like an old, old woman."

"Do you think," he asked, after a moment's silence, "that you will always feel the same?"

"I think so. I don't believe when men and women have passed through great storm and stress that they can ever again become as placid as they were before. When you once feel old, I doubt if you ever grow to feel really young again."

"But don't you think," he said wistfully, "that it would be very dreadful to your husband if he could know that your entire life was given up to a desolation of unavailing regret?"

"I have never thought of that," I returned simply.

" If he really and truly loved you," he went on, " don't you think that he would rather you were happy, even if you were not quite so happy as you had once been, than that you should live out the rest of your life practically alone ? "

" I could not imagine my husband wishing—*wishing* me," I repeated, with a certain feeling of outraged dignity, " to marry again. He was so unselfish, Prince, that, if it would make me happier, I know he would be the last, if he could give an opinion, to set himself in the way of my attaining any measure of happiness. I won't pretend that I do not know what you mean. It would be foolish, and while I am as I am with your mother, it will tend to make us less good friends than we should otherwise be if we only make-believe to understand each other in a half-and-half kind of way. I thought the other day when you spoke on this subject that you understood me ; that you realised, not that I felt I was tied by the wishes of my husband, but that I myself had no wish to alter existing arrangements."

" Mrs Hamlyn," he said — " may I call you Dorothy ?—I had no intention of speaking to you again, because I feel that in a sense I have violated the sanctity of my hospitality. Forgive me ; it is only Wyndham's presence here which has made me speak. Forgive me, and believe that I am moved by a desire first and foremost for your happiness."

He rose from his chair as he spoke, and so did I from mine. He took my hand for a moment in his, and raised it to his lips, and as he turned away he trod upon one of the great hounds which was lingering very near to him. I remember when he first came home that I had thought there might be some-

thing of the brute in him, yet even in what I saw
was a moment of deadly pain, he stopped and patted
the great dog on the head with a word of regret upon
his lips. I had never liked Prince Barzadiev so much
as I did at that moment. I don't know that I had
ever felt so sympathetic towards him, so completely
at home with him; that I had ever before felt so little
of his nationality—I mean that I had never felt so
nearly as if he were indeed an Englishman.

I don't think that the princess ever suspected that
matters had gone as far between us as they really
had done. For months after that little visit of
Colonel Wyndham's we went on without very much
change in our every-day life. It was marvellous to
me that they did not wish to travel more, to leave
Ischelstein more often. More than once the princess
told me that for several years her son had not been at
home for so many months at one spell.

"Louis is very much changed," she said to me one
day. "He used to be always longing to roam about,
to travel abroad, to shoot big game, to live a life of
adventure and change, but since he came home this
time he seems to have altered, he seems to content
himself with such placid and domestic things in comparison with his past life."

"Perhaps he feels that he must stay more with you
now," I suggested.

"Now that I have not Elisabeth for a companion?
Yes, perhaps that is so."

"No doubt that is it, dear princess," I said, in a
tone of acquiescence, although in my heart I knew
perfectly well that such was not the reason.

"Perhaps," said she, musingly, "he has another
and a different reason. Be that as it may, it is
delightful to me to have my son always with me,

even while I wonder that he does not grow tired of Ischelstein."

"I wonder that you do not travel more," I said, perhaps rather incautiously.

"You would like to travel more, Dorothy; you would like to move about, to go to Paris—to Vienna? Well, our year of seclusion is over now, and there is no reason why, if you would like to have a change, my dear, that we should not take it."

"Oh, no, I did not say so!" I cried.

"Perhaps you did not say so, but you are young and change is good for young people. You have never been to Vienna; you would like to see it?"

"Oh, yes, if it would please you to go."

"Certainly it would please me. I shall speak to Louis about it."

The result of this conversation was that we very shortly left Ischelstein and took up our abode in their house in Vienna. Just at first I was half reluctant to undertake even so short a journey, and yet when I found myself in the beautiful, bright city, where I found myself in the very cream of social life, I wondered how I had ever been able to support with equanimity the deadly dulness of existence at Ischelstein.

I had no lack of gaiety. I went here, there and everywhere, meeting Colonel Wyndham continually, and, I needs must confess it, winning a great deal of admiration. I was very circumspect in my behaviour, however, for I gathered very early during our sojourn in the gay capital that the sight of me in the world of fashion was neither more nor less than torture to my adopted mother's son, and as I had no wish either to torture him or to give other men the impression that I was perchance for them, I shut myself up, as it were, within a high wall of reserve, and never did a poor nun in a convent seek less to attract the attention of the other sex than I did.

CHAPTER XXII

THE WEAVING OF THE NET

AFTER we left Vienna, which we did rather earlier than we had originally intended, owing to an unconcealed restlessness on the part of Prince Barzadiev, we went for a few weeks' cruise in the yacht *Kaiserin Elisabeth*.

This time we were not quite the family party which we had been during so long a period at Ischelstein. Several intimate friends of the prince's accompanied us, and also two married ladies, both Austrian, and of distinguished position, and the charming young daughter of one of them.

For some weeks we cruised about, starting from Venice, going down the Adriatic and skirting the Dalmatian coast, among the islands of the Greek Archipelago and along the Bosphorus as far as Constantinople. It is not part of my story, at least I would be more correct in saying that it is not necessary to the unfolding of my story, to give much detail of the life which we lived at that time. We fared as the Barzadievs were accustomed to do, with every luxury that money, wealth and position could give. Each day's doings partook of the nature of a picnic, excepting when we were actually at sea, when we were entirely dependent upon the resources of the yacht's company for amusement and occupation. The moment we came within reach of land, our whole days were occupied with excursions and sight-seeing. Each evening's dinner was a banquet, and when in port many visitors came to join us at that meal. After dinner we had music and dancing, and in all these festivities I was given the honoured place of daughter of the princess. I often used to think that a perfect stranger coming in among us would hardly have known, except by my speech, that I was not really Princess Barzadiev's own daughter. It was wonderful to me how she seemed to have got over the loss of the Princess Elisabeth. I hinted as much to her one day when we were talking together upon a kindred subject.

It happened that I had been suffering for some hours from a violent headache, one of those semi-neuralgic, semi-nervous headaches from which I had occasionally suffered during the whole of my life. The rest of the party had gone off to visit some ruins a few miles inland from the port in which we were lying, but the princess remained with me, and when, in the cool of the evening, I was relieved of the pain, and was able to rise from my couch, I went up on deck and joined her, where she was sitting under the gaily-striped awning which protected us from heat and mist alike. There we sat in luxurious deck chairs, and she ministered to me with fresh and fragrant tea, dainty cakes and luscious fruit.

"You really are better, Dorothy?" the princess asked me anxiously.

"Oh, yes, dear Princess, my headache has quite passed away now. I am only so annoyed that you should have stayed at home because of my being out of sorts. You ought not to do it; it does make me feel so uncomfortable."

"My dear, I could not possibly have gone off for a whole day leaving you alone and ill. After all, what is a day's outing to me? I am not like the young people, who cannot bear to miss a single pleasure. It has been more pleasure to me to stay here with you."

"That is so good of you!" I said gratefully. "Only it makes me feel so selfish and so troublesome to you."

"You would have stayed with me, would you not?" she asked, laying her hand upon mine, and looking at me with her sweetest smile.

"Yes. But the case is different. I am delighted to do things for you that are not necessary for you to do for me. It would be most unkind if I were to leave you feeling even a little dull; but that you should sacrifice yourself for me is preposterous, or it seems so to my mind, at all events."

"My dear Dorothy, sometimes you talk great nonsense!" she said, smiling again, and surely she had the sweetest smile in the whole world. "At all events, I stayed, and I cannot undo the day's work now, so it is useless to talk about it any more. You are enjoying this trip, dear child?" she asked me, with a change of tone.

"Oh, yes, I have enjoyed it more than anything that I have done since I came to Europe."

"Not more than anything you have done in your life?" she asked, speaking in a very indifferent tone, and looking away over the horizon as she did so.

"No, not more than anything I ever did in my

life, dear princess," I replied. "That would be saying too much, but certainly more than anything that I have done since I came to Europe."

"Dorothy," she said, speaking in a very low voice, and keeping her eyes averted from my own, "tell me one thing. I would not pain you, dear, for the world, but tell me, are you getting a little more reconciled to your existence than you were?"

"A little more used to it," I said guardedly.

"But not reconciled?" she persisted.

For a moment I did not, could not, answer. "Princess," I said at last, "do not think me ungrateful or fault-finding or carping, but I do not believe that I shall ever be really reconciled to my life as it is."

"Tell me," she said eagerly, "is there nothing that we can do—Louis and I?"

"Oh, no. You have done so much; you have won all the love that I have to give, all that is left of my starved heart. You could not do more for me. There are some things which no human being in this wide world could do for me. Don't think that there is anything more that you could do— dear princess—my more than mother. Never in this world was a stranger taken in and cared for, and loved and protected, as you have cared for and loved and protected me. I am not ungrateful. I have tried so hard not to seem to repine; indeed, I tried not to do so. I have tried to believe that it is all for the best, and it is only when you ask me outright whether I am really reconciled that I allow myself to think of the past at all. We cannot shut the past right out of our lives, out of our hearts and our memories. You have not forgotten the dear daughter you left alone in Florestella under the orange trees and the rose bushes. It seems sometimes to me, Princess, as if you have quite got over her loss; but I know by myself that you cannot have done so; and then there comes some chance word which tells me that your memory is just as keen and your regret just as bitter as on that sad day when we left Florestella together."

She caught her breath with a short, gasping sigh. "Oh, yes, yes, you are right," she said; "you are quite right. There are times when I smile and laugh and try to enter into the young life that is going on about me, partly for Louis's sake and partly for yours; and sometimes not a little because I feel that it would make my girl so unhappy if she knew that I was fretting and grieving for her; but I have not forgotten—I have not ceased to regret."

"Oh, no! How could that be? And yet, dear Princess," I said, "you ask me if I am reconciled."

"Ah, my dear, you don't quite understand. You are so young, and I am so old—"

"Oh, no, Princess!" I broke in.

"So old in some ways, dear. I feel sometimes as if I were ninety instead of being only fifty-five. Some women are comparatively young at that age—barely middle-aged; I feel old—old. But with you, dear; you are a girl still, and the young forget—mercifully, they forget. Life would be unendurable if the young and the very old felt things quite equally, and no relief came to them. It is we people in middle life who feel the most keenly. The young have a chance of fresh happiness; the old—I mean the physically old, who are almost done with this world—very often feel that it is no use dwelling upon their troubles, that the partings of death are only for a day, or, as your English poet puts it, a 'going out of this room into the next.' But we who have not outlived our most precious emotions, who have to look forward to possibly twenty or thirty years of dead, blank want—heart-want—we are the ones who suffer, and suffer the most deeply. I feel sure that some day," she continued, "you will find the flowers of your love bloom up again on the grave of your past sorrows. I hope so, Dorothy—I hope so."

"You may be right, Princess," I said, not looking at her, but twisting my rings round and round my fingers, "you may be right; but I do not feel like it now. I have got over the horrible yearning to get away from everything and everybody about me; I have got over the feeling that I must wake up one day and find that this has all been a dream and that I have never been away from India or from—him; but I am afraid that my heart-want is just the same as it was, and nothing on this side of the grave will ever fill up the blank that he left."

"And yet," said the princess, significantly, "there may be other hearts as loving, as faithful, as true; other hearts that *want*, just as yours does. Have you no pity for any such?"

"I don't know. I don't feel that there are such hearts for me."

"But I think," she said, in a very gentle voice, "that I could tell you of one—"

"Don't tell me!" I broke in. "Don't tell me, princess; I would rather not know it."

"My dear, don't you think it is best you should know it—that you should face the truth, that you should try to build up the damaged fabric of your life; and, if you have lost the highest happiness of all, that you should try to give that happiness to another who has not yet found it?"

For a few minutes I did not, could not, speak.
"Dear Princess," I said, at last, "may I speak quite
plainly to you?"

"Assuredly."

"Then don't speak of this again to me; don't, when
you have been so good, take away my one harbour
of refuge from me and make my life, which is almost
contented and happy, impossible for both of us. I
won't pretend that I do not know what you mean—
that would be foolish—but I do so dread having my
life upheaved yet once again. You could not understand, I think, how much I have been the victim of
strange circumstances in my past. I seem to have
been taken up right out of my life and thrust down,
without any will power of my own, into a totally new
existence among new scenes and among strange people.
This has happened to me twice already. When I
was first married I knew nobody that my husband
knew, not a soul, and yet no sooner did I go into this
new life than the old one was swept absolutely and
utterly away. I have told you, have I not, how my
dear father died immediately after my marriage?
So, when I came to Europe, I stood out, oh, so stoutly,
against leaving India without my husband; but it
was of no avail. I came, as you know, alone. Not
one soul that I had known in my past life was there
about me, excepting poor ignorant Ayah, who is more
dependent upon me than I upon her, to whom I am
of much more use than she is to me, much more use
and support; yet my whole life was upheaved once
again, and I was taken up and cast down in a strange
country among those who knew me not, as if I were
some child of Fate, some ball of chance with whom
the gods were playing as they would. Don't you
understand how I dread that this should happen once

again, and that I should be taken up and flung heaven knows whither?"

"But, my dear child," said the princess, "you have it in your power to make your future so secure that you need never fear that such a change could happen to you again."

"I thought so once before," I replied. "I thought when I married my dear husband that I was safe for the rest of my life, and yet in a few months all was swept away from me—husband, child, home, position, everything."

She laid her hand upon mine again. "That shall not happen to you again while I have it in my power to prevent it, Dorothy," she said quietly and yet very firmly. "In any case, whatever happens in your life here, you will be amply provided for. I have made special provision for you in my will."

"Oh, Princess, don't talk about your will," I said hurriedly.

She turned and looked at me with a new light in her eyes. "I wonder," she began—then checked herself abruptly. "But there, never mind — a thought crossed my mind, that was all," she said, a little confusedly. "I was saying, dear, that you need be under no apprehension as to your future. I am very rich, you know, apart from the Barzadiev property, and I have left you an ample provision, so that if anything should happen to me you will be quite independent of—of Louis, for instance."

"Dear Princess," I said, "you are too kind— far more kind than I deserve. I don't know why you should have picked me out as one upon whom to lavish such thought and kindness as you have done. I am afraid that I repay you but badly."

"No, no, it is I who can never repay you," said the princess, "always remember that, Dorothy; what I do for you is but a recompense, a small recognition of an inestimable service which you have rendered to me and mine."

I had been so unstrung and nervous all day that it was with the greatest difficulty I could keep myself from breaking down there and then into a violent fit of weeping. "I wish that you had not spoken of this," I said at last, "because it is dreadful to me to contemplate a time when I shall be separated from you by any cause. The one of which you speak may be many, many years away—I hope so, oh, I hope so. I have lost so many of my dearest in that way that I begin to think there is a fate upon me, that I am something like the upas tree, deadly to those that love me, for I seem to bring ill-luck upon all who attach themselves to me."

"No, my dear, no," she said, with gentle yet firm decision, "you must put that notion out of your mind at once; you are so good, so kind, so gentle, there can be no ill-luck about your affection. At all events, you have never brought ill-luck to me, quite the contrary. My poor Elisabeth was doomed before you ever saw her. You added much to the joy and comfort of her latter days, and I have never had so much pleasure in my son as I have had since you came and proved yourself the magnet which has kept him so long with me. I won't speak about him again except to say one thing, Dorothy: that if you and he should eventually make up your minds to cast in your life's lot together, I want you to know beforehand that such an arrangement would not only have my consent, but that it would be the fulfilment of what at present is the dearest wish of my heart.

CHAPTER XXIII

REST AND UNREST

MORE than a year went by after the princess had laid bare her heart to me on board the yacht *Kaiserin Elisabeth*. Prince Barzadiev was not with us during the whole of the year following our first cruise. When the gay party broke up and severed company in the middle of September, the princess and I went immediately to Aix-les-Bains for the benefit of her health, which was a good deal troubled by a tendency to rheumatism.

"Do you go with us to Aix, Louis?" the princess asked her son when our journey was first mooted.

"I think not, Mother. I have made several shooting engagements for this autumn," he replied, "and I will take the chance of your having an occupation to get through them. Of course," he added, "Dorothy will take a cure also?"

I laughed outright. "I don't think, Prince, that I need a cure," I said.

"Well, now," he said, "there I don't agree with you. Aix is a great place for curing neuralgia, and you are always having some form of it or other. It will be very much better for my mother if you are baking yourself in a vapour bath and going through a cooking process at the same time as she

O

is. It will do you as much good as it will do her, and if you are wise—I won't say I consider you wise, Dorothy—but if you are wise you will take the opportunity of the cure at the same time."

I had no objection whatever to taking a cure. I was perfectly willing to do anything so harmless as that, if it would please them. So I consented to be parboiled and half baked as regularly as the mornings came round.

I am bound to say that the sojourn at Aix did me a great deal of good, and when I found myself in Paris, which was the princess's next idea, I was both physically and mentally able to enjoy myself exceedingly. From Paris, where we remained a couple of months, we went on board the yacht again. I think that in the ordinary course of events the princess would have wished to spend the winter upon the Riviera; but our mutual experience at Florestella had been so terrible, that when the idea was mooted, she vetoed it with a decision which was very unusual for her sweet and yielding character. In a general way, the princess always gave one the idea that she was a woman of few preferences, who cared little or nothing for having her own way. At any moment, if she could yield to the wishes of others, she seemed to find her highest happiness in so doing.

But to the suggestion that it might be wise to spend the winter on the Riviera, her reply was at once determined and even abrupt. Eventually it was decided that we should spend the coldest of the winter months on the yacht, that we should explore the south of Italy, and, if we felt so inclined, go further afield and take a run along the African coast.

I inquired of the princess what guests were

likely to be invited, and whether there would be
any of the same friends who had accompanied
us on our Eastern cruise. She told me that the
prince had already invited several of his men
friends, and that he was rather anxious she should
include a certain Italian marquesa in the party.
"Otherwise, Louis is quite indifferent as to what
ladies are asked. If the Marquesa de Canturce
accepts our invitation, I shall ask two ladies
whom I know she likes, and with whom she is
good friends."

"And won't you ask that charming Madame de
Furstang?" I inquired.

"No, I think not. Dear Louis did dislike the
daughter so much."

"But she is so extremely pretty," I protested.

"Yes, I thought her very pretty and accomplished, and charming, and all that, but Louis
disliked her immensely. He begged me not to
ask her this time. He declared that she quite
spoilt his trip before. So that, of course, makes
it quite out of the question that she should be
included again. I am sorry, because Madame de
Furstang is a very agreeable woman, and always
seems to be in the right place under whatever
circumstances you find her. It is a pity that
her daughter has not more of her natural manner
and adaptability. However, there it is, and, of
course, I cannot go against Louis in this respect."

Eventually the marquesa did join our party,
which was further supplemented by the two intimate friends of hers of whom the princess had
spoken, both charming married women, who took
full advantage of the situation. The cruise was
even more successful than the one to the Bos-

phorus had been. So successful was it, indeed, that although we were bound to go back to Ischelstein for the New Year, the princess and her son having faithfully promised to be with their people at that time, we all assembled again during the cold spring days, and made the *Kaiserin Elisabeth* our home some weeks longer.

Then we went to Vienna, and once more to Aix, and in the October we found ourselves settled at Ischelstein for a spell of at least three months. By this time I had grown quite accustomed to the life which I lived with the Barzadievs. I will not say that I had, in any sense, forgotten my past, or ceased my regrets for the husband of my youth, or the dear love of my whole heart. Oh, no! Does one ever forget one's first love, one's only great love? I think not. But I was very young, and one cannot go on feeling the same poignancy of grief for ever. Time, if it does not actually heal our heart-wounds, does most assuredly deaden our keenest sensations, and I, with no feeling of unfaithfulness in my bosom, with no desire to re-people the blank chambers of my heart, yet had come to take a pleasure and an interest in the events of everyday life. I did enjoy beautiful scenery; I did revel in fine music; I took an interest in my appearance and a pleasure in my wardrobe. I had in a great measure lost the dreadful feeling of age which had so oppressed me on my first going to Ischelstein. When I sang to please those who wished to hear me, it was without the great effort which I had made in the beginning; when dancing was going on, I danced like any other young woman of my age, from sheer love of the exercise and the pleasure of attuning my feet to the rhythm of the music which reached my ears.

During those three months at Ischelstein, a continuous stream of guests came and went from time to time. I had never been one of a large house-party before. You see, my experience of English life was very small, almost, indeed, amounting to nothing; and although I had heard a great deal from my husband, and from various English ladies whom I had known in India, of the joys and pleasures of country-house life, I had never known it for myself. I think it would have been hard to find any English house-party where more trouble was taken to promote the welfare of the various guests than was taken by Princess Barzadiev and her son for the edification and amusement of those who came to stay at Ischelstein. The castle was such a palace of a place—so vast, so filled with luxury and convenience for the entertainment of a great crowd of people—their acquaintance was so large, and their place in the world so high, that they were naturally able to command the very best in the way of company as well as of service. All that was best and brightest in the world of European fashion and wit seemed to find its way to Ischelstein during those few months. I had constant hopes that the attractions of some fair lady would prove too much for the peace of mind of Prince Barzadiev, but, alas, he remained inconveniently faithful to me.

And certainly Prince Barzadiev was not without many opportunities of marrying. He might, as a matter of fact, have married anyone. He was one of the most eligible matches in Europe, his age, wealth, position and birth all combining to make him so. He was a favourite with women, too. They liked him because of his lack of effeminacy, his simple, direct manliness, to say nothing of the proud

position which he would have been able to bestow
upon his wife. But they spread their charms for
him in vain. He had beautiful manners, and he was
very polite, but unfortunately he was too polite for
anything approaching to that sweet intimacy which
so frequently precedes serious love affairs. He did
not actually propose to me again, and only once or
twice was he betrayed into letting me perceive
clearly that he still was not without hope that one
day things might be different between us.

At last we were left alone, we three. "Do you
know," said the princess to me when we found ourselves together in her boudoir, "that it is a great
relief to my mind to have got all these visitors done
with ? "

"You are not feeling well, Princess," I said
quickly.

"No, dear, I have not felt well for some weeks,
and the last few days it has been almost more than
I could bear. I almost think that I shall not go
away just yet. Would you be very much disappointed if I cried off our visit to Paris for some
little time ? "

"Oh, no ! " I exclaimed. "What difference can
it make to me ? Besides, if you are not well enough
to go, that puts it out of the question. Here is the
prince. Let us see what he says."

Prince Barzadiev came into the room just in time
to catch my words. He sat down on the end of his
mother's couch, and asked what we were talking
of.

"I was saying to Dorothy that I do not think I
feel fit to go to Paris at present," said the princess,
half apologetically.

"Then don't go," he returned, without hesitation.

" You would go, Louis ? You will not remain here because I am not quite well ? "

" Well, I would much prefer to stop at Ischelstein," he replied promptly. " You know, Mother, I am never tired of Ischelstein, and if you are not feeling well, I would much prefer to remain with you. I am afraid all these house-parties have been a little too much for you."

" Well, dear, perhaps they have been a little too much ; and yet, I don't know, they have been a great pleasure in their way. No, I don't think it is the house-parties. I have such a curious feeling of faintness, a kind of sensation as if I were slipping out of life altogether. It comes over me from time to time almost irresistibly—I mean, that I have to make such an effort to go on living, as it were."

" You want rest and quiet," said the prince, in a tone of decision. " I shall certainly not leave Ischelstein whilst you are like that. Nor is there any reason why we should do so, unless Dorothy here is craving for excitement."

I laughed outright. " I am not craving for excitement," I replied immediately. " Never was a more humdrum and contented nature than mine, as you must know perfectly well."

" I believe that that is so," he said, half gravely and yet half lightly. " Then we will both sacrifice ourselves and stay here with my mother, in order that she may rejuvenate herself. For my own part," he went on, " I must say that I am thoroughly glad to be rid of all these people. One has to entertain, of course. When one has a large acquaintance one must keep it going, and pay one's debts of hospitality ; but a succession of big house-parties is a great tax, and be as easy-going as one will, they are bound to take it out of one's nerves.   If I were you, Mother, I should think twice before I asked a fresh succession of visitors to Ischelstein."

So it was decided that we should remain at the castle for some weeks to come.   But the princess did not recover as quickly as she ought to have done. Those curious spells of deadly faintness recurred from time to time, making us more anxious and uneasy with each one that came upon her, and she began to look very transparent and ethereal, as if a breath would blow her away.   I confess that I watched her from day to day with my heart in my mouth.   I had not had an experience of illness such as would tend to make me hopeful in the face of long-continued ill-health, and I think at that time that I had become so apprehensive and so nervous about my adopted mother that, if she had asked me to cut off my hand, I should cheerfully have complied with her request.

CHAPTER XXIV

ON THE THRESHOLD

WE seemed once more to have gone back to those first quiet days which had been our portion after the return of Prince Barzadiev to the home of his ancestors, that is to say, when I had first known him. The spring was an unusually cold one, and the princess lived in an atmosphere more resembling that of a hothouse than anything that I had ever known in my life, even in far-away and sultry India. To one in her extremely weak condition this was an actual necessity, but to us younger people it was extremely trying.

"Dorothy ought to ride with me every day," said the prince to his mother, when he entered her boudoir one afternoon. "She is getting to look very peaked and pinched, and I believe it is nothing but the fact that she lives in this hothouse atmosphere."

"She is certainly looking very wan," said the princess, turning on her couch and looking at me anxiously. "You know, dear child, there is no reason, because I cannot breathe the chill air, that you, who are, or should be strong and well, should remain cooped up all the day with me. Do take her out as much as you can, Louis. It is good for her and it is better for me that she should be well looked after."

So we began our old system of daily rides, drives and walks together, and I believe that we should have gone on so indefinitely, without any idea of after consequences, if it had not been for the princess herself. Just at first she seemed only relieved that I was being looked after and my health taken care of, and her son kept amused and free from *ennui*. Then I began to notice that each time I came in her eyes wore a searching look and she would ask, " Well, dear child, what news ? " in a tone as if I might have something very unusual to impart. I seldom had anything unusual, for our life was as uneventful as the life of people high in the world possibly could be. I do not mean to say that I was of any importance, for I was not, and I never flattered myself with any different idea ; but the Barzadievs were a family of almost regal position, upon whose nod the weal and woe of the population of several very large districts depended.

Prince Barzadiev spoke to me one day about his mother's state of health. " Dorothy," he said to me suddenly when we were out riding, and were miles and miles away from the castle, " what do you think of my mother ? "

" What do I think of the princess ? Why, how do you mean ? "

" I mean of her health."

" Oh, I think her health is extremely delicate. I think she will have to take great care for a long time to come."

" Yes, but do you think that care will do all that is necessary ? "

" How do you mean ? "

"What is your candid opinion of my mother's state of health?"

"I think it is very bad."

"Does that mean that you think she is going to die?" He put the question exactly as if he had been nerving himself to do so for a long time.

"I don't know," I replied. It was true. I did not know. And I did not like to think.

"I don't know either," he said, looking hard over his horse's head, "I don't know either, but one cannot help thinking, and I have been thinking pretty often lately that there is a look in her eyes which I do not like."

"I too," I murmured.

"A far-away kind of look. She was always more of a saint than a human being—that she has been ever since I can remember anything—but she never looked so heavenly as she has looked during these last few months. Have you, too, noticed it?"

"Yes, I have noticed it, Prince," I replied, almost under my breath.

"Dorothy," he said, "I don't want to disturb you, but has it ever struck you that in the event of my mother being taken away your relations and mine must of necessity be altered?"

"I don't see why," I replied.

"You would not be able to remain at Ischelstein."

"Oh, no!"

"I mean you would have to make a new home for yourself."

"Yes, I know that."

"Not by my wish, you know, Dorothy; you

know what my wishes are and have always been, but we could not fly in the face of the world—of the whole world—you understand that?"

"Oh, yes! But need we think of that contingency before any actual necessity arises that we should discuss it?"

"It is always best," he said quietly, "to be prepared for any emergency that may arise. I have always found it so, and my experience has been corroborated by watching the lives of others as well as of my own. You would be sorry to leave Ischelstein?"

"Oh, yes!"

"And sorry to leave us?"

"Yes, undoubtedly, I should be very sorry."

"Then why," he said, "can you not make up your mind to remain here for always—to remain in the one position which will be unassailable, the position of my wife? You know," he went on, "that I think nothing in this world would give my mother so much pleasure as to know that you and I had come to an understanding with each other."

A thought flashed into my mind that we had come to an understanding with each other, or, rather, that I had come to an understanding with myself as regarded Prince Barzadiev, but it was one of those situations in life in which quite plain speaking was almost an impossibility. I could not shut my eyes to the fact that he was paying me the highest compliment which lies in the power of any man to offer to any woman. I could not shut my eyes to the fact that probably not another woman of my age in Europe would have hesitated to accept the proud position which he was able to offer, and was then offering to me. It was not only a proud position, it was a loyal and faithful love, which had borne the test of nearly three years' lack of encouragement.

"I have been very patient with you," he went on, "because I felt that your life had been so cruelly shipwrecked, that a hasty or impatient word of mine might not only undo all my wishes, but give you what I would not give you for the whole world—an infinitude of pain. But nearly three years have gone by since I first hoped to be able to win back the sunshine to your heart and the real smiles to your lips. I cannot shut my eyes, nor can you shut yours, to the fact that my mother, whose presence renders your position here possible and bearable, is in an extremely delicate state of health. She may be taken away at any moment. I cannot wait until that contingency arises to, as it were, force myself upon you and take advantage of your natural reluctance to go into a world that is unknown to you, and to form fresh ties for yourself, with your heart sore from the loss of your best friend. I am not taking advantage of my position as your host —your willing host, grateful for the privilege of being able to stand between you and the world: I say I am not taking advantage of that position, it is from a feeling that you shall not be taken by surprise later, when you are less fit to discuss such a question, that I have allowed myself to speak now. But, Dorothy, I do ask you to consider that I have been for nearly three years absolutely at your feet. I won't attempt to compare my love with that of the man whose name you bear; I neither laud mine nor decry his, but

I think if he knew the circumstances in which you are placed, and if he really loved you as much as I do (and your faithfulness to him gives me no reason to doubt it), that he would be the first to advise you, to counsel you to listen to me. I cannot understand any man with a real love for his wife who would not, if he were taken away from her, prefer that she should be sheltered and shielded from a hard world by a man whose love was as great as his own. Will you promise me to think over this during the next few days?"

I did so promise—I had no choice—and I told him that I would like to go home. "Let us turn back," I said. "In a measure you have taken me by surprise. Oh, Prince," I went on, and I turned and held out my hand to him, "I don't know what you must think of me. I must seem to you so ungrateful and so hard, but it is not that which makes me hesitate; but truly it is because I have never forgotten my first, last, dear love whom I left broken-hearted far away in India. I feel as if I never could put anybody else into his place. Don't think me unkind or slighting. Perhaps if I had seen you first I should have liked you best, but he was my husband, my love, I gave him all my heart, and I do hesitate, both for his sake and yours, to give you what is left of my life, because I could never, oh, not if I lived to be old—old—old—give you the same love that I had and still have for him."

"Nay," he said quietly. "I don't ask that, I don't expect it. There was a time—I mean a time when I would have said that I would be all or nothing to the woman I loved, but that is gone by. This love of mine for you possesses me so completely that I would cheerfully and gladly take you on any terms, short of their being terms of dishonour. I don't mean, Dorothy, that I would win you by a trick—no Barzadiev has ever descended to a trick of any kind, not in the whole history of our race— I do not mean that I would take you for my wife if you showed me repugnance or distrust, or hatred, or fear; but you have none of these feelings for me?"

"Oh, no!" I cried hurriedly.

"You like me. If you had not met that other one, you might have loved me as you loved him. He is dead, I would not say a word against him for the whole world, I would not say one word even in the faintest disparagement of him; and besides that, I have never had such sympathy for any human being as for that dead husband of yours, because he loved you, and I love you; but when it becomes a question of being eager, and proud, and glad, and willing to have you for my wife, with no more on your side than a feeling of liking, that is different. I would rather have your liking than the love of all the other women in the world. So you see, Dorothy, it is no light love which I offer. You will think it over, won't you?"

"Yes," I said, "I will think it over. I can promise you nothing—I must think. I don't believe," I went on hurriedly, "that I can say yes. You don't know what an upheaval it seems to make to my mind to even contemplate such a change. If I say yes, it will be as much for your mother's sake as for yours—it will be for both your sakes rather than for mine. I know that it is hateful of me to say this, but it is true. As my dear adopted mother's son, I like you, and respect you, and admire you,

Prince, but I do not love you. It is no use letting
you buoy yourself up with the idea that I might
come and lay my hand in yours, and tell you that
I love you. I don't love you the least little bit in
the world. I like you—nothing more. It is not
that you are not lovable—nobody who has seen
what a son you are could feel that—but you do
not touch me. Perhaps, I ought rather to say that
all my power of loving seems to have died, to
have been dead within me before I ever saw you.
It is only a dead heart that I have here," touching
my breast; "not the kind of heart that ought to
be given in return for such a love as yours. I do
not try to excuse myself; I do not try to gloss it
over; it is something I cannot help; something for
which I am not responsible. Perhaps, if my husband
had died in my presence, I might have felt differently
by this time, but he has never seemed dead to me;
it has always been to me as if he was just out there
in India, and I must get along without him as best
I can until we shall meet again. My reason tells me
and has always told me that in this world there can
be no meeting, no coming together again; but I have
that curious feeling that if I go out of this world
as he left me, that I shall find him somewhere or
other. I have lived for that, and in that hope, all
these three weary years. Supposing that I were
to marry you—to say yes, to become your wife, and
you ever reproached me that I did not love you as
I loved him—Oh, I should kill myself!"

"But I never should so reproach you," he said
gently, and yet in a tone of deep conviction, "it is the
last thing in the world that I should dream of doing.
I could not reproach you with what you had warned
me previously would assuredly happen. I ask you

for no love; I do not even ask you for an immediate answer. I only wished, for your own sake, to lay before you, clearly and distinctly and dispassionately, certain contingencies which may arise before very long. I want you to think it over for my sake, whom you like, for the sake of my mother, whom you love, and, most of all, for the sake of your own welfare, though I know that you think of yourself last and least of anybody in all the world."

I bent my head, and presently nerved myself to say that I would think over all that he had said to me, carefully and dispassionately. In truth, I had never liked him so well as at that moment. There was something so manly and so brave about him, so unselfish and so considerate, that my very heart smote me that I could not love him as he deserved to be loved by the woman of his choice.

We rode back to the castle almost in silence, not referring to the serious subject of our conversation at all, and when we reached the great entrance we were met with the information that the princess had had a very serious seizure of faintness, and that the servants had sent in haste for her doctor. They told us that she was still in the boudoir, the doctor not having thought it advisable to move her even to her own chamber.

"And who is with her?" asked the prince.

The servant told him that the doctor was still in attendance upon the princess, and that he had given orders that on our return we were to go in as quietly and in as ordinary a manner as possible.

"I will go in without changing my habit," I said; "because the princess is so accustomed to that that she would notice it if I stayed to change my things."

I, therefore, went straight to the boudoir, where I found the princess lying back upon a large couch,

Ayah was in attendance upon her, and, sitting beside her was the doctor, who had general charge of her health.

"Why, dear Princess," I said, in as cheerful a tone as I could put on, "have you had another attack of faintness?"

"Yes. I am not very well," she said in a feeble, far-away voice.

The doctor briefly explained to me that the attack was not serious, a merely temporary indisposition which was already greatly relieved.

"Ah! I suppose the servants were frightened," I said, taking my cue from him and speaking very carelessly, far more carelessly than I was feeling.

"Yes, I think that that really was the state of the case precisely," said the doctor. "Her highness is much better, greatly relieved. Fortunately, I happened to be within reach, and was able to come immediately. Mrs Hamlyn, I would like to give you various little instructions presently in case the attack should return."

"Certainly. I shall be at your service when you wish to speak to me."

I don't think that the princess herself was at all alarmed by her sudden illness. "Don't let them fuss over me," she whispered, when I had brought her a cup of tea, and the prince had come in and heard the full account of her seizure. "It is the fuss I cannot bear. Doctor Rathalder is coming back presently. Now that you and Louis have come, he need not trouble to remain longer. He can come back presently."

"Then I will run upstairs and take off my habit. Ayah will remain with you until I return. I shall not be more than a few minutes, and then I will read that story that you were so anxious to finish this morning."

I was out of my habit and into a tea-gown as quickly as possible, and, on my return, despatched Ayah out of the room. The prince had followed me into the boudoir, but when he had seen me ensconced in a low chair beside his mother's couch, with one of the new English magazines in my hand, he asked her if she could spare him for half-an-hour that he might send an important letter away by the next post. She gave him the required permission, and as soon as the door had closed behind him, turned eagerly and said to me, " Dorothy, have you any news for me ? "

" News, Princess ? "

" Yes, news. Has anything happened between you and Louis ? There is a look on his face that I have not seen there before. Don't keep me in suspense. Oh, Dorothy, Dorothy, if anything in the world will save my life, it will be to know that you have promised to make my son happy."

CHAPTER XXV

MY MEMORIES

I ADMITTED to the princess that her son had spoken to me during the course of our ride, and that I had promised to give him a definite answer during the next few days. She held my hand in her hot, frail clasp and looked at me wistfully. "My dear," she said, "I don't like to say anything to urge you one way or the other, and yet I must tell you that if you consent to become Louis's wife it will make me more happy than I think anything else in the whole world could possibly do. If I know that your future is assured, and his, I can lie down and die, oh! with such content! And if anything will keep me alive a little longer, it will be the pleasure of seeing my son's happiness, and, I truly believe, your contentment."

"I will think it over, Princess," I said. "I must think before I can promise anything definitely. Don't try to force me into it, don't hurry me. You see," I went on, pitifully, "I am not in love with him, and I was with my husband, and still am with his memory."

"And yet Louis is very lovable," said the princess, wistfully.

She was still holding my hand, and I pressed

hers tenderly. "Dear Princess," I said, "I know how very, very lovable your son is. It is that which makes it so hard for me. If I had known him first, it might have been otherwise; as it is, I think that my heart was dead before I ever saw him."

"A dead heart may bud and bloom again," murmured the princess.

"I don't think so," I replied. "I don't feel like it. I feel hopeless and full of despair, not knowing what to do for the best, not knowing which is the right course for me to take. I want to do what is best, I want to take the course that is the wisest and the best for all of us. But you must leave me to think it out for myself. I can neither seek nor take advice; it is a subject that I must decide for myself and of myself. Don't speak to me about it again, princess. Leave me alone the next few days, and perhaps the light may come in upon my brain, so that I may be led to do what is really the best and the wisest."

"I will not speak of it again," she said, with quiet decision. "I am sure, dear, that you will do what is the best and wisest, or what you believe to be so, and if you decide against Louis I promise you that I never will reproach you or feel any differently towards you—my dear, dear daughter, Dorothy."

The princess remained in the boudoir during the evening, taking there the light meal which the doctor had ordered for her; and Prince Barzadiev and I dined alone together in the smaller of the two dining-rooms. I think that any stranger watching us would have believed us to be brother and sister; most assuredly no onlooker would have believed that a grave question affecting the whole of our after lives had arisen between us that very day, and was still pending decision.

We went back to the boudoir immediately the meal was over, and very soon the princess was carried to her own chamber by the servants, when I at once turned to the prince and held out my hand to him. "You will forgive me if I retire now," I said. "I must see your mother settled for the night, and then I wish to be alone."

He bent and kissed my hand, bade me his usual parting of "Sleep well," and I left him.

I was not long in the apartments of the princess, for she was naturally very much exhausted after her attack, and was already in bed when Doctor Rathalder came to pay his second visit. When he had gone, I bade her good-night and went at once to my own apartments. Once there, I told Ayah to go to bed, to go away, and not trouble about me any more, that I would be my own maid for the night; and when she had departed and I found myself alone at last, I drew a chair up to the tall white stove by which my sitting-room was warmed and sat down to think over the events of the day.

Well, I had come face to face with the end at last. I must either consent to marry Prince Barzadiev, to make him and his mother happy, to make that return for all the kindness and care which they had lavished upon me, or I must face the certainty that, at no very distant date, I must turn out of the home where I had spent three safely-sheltered, if not altogether happy years, and seek a new life in a world that was utterly strange to me. Long, long did I sit there, conning over my remembrances

of him whom I had lost, looking with dry sad
eyes at the many photographs that I had of him,
turning over the souvenirs and gifts that he had
given me from time to time during our short and
happy married life, trying to pierce the unfathom-
able future with my tired eyes and to see light
where there was no light. Oh, it was so hard, so
hard! If I had followed my natural instinct I
could have decided the question in a single moment,
for my soul turned sick within me at the thought of
putting another man into my Eddy's place; but there
were other considerations in the matter than my own
personal feeling. There was the thought of a man's
whole life then trembling in the balance of fate, a
man who for three years had done everything that
lay in his power to show me honour, respect, consideration and true affection; there was the long
record of his mother's love for me, the fact that
in the darkest hour of my life's tribulation she had
stood between me and the evils and hardships of the
world; the equally indisputable fact that she was
lying just across the corridor in an almost dying
condition, that it was the desire of her life—of this
part of her life, at all events—that I should become
her son's wife. By that one act I should amply repay all that I had received. It was no light price
to pay for kindness, but it was a price the value
of which, to my creditors, was indisputable. Then,
on the other hand, there was the awful contingency,
alas! drawing painfully near, that I should have to
turn out into the world alone. I think that anyone who has lived a safely-sheltered life, full of
family joys and ties, would scarcely be able to
understand the unutterable loneliness of my position, and the extreme dread with which I contem-

plated even the possibility of beginning life afresh
for the fourth time. And yet, in spite of all this
there was the thought of the dear sweetheart of
my girlhood, so cruelly taken from me ere our
love had lost its first youth. I could not make
up my mind to set him and his dear memory on
one side.

"Eddy, Eddy, what shall I do?" I cried. "Can
you not give me some sign from where you are?
Have you so forgotten me, have you been so
happy during these years that you have been up
in heaven that you have no thought or care for
what I have been suffering? Or are you not able
to come to me for a single moment to tell me
what I ought to do, to help me to guide myself?
It is so hard for me to have to decide everything
for myself, who once rested upon you."

But there was no sign. My Eddy's photographs
smiled at me with the same careless, bright look
that had been his when in life. There was no
guidance in the poor bits of paper, there was no
longer any comfort in regarding them.

At last I went to bed and slept, and in my sleep
my lost husband came to me—came just as I had
known him in this world, with a smile on his
lips, with the old pleasant light in his eyes, and
he greeted me with the same firm yet tender hand
clasp that had been one of his most delightful
characteristics. I don't think that I have a very
clear idea of what he said to me, but I awoke in
the dead of night to find my room only illumined
by the little silver lamp which burned near my
bed, and I awoke with the impression that my
husband had been with me, and that his advice
to me was to go on and make those about me

happy. I lay awake for a little time, feeling perfectly tranquil and at ease in my mind, and then I fell asleep again, and knew no more until Ayah arrived with my early tea.

I learned from her that the princess was decidedly better; that she had passed a really good night, and that the doctor had been with her and had just taken his departure, having expressed himself extremely satisfied and pleased with her progress.

The regular breakfast hour at the castle was ten o'clock, and I arose leisurely and dressed so as to be ready by that time. Strangely enough, all the perturbation, doubt and dread of the few previous hours seemed to have left me. I dressed myself with care and went down to the cosy little breakfast-room just as the bell had sounded for the meal. It was the only absolutely informal meal of the entire day. It was the custom for the servants to serve the first course and then to leave the room, so in less than five minutes the prince and I were alone together.

"I hope you slept well, Dorothy?" said the prince, as the door closed behind the last of the attendants.

"Oh, yes, I slept fairly well, thank you," I replied. "I am so delighted to hear that the princess is better, that she has had a good night."

"You have not seen her?"

"No. I went across to her rooms, but she was dozing, and I told Louise that I would go to her when I had breakfasted."

"I just saw her for a moment," he said. "She looks decidedly better. I don't think her attack was as serious as the servants seem to have done. I suppose they got frightened."

Then we talked of other things, looked at our

letters and at one or two of the newspapers, and when he had finished breakfast and left the table, and I was leaning back in my chair wondering how I should break the ice and say what was in my mind, an opportunity presented itself to me, for the prince suddenly looked over the top of his paper at me and said, "If you think my mother is really better when you see her, I shall take the opportunity of going over to Molderberg for a long business talk with Schiff. I have promised him for some time that I would give him a few hours to discuss certain alterations necessary on that part of the property. I may as well do it to-day as any other day."

His manner revealed to me as clearly as if he had put it into plain words that he was anxious to betake himself out of my way as much as was possible during the time that I was trying to arrive at a decision concerning our future. My heart smote me. How considerate, how unselfish, how delicate-minded he was!

I got up from my chair and went nearer to the great porcelain stove, holding out my hands that they might catch something of the warmth which radiated from it. For a moment I hesitated to speak, then my eyes fell upon the chill and wintry landscape which was to be seen through the double windows. Molderberg was at least ten miles away, and his going over there meant driving that distance and home again. "Prince," I said, half hesitatingly, "I have something to say to you. I understand what you mean about going to Molderberg, but I do not think that you need go. Your mother may want you, and there is no occasion for you to get out of my way.'

He just touched my hand with his. "How very keen you are, Dorothy," he said, with a half laugh.

"Oh, it does not need any very keen perception to see your meaning in that," I said, smiling; "but the truth is I spent a long time last night thinking over what you had said to me, and if you are prepared still to—to—take me upon the very unequal terms which I told you were the only ones that I could—"

"Dorothy!" he exclaimed.

"I cannot say anything more," I said hastily, and went on hurriedly, for I felt that I must make a last protest as to my own unworthiness. "I am afraid that I can feel no differently, that I shall never be able to feel differently, but if you like to take me, knowing that my heart is practically dead, that I have no real love to give you—"

He caught my two hands in his without giving me time to say another word. "Dorothy!" he cried, "is it really true? Can I believe what I hear? If I will take you! Why, I would take you upon any terms—thankfully, gladly, reverently. And may my life from now forward be used in no better cause than to make you happy, to reward you for your goodness and your generosity to me."

In spite of his tremulous earnestness, I could not forbear from laughing outright. "Well, prince," I said, and perhaps my perception of the quaint side of the situation saved me from making anything approaching to a scene, "I do not know where my goodness or my generosity are to be found. I think it is you who are generous, you who are good. With me it is take all and give nothing."

"But you have given me yourself."

"Yes, I give you the husk of myself, that is all."

"Still, it is the best that you have."

"Yes, it is the best that I have."

"And perhaps, who knows," he exclaimed, "some day you may find that your heart is not so dead, after all; you may find a love, as fresh and sweet as the old love, bloom up again."

"But you will never reproach me if there is no such blooming?" I protested.

"I will never reproach you at all. I will never reproach you with anything," he said passionately. "And yet, Dorothy, my dear, dear love, I do feel that a young life like yours cannot be all past. There must be some future, there must be some fertility left in your heart. I have great faith in the flowers that may bloom of their own free will by-and-by."

Oh! if we could have looked forward, we two —forward to the time when the wellsprings of love would gush up once more in my heart with tenfold the strength they had ever gushed forth with in the days gone by. Oh! if we could have looked forward — as we were able to look back! But that is what poor mortals cannot, may not do.

And so we plighted our troth to each other, and he kissed me for the first time in our lives.

CHAPTER XXVI

MY SECOND MARRIAGE DAY

AFTER having once imparted my decision and my consent to Prince Barzadiev, I seemed to have no time even to breathe. Naturally, the princess was immediately informed of what had taken place between us, and from that moment her health began steadily to mend.

"You will not keep Louis waiting?" were her first words.

He had not asked me to hurry on our marriage, yet I felt that this was an additional reason why I should put no obstacle in the way of everything being clearly settled. "Oh, no," I said. "I will do anything that you and he like, now that I have really made up my mind."

"Then I must make haste and get well," she said, with feverish eagerness. "I shall have something to get well for now. Has Louis mentioned any time?"

"No, he has gone into no details whatever."

"Ah! I expect that his happiness was enough for him for the moment. I must make haste and get up my strength again. There is so much for me to do."

"Dear Princess," I said, "why is there so much

for you to do? Why need you make an extra-ordinary fuss about this new arrangement?"

"My dear," she said, "you forget that there has not been a Barzadiev marriage since my own, and that you are going to marry the head of the house. There are endless things to do. There will be your apartments to entirely refurnish, your trousseau to order, the jewels to be re-set, the entire house to be rearranged, to say nothing of the intimations to our friends, and the pre-parations for the actual ceremony. There will be great rejoicings all over the estates. A Barzadiev cannot be married as if he were a mere notary or other unimportant person, and if Louis is not to be kept waiting very long, we shall have all our work cut out to have things in train by the time that the ceremonial day is upon us."

I half hesitated for a moment. "Dear princess," I said at last, "don't you think that for once things might be done a little differently, arranged somewhat out of the ordinary course? Is it really necessary to have so much fuss made over the wedding? Could there not be some stress laid upon the fact that I am a widow?"

"No, my dear child, that is the one thing which you must not ask," she said with firmness. "I know that if you ask Louis he will consent to anything to please you, but the disappointment to hundreds and hundreds of people would be enor-mous. It would make a bad impression upon everybody connected with us. You would start wrong. It would be extremely bad for you to have anything unusual about your marriage. You see, you must not forget—at least, I cannot let you forget — that you are an Englishwoman, and it

would probably be set down at the door of your
nationality if a Barzadiev, and the head of the
house, was to be married without the ceremony
which is his due and his right. Believe me, it
would be most short-sighted policy. Rather, under
the circumstances, would I advocate that you
should be married with even more ceremony than
if Louis were marrying a country woman of his
own."

I felt that there was reason in what she said,
and so my hopes of a quiet wedding died out and
faded away. Oh, I knew that she was right, and
when she mentioned my wishes and her advice to
Louis himself, he at once unhesitatingly declared
that she was perfectly wise in all that she had
said; so, from an existence of tranquility, almost
indeed of dulness, my life became most of anything like unto a whirlwind, and truly I frequently found myself longing for the time when
I should be safely on board the *Kaiserin Elisabeth* which we were to use for our honeymoon
cruise.

The improvement in the princess's health was
little short of miraculous. The fact of our engagement seemed to have put new life into her.
"Dear child," she said to me one day, "you have
done me more good than all the drugs in Doctor
Rathalder's surgery. I told you if anything would
save my life it would be that you should make
Louis happy. Oh, my dear, it must be an untold
joy and satisfaction to you to think that you
have it in your power to make any mother and
son so supremely and blessedly contented as you
have made us."

"It is quite incredible to me that I have any

such power, dear princess," I told her.   On the whole,
she did not talk very much either about her feelings or mine, for her time was all taken up in
preparations for the great event.

I had never seen the Barzadiev jewels gathered
together before. I had seen many jewels belonging to the princess, but she told me that, excepting on a few State occasions, she had not once
worn the family jewels since the death of her
husband.

"I think it is dreadful to take your jewels from
you!" I exclaimed, as a couple of servants brought
the great chest into the boudoir.

"My dear, they are not my jewels, they belong
to the family. I have more jewels of my own
than I shall ever care to wear. They will be all
yours some day, and many of them will be
yours from this time. I don't think that any
woman has too much satisfaction in family dia-
monds and family gems; they are not like her
own, that she may put into the fire if she so
pleases. You will only wear these for Court use
and on occasions of State; they will be no personal satisfaction to you. I always felt the same
about my engagement ring. You know that ring
which you are wearing now has been used by the
affianced brides of the Barzadiev family for more
years than I like to tell you without consulting
the archives of the house. I fancy that you are
the twenty-third wearer. I wore it, as in duty
bound, myself; but it gave me no pleasure, no
satisfaction, and I never put it on after I was
married. I put it away on the morning of my
marriage, and it was never worn again until Louis
gave it to you at the time of your betrothal. I

made my husband give me several other rings, one of which I always regard in my own mind as my real engagement ring, and I expect that Louis will wish to give you others that will be more pleasure both to him to give and to you to receive than that hideous old black diamond which has sealed the fate of so many Barzadiev men and so many Barzadiev brides."

Of a truth, it was rather a relief to me to find that the princess did regard the famous black diamond as a hideous old thing. I had seen it slipped on to my finger with a shudder, and in my ignorance had feared that I should be compelled to wear it during the rest of my life. I said nothing to her, but I determined that I would follow her example, and that on my wedding morning I would leave it off never to wear it again.

Of rings and other jewels, the prince gave me galore. Never a day went by during the whole of our engagement—and it lasted for two months— that he did not lavish some fresh gift or offering upon me; he gave me black sables of almost priceless value, laces worth many thousands of pounds, jewels of all kinds, and I do believe that I had more clothes bought for me than I should ever be able to wear out if I lived to be a hundred. I protested from time to time that it was extravagant, that it was wasteful, that it was making my life a burden to me; but it was all of no use. The princess told me, and Louis himself backed her up in the assertion, that it would be necessary to my position to have all these belongings, and also that there were certain tradespeople in Vienna, Paris and elsewhere, who would expect as a sort of right to be remembered

in the parcelling out of a Barzadiev trousseau. I
felt that they could have left out nobody, that
none of their tradespeople could have the least
justification for feeling themselves aggrieved on
the score of having been slighted; but the sense
of possession was in no wise pleasant to me,
rather, on the other hand, was I oppressed as by
an intolerable weight.

As the time for the wedding drew near, the
Castle of Ischelstein began to fill with guests.
Remembering how ill the princess had been but
a few short weeks previously, it was wonderful
to me that she could have sufficiently pulled up
strength again to be able to bear the great strain
which was put upon her at this time. I had
fancied that the Barzadievs were rather a small
family; that the mother and son stood almost
alone in the world and were not troubled by
many relations. True, there were not many who bore
the name of Barzadiev, but of their relations there
seemed to be no end. They came thick and fast;
I was positively bewildered in trying to grasp the
different degrees of kinship. They were all titled,
all noble, all rich, apparently all equally powerful.
They came, whatever there might have been in
their hearts, with honeyed words on their lips
and valuable gifts in their hands. I was *fêted*,
caressed, loaded with compliments and many marks
of honour, but it seemed to me that in the midst
of all this adulation and flattery, there was only
one real simple soul, the princess herself, and
besides her only one really well satisfied person,
which was my bridegroom.

I had no time for thought, no opportunity for
repining; no, there was not the faintest chance of

my being able to go back on my word. I had
passed the Rubicon, and whether my mind mis-
gave me or not, there was no withdrawal possible
to me. I was bound to go on, to carry my resolve
through to the very end. In the face of that
gay and brilliant assemblage, it would have needed
a woman with a stronger nerve than mine to have
done aught but carry out the compact in its
entirety.

Perhaps it was as well for me that there was
as much preparation made for the marriage as the
family thought needful, because I seemed somehow
to turn to Louis as to a haven of refuge from the
endless flattery and turmoil which the wedding
had entailed. He always spoke of the various
arrangements as of an intolerable nuisance, out of
which, unfortunately, we could not hope to escape,
excepting by going bravely through them.

"When we are once on board the *Kaiserin
Elisabeth*," he said to me, a few days before that
of the wedding, when I was groaning under some
fresh tax upon my strength, "we will pass a few
weeks in doing nothing. We shall see nobody
unless we choose, we shall receive no letters except
by our own fault, we shall have gone away
perfectly secure in knowing that the mother is
absolutely happy and that nothing more can be
expected of us. Why, if it will please you, Dorothy,
you can wear one frock the whole time that we
are away."

"My dear Louis," I said, "I have had so many
frocks fitted on me that I feel I shall positively hate
every one of them when I come to wear them. I am
so dazzled with jewels that at the present moment
I feel the greatest luxury would be never to possess a

jewel again.   You know one may have too much even
of a good thing."

" Oh, my dear," he exclaimed, " there will come a
day when you will value your jewels like any other
woman.   It is because all these people worry you so,
and everything has been rushed on in a hurry, that you
feel so impatient.   In a few months' time you won't
know yourself, and you will tell me you want to go
to Paris because you have nothing to wear, and you
must have your wardrobe attended to."

" Yes, I may; nothing is impossible.   I shall never
believe in the impossible again," I replied with a
smile.

So the days went over, each one seeming to go more
quickly than another, because each one was more
filled with occupations and duties than that which
had gone before it.   And at last my second marriage
day dawned.   Oh! how different it was to the other
one; and yet in some things how like.   There had
not been present at my first marriage one single
relation on either Eddy's side or my own.   On the
day of my marriage to Prince Barzadiev there was
not present one single person, excepting my Indian
ayah, who had known me longer than my bridegroom
and his mother.

We were married in the great chapel of the castle
—married by a cardinal of the Church of Rome, to
which the Barzadievs belonged, and into which I
myself had been received during the period of my
engagement to Louis, not so much from conviction as
from a desire to start fair in my new life, and a
feeling that nothing would so far tend to make me
one with the new life which I was entering than
to have the same outward expression of religion.
Neither Louis nor his mother had asked or even

suggested that I should take this step, but I saw very plainly when I first hinted at it that nothing could have given them greater pleasure and satisfaction, or have tended to make my future path more smooth.

Being a widow of course I did not wear the orange blossoms and dress of a bride, but my gown was a marvel of beauty and costliness—a triumph of the dressmaker's art, a delicate shimmering grey in tint, almost hidden in clouds of priceless lace, one of my adopted mother's wedding gifts to me. I only wore such jewels as Louis had given to me for my own, and I carried a bouquet of yellow roses, which kept me in mind of a little grave in the churchyard on the hillside in far-away Florestella.

A marriage ceremony once begun is soon an accomplished fact. Almost before I realised that I was walking up the aisle of the chapel I was conscious that the ritual had come to an end, that I was no longer Dorothy Hamlyn, that I was Prince Barzadiev's wife.

For one wild moment when that realisation came to me I was tempted to fling down the yellow roses from my hands, to tear off the glittering jewels and cobweb-like laces with which I was bedecked, to cry that a great, an awful mistake had been made, that I had not meant to go so far as this, that I had not really thought what I was doing, that I belonged body and soul to another man! But in the midst of a fashionable crowd one does not follow out even one's most natural inclinations, and when after my new husband had kissed me and murmured in my ear that he was the happiest man in the world, and that, God helping him, I should never repent the step I had taken, and when my dear adopted mother had come in her turn and kissed me, blessing me, while her kind arms were clasped about me, I came to my full senses with a gasp and a shudder of remembrance. I realised that there was no going back again in this world, that I had come to one of those epochs in my life's journey from which there could only be a passing onward.

Then we went back into the castle, to stand the centre of a brilliant throng of guests, to receive more flattery, more adulation and many good wishes for our health and prosperity. There was a great banquet at which Louis and I sat side by side, when the laughter and mirth ran high, to be suddenly broken by an authoritative knock upon the high table.

" Ladies and gentlemen," cried a voice, the voice of the chief servitor in the establishment, "you are asked to charge your glasses and to drink to the future health, happiness and prosperity of their High- nesses the Prince and Princess Barzadiev."

CHAPTER XXVII

TRANQUILITY AND CONTENTMENT

LOOKING back from my present standpoint, it has always seemed to me that the few weeks which Louis and I spent on board the *Kaiserin Elisabeth* after our marriage was one of the most happy and tranquil times of my whole life. During the time that we were aboard of her we entirely shook off all the irksome pomp and ceremony with which we had been surrounded during the previous two months, and we lived again the same simple and easy existence which had been ours from time to time previous to our engagement. It was, and is still, surprising to me that I was able to settle down into my new life with so little personal effort to myself. I must lay stress upon the fact that I was not in love with my husband; and yet he satisfied me. He was so thoughtful for my comfort, so restful, so strong. He seemed such a haven of refuge from all the storm and stress of the world, and I grew so to depend upon him that long before our cruise was over I was fain to acknowledge to myself that if I missed something of my earlier experience I was yet a supremely contented and fortunate woman.

He was very wise with me. He never worried me with questions about the state of my feelings;

it seemed to be enough for him in those golden days
of spring sunshine that I was his; it seemed to
be sufficient joy for him to lavish his love upon me
without exacting impossibilities of love on my side.
Before our marriage it had been one of my principal
fears that he might give me no peace nor rest until
I should be able to assure him that I really preferred
him to my first husband. Had he chanced to have
taken that course all hope of happiness would have
been at an end for me; but he was wisdom, discretion and kindness itself. He never referred to
the past in any way. He took me as I was, and
my gratitude for his consideration was beyond all
expression of words. Unfortunately, in our position,
our honeymoon cruise could not last for ever, and
we were obliged at the time we had originally
fixed to go back to Ischelstein, there to be present
at many *fêtes* given in honour of our marriage, to
pay and receive many visits—in short, to justify the
marriage as it were.

The princess struck me as a marvel of recupera-
tive power. We found her looking better and
seeming stronger than she had looked or seemed
at any time since I had first known her. There
had been some question of her leaving Ischelstein
and taking up her residence in one of the other
castles belonging to the family, but I had set my
face resolutely against this plan from the very
first.

"There is no reason, dear Princess," I said to
her, "that because I have married Louis you should
be taken out of your natural place, your real home,
the one part of the world you are really fond of,
and I warn you distinctly that if you leave Ischelstein on my account, I will never set foot in it

again. I hope that that is plain enough both for you and for Louis."

"There can only be one mistress of a house," said the princess.

"Oh!" I exclaimed hastily. "The mistress of a little villa with half-a-dozen servants is of importance, and her position a serious matter; the mistress of a township is quite another thing. We can quite well have our separate establishments under the same roof. It would be no pleasure to me to use your apartments other than as I have always used them, as your daughter; and as neither of us has ever ordered a dinner at Ischelstein since I first knew it, I don't see that we need ever fall out upon that subject. At all events, I simply and flatly refuse to have anything whatever to do with Ischelstein if you leave it."

"But, my dear—" she began.

"No, I have never set myself up against you before, dear Princess; but in this instance I must and will have my own way. It is no use talking to me and calling me 'my dear,' if you make me feel that I have driven you out of your home, the place you love. I won't have it. Louis, I am quite sure, does not wish it."

"Decidedly not," said Louis, thus directly appealed to.

"Why, when you consider the peculiarities of the people, the charities, the little ins and outs that have to be considered, it is perfectly preposterous to think of setting down an ignorant Englishwoman, who has lived all her life in India, to manage everything."

"But what would you do if I were taken away altogether?"

"Well, you see I should have no choice then, I should have to do the best I could; and how much I might try Louis's patience, under those circumstances, it is impossible to tell beforehand. But while you are alive and in such wonderful health, I cannot see that anything would be gained by your leaving your own home and going to live in some unaccustomed place all by yourself. You would be a continual anxiety to us; we should spend all our time trotting to and fro to make quite sure that you were not dull and lonely, and we should have no comfort in your society, and I won't have it! So, my dear, sweet Princess, I must ask you at once, now, from the very beginning, not to mention this matter again, because I shall never give you any other opinion, and I don't want to hear anything more on the subject whatever."

So she gave in to our wishes, and remained at Ischelstein on precisely the same footing that she had always occupied there. My position was necessarily altered in this way. In place of Ayah I had several maids, who attended wholly and solely to my personal needs. I did not get rid of Ayah, of course. She remained a picturesque figure, doing nothing (or next door to it) with admirable grace and tact. She still occupied a room somewhat near to my own; but not the actual apartment which had been hers first on our arrival at Ischelstein. I had an establishment of my own; I mean my own footmen, who waited upon nobody else, my own horses, carriages, coachmen, grooms, and so on; and these people were all naturally under my immediate orders. With the conduct of the house, neither the princess nor I much troubled ourselves, as the vast establishment was under the charge of a house-steward, who was responsible to Louis for all plans and arrangements. We dined together always, and a copy of the *menu* was laid upon my desk every morning—a similar compliment being paid to the princess. I have no recollection of ever troubling to make any alteration therein; whether my adopted mother did or did not was a matter of profoundest indifference to me. I visited her at regular times, always going to her apartments for a few minutes after the ten o'clock breakfast, if she had not appeared at that meal. For the rest of the day our interests were in common and never clashed. I was no drag upon her, and she no tie upon me.

As the summer wore on and the time drew near for the princess to once more take her cure at Aix, the question arose as to whether Louis and I should accompany her or not. For my own part I was absolutely indifferent. I liked Aix as well as any place I had ever been in in my life, and I was perfectly willing to go there with her if such a plan would suit Louis; but for once in his life he did not seem inclined to lend himself to the plans and the wishes of other people.

"I think Aix is the most detestable place in the world," he said, when the subject was first mentioned to him. "Could you not take some of your people and put in your cure without us?" he asked of his mother.

"Most assuredly," she replied. "I know so many people who go to Aix; and it would be quite easy for me to go without you two. Where do you propose to take Dorothy?"

"I have not proposed to take Dorothy anywhere. There is a big shooting party at the De Furstangs,

but that will come a little later on.   It would be best
if we went to it."

"What are you wanting to do, Louis ?" I asked.

"I would like to go to Switzerland," he replied.
"And after we leave the De Furstangs, I think
nothing would please Dorothy so much as another
little tour in the yacht.   Am I not about right,
dearest ?"

"Yes, I should like a cruise immensely," I replied.
"Between ourselves, Louis, I would rather, if it is
practicable, go for a cruise before the De Furstangs'
big shoot as well as afterwards.   I should so like to go
right along the French coast—not the Mediterranean
coast, not the Riviera, but Normandy and Brittany
and as far as Ostend.   I hate these big hotels where
there are always people trying to scrape acquaintance with us.   They are so trying."

"You would not like," he said, "to go over and
see a little of the English coast ?   You know, it is
really preposterous that you should know so little
of your native country."

"I don't know that I specially mind—I mean that
I should specially object to do so ; but England is only
a name to me," I replied quickly.   "I know nobody
in England, and I don't feel in any way drawn towards it.   I will go with you there if you would like
it."

"We can leave that open," he said indifferently.
"But certainly, if you would prefer a short cruise in
the yacht to a tour in Switzerland, your wish is a
very easily-gratified one.   I would much prefer it myself, but I thought you might be bored, and I did
not like to suggest it.   Shall we take anyone with
us ?"

"Oh, no.   Let us go just by ourselves ; we have

seen so much of other people. There is no tranquility, no rest in a large party, even on a yacht.
I would much prefer for us to go together."

So we arranged our summer. In due course of
time the princess went off with her own people to
Aix, and Louis and I, on hearing of her safe arrival
there, at once joined the yacht, which was lying at
Trieste. Louis had been rather anxious that I
should go overland and join her somewhere on the
Breton coast, but I loved the sea, and in spite of
the heat much preferred the longer sea journey.

So the pleasant weeks went by until it was time
for us to retrace our steps in order that we might
pay our promised visit to the De Furstangs. I do not
need to tell very much of my life at this time. It was
very gay. Visit succeeded visit, and with every day
that went by Louis became more and more devoted to
me, and his mother more tenderly attached to me. I
never for one moment regretted that I had consented
to their wishes and married Louis. I was calmly,
quietly, peacefully happy, and, above all things, I
had that tranquil feeling of assuredness which was
most of anything satisfying and delightful to one
who had suffered as cruelly and bitterly from un-
looked-for change as I had done in the past. I
never in any way thought of putting Louis in the
place which my first husband had occupied. When
I thought of him, which was very often, it was of
some sacred past too bright for human hopes to hold
on to for ever. I never talked about him, and Louis
never mentioned him, never spoke of him in any
way, asked me no questions, never sought to open
the door of my past love, never treated me other
than as if he were the first and only man who had
possessed my heart. I was more than glad of this,

because I had never in any way sought to parade
the fact of my first marriage before the face of my
second husband. Immediately upon my betrothal to
Louis, I gathered together all my photographs and
souvenirs of Eddy and put them away. It would
have been terrible to me to have had to answer
careless questioners who might have seen them in
my apartments, and to me it seemed that it would
have been terrible to Louis to see continually before
him the face of his dead rival. So we had begun
our new life without any evidences of the old one,
and the only remembrance of my first love that I
had allowed myself to retain in daily use was that I
always wore a little gold ring, set with a single
diamond, like a dewdrop, which Eddy had bought
for me in Bombay on the evening before we parted;
a little ring for which he had given something like a
couple of hundred rupees, and which he had bought
as a last souvenir of India, and not with any idea
that an immediate parting was upon us. I never
explained that ring, and Louis asked no questions
about it; indeed, I knew not then and know not
now whether he ever noticed that it was always
upon my hand.

So our life glided peacefully on, a life that was
peaceful, and yet very full of interests and occupations. We visited during that winter each one of
the different estates belonging to the family, the
princess remaining at Ischelstein, partly because she
thought it would be better if we went alone, and
partly because she was afraid to face long journeys
in the midst of a rigorous winter. Wherever we
went we were *fêted* and belauded. Great enter-
tainments were got up in our honour, and we
came back to our ordinary every-day life again,

on my part, at all events, with sighs of satisfaction and relief.

The following spring was taken up by visits to Vienna and Paris, and when the time came round again that we should think of the cure necessary for the warding off of the princess's rheumatism, Louis suggested to her that we should all go together to Homburg, rather than that she should once more take a cure at Aix. She was absolutely indifferent as to her place of cure.

"I don't think that it is quite the right place for me," she said to me, "because it is more for gout than for rheumatism, but if we find that it does not agree with me, we can very well go to Wiesbaden, where I should be very near to you in case I were not so well."

"From what I can gather," Louis replied to her, "I believe that Homburg would suit you even better than Aix, and I think you would like the place itself much the better of the two. I am anxious for Dorothy to see it, and I have not been there for a long, long time, so that if it makes no difference to you, Mother, we may as well try it for once."

"I have not been there for nearly twenty years," said the princess. "I shall be delighted to renew my acquaintance with the picturesque little spot. Shall we then regard it as a settled thing?"

So it was quite decided that we were to spend a little time at Homburg. For myself, I cared little or nothing. I was in excellent health at this time, and had no need of taking a cure at either one place or another. Indeed, so far as I knew, there was at this stage of our life together only one thing which seemed possible for us to want, and that was an heir to the great house of Barzadiev; and I confess that I should have hailed the coming of such an event with untold satisfaction, for it seemed to me that to give Louis an heir would be the only adequate way in which I could in any sense repay him for all that he had given to me.

CHAPTER XXVIII

A THUNDERBOLT

IN due course of time we three found ourselves comfortably established at Ritter's Hotel, overlooking the pretty little park at Homburg. Then, not a little to Louis's chagrin, we discovered that he had done absolutely wrong in persuading his mother to accompany us. The place did not seem to suit her at all, and the doctor who was called in to attend her at once told us that we had better remove to Wiesbaden. The princess, however, with that rare unselfishness which so distinguished her, flatly refused to change her quarters unless we would promise that she should go alone—that is to say, only with her attendants.

"I shall be quite wretched if I know that I have taken you and Dorothy with me," she said to Louis. "After all, the cure is a short one, and I should be perfectly happy and comfortable by myself. I shall be neither happy nor comfortable if I know that I have altered all your plans and arrangements."

She spoke with so much decision that we did not argue the point. Louis went with her to see that she was suitably domiciled, and then returned to me at Ritter's Hotel.

I do not know that I had ever been so much

R

charmed with any place in my life as by Homburg. We found many acquaintances there, and made many more. We lived the same simple, everyday almost commonplace existence that was lived by everybody else, rising early in the morning, going to bed early at night, dining most times under the trees, and always sauntering up and down for a while listening to the strains of the band on the terrace of the Kursaal.

It was a life in which one could not be dull, and yet in which there was no strain, which is, I suppose, the reason why Homburg is such a favourite place with those who live the gay life of the great world.

Louis, who had only one fad regarding his health, had taken it into his head at this time that he was likely to develop symptoms of gout, and he religiously dosed himself with the waters, and went through the entire treatment of the baths every day with the regularity of clockwork. He used to disappear from the tennis ground, or whatever part we might chance to be in, and go off for a bath of the wonderful pine-needles. Certainly the treatment was good for him, and every day that we remained at Homburg he became more healthy-looking and more contented with himself and his surroundings. Our only trouble at that time was that the health of the princess began to fluctuate again. It was not that Wiesbaden did not suit her; that certainly was not the case, although Louis daily reproached himself that he had persuaded her to abandon her usual stay at Aix. Twice or three times during each week he ran over during the latter part of the day in order to satisfy himself that she was not losing ground. Once or twice I went with him, but the princess so scolded me for putting an unnecessary strain upon myself that at last I gave up these trips and remained quietly behind by myself. At first I had felt a little lonely, for this was the first time since my marriage to Louis that I had been left anywhere by myself, but as the occasions went by, and I became more accustomed to my surroundings, I began to regard Louis's frequent absences as being altogether a matter of course. Already his cure had come to an end, and we had agreed that, on leaving the neighbourhood, we would go to the Engadine, which the doctors said would be good and even necessary, both for the princess and for Louis.

Then one morning there arrived an exceedingly disquieting letter from the princess's head maid. She wrote to Louis saying that madame had had an alarming seizure of faintness the previous evening, that is to say immediately before her letter was written, that they had called in the doctor who was attending her, and he advised that she should communicate with her son immediately.

"Madame la Princesse," Louise wrote, "recovered very quickly from the attack, much more quickly than from any previous attack in which I have seen her, but she still looks very drawn and very pallid, and I should feel more comfortable if your highness will come and see her at the earliest possible moment. Madame la Princesse forbade me to communicate the news to your highness, and I humbly beg of you to exonerate me from blame should she be angry on finding that I have written to you. I had orders to do so from the doctor, but had he not so instructed me, I should have ventured to take the matter into my own hands, as I feel it is not right that your highness should be left ignorant of the condition of your high-born mother."

"There is nothing for it but my going over at once, Dorothy," said Louis, on receiving this letter.

"Oh, yes! You must go. But if I were you I should go as if you knew nothing. I will go with you, I think."

"I fancy you had better not," he said, looking at me doubtfully. "My mother will realise in a moment that Louise has written us a disquieting letter if you go without any explanation. She was so annoyed the last time that you went, because she thought it was undergoing unnecessary fatigue, and as we are really on the eve of rejoining her, she would naturally look for an explanation as to why you troubled to come over to-day. I think you had better let me go alone. If I find her not so well, I will remain the night; but, of course, I will apprise you if I do that. You would not mind my remaining away a night, would you?"

"Oh, no, I will manage to exist," I said, with a laugh. "I think you are right, you know, Louis. There is no need to make her nervous for nothing. She is not at all nervous about herself; but it may disquiet her if she thinks that Louise is unduly so. Of course, I would much prefer to go with you, but I think, perhaps, under the circumstances, that it would be wisest if I remained here."

So we settled it, and immediately after luncheon Louis took leave of me and started for Wiesbaden. By this time I had got quite accustomed to his leaving me for short absences, and I set about employing myself quite happily and contentedly.

I had promised to take an English friend, a Lady
Stewart, for a drive among the picturesque pine
woods. She was in quest of some curious little jugs
—mere toys, which she had promised to take back
to England with her for the benefit of some small
nieces.

"I don't know," said she, as we started, "exactly
where they are to be bought, but my sister's
children had a few of them taken to them last year
by a friend who was staying here, and they were
most eager that I should get them some more, as
their doll's house was not sufficiently stocked with
them."

"We can easily find out," I told her. "The people
in the villages we are passing through will be able
to tell us. I am sure we shall find no difficulty in
meeting with them."

We made several inquiries as we drove along, but
either the people were very stupid or they did not
understand exactly what we wanted. At last, however, when we were both in despair, we inquired at
a little inn in a small stone-built village, apparently
the most unlikely spot in the world to find anything
of such a nature.

The good woman of the inn told us that if we
would condescend to enter she would send for a
neighbour who had many of these little jugs and
pots for sale. "If the ladies would like refreshment,
I can offer it," said the good woman.

We asked her what she could give us. She told
us we could have milk, coffee or beer, and also excellent sweet cakes. "Let us have some coffee and
cakes while she fetches the woman with the little
pots," said Lady Stewart, in English, to me.

I was perfectly willing, and we alighted from the

carriage, telling our coachman and his fellow-servant to refresh themselves while we were waiting.

The busy house-wife was as good as her word. She brought us very soon a delightfully homely repast, consisting of coffee, cream, delicious sweet cakes and honey, and while we were partaking of it the friend for whom she had sent arrived with a large basket of tiny jugs and pannikins of glazed earthenware of every conceivable shape and colour. My English friend was enchanted with them. "Did you ever see such darlings?" she cried. "Why, my little nieces will be wild when they see them! Those they had brought to them last year were nothing like this —mere black and brown things, quite ordinary and ugly. These are delicious, delightful! Look at those brilliant greens and those vivid oranges! How quaint the shapes, how charming the colouring! What dear little jugs and pannikins! Upon my word, I think I shall take a store back for my own pleasure and edification!"

I could not help laughing at her, indeed, she laughed at herself as she turned over the quaint little jugs with the delight of an unspoiled child, while the stolid vendor herself laughed from sheer sympathy; and we picked from her great basket all that were at all quaint in shape or brilliant in colouring, paying her in the end an absurdly low price, though I fancy from her look of satisfaction as she bade us good-day that she had suited her prices to the appearance of our carriage.

As we drove home together, Lady Stewart professed herself very much my debtor for the afternoon's doings. "I feel quite convinced, my dear Princess," she said to me, "that but for you I should have gone home to England without finding out these

treasures. You see, I only speak French. In my
young days German was not considered an essential
part of a girl's education, and one is at such a dis-
advantage in dealing with people a little off the
highways if one cannot tackle them in their native
tongue. If I had daughters of my own, I should
insist upon their learning as many languages as
possible. I always think," she went on, "that it is
such a waste to set girls strumming on the piano
whether they have any talent for it or not. Now,
for my part, I never had the smallest gift of any
kind in the direction of music, and yet, from the
time I was six years old until I was eighteen—twelve
years of woe, twelve of the best studying years of
one's life—I was made every day to do a certain
amount of music. The result? Oh, it was pitiful.
An every-day school-girl of twelve years plays better
than I did when I gave it up for good and all, and I
often think that if I had had a sensible mother—I
do not wish to say a word against her, poor dear
soul, she did her best for me, I have no doubt—but
if I had had an enlightened mother, who would have
studied me a little, and found out in what direction
my talents lay, she would not have allowed me to
waste a single day on music, and she would have
made me put all my energies into the acquisition of
languages. I speak French really well," she went
on, "really well; and I am quite sure that if I had
had the opportunity I should have spoken German
just as fluently and just as correctly."

"Why don't you learn German now?" I suggested.

"Oh, my dear, it is too late in the day, much
too late in the day. An old woman of my age
does not thank you to go to school again. No, no.

Girls ought to learn their lessons while they are girls. When you get to womanhood and to middle age, as I have done, you have other lessons to learn which take up all your time. Ah, here we are at home again. Oh, there is the prince!"

I looked aside, expecting to see Louis, but instead perceived that Lady Stewart was speaking of the most distinguished visitor who ever sheds the light of his countenance upon the pleasant little Bad.

"Now you will remember that you are dining with me on the terrace to-night at a quarter past seven!"

"Oh, yes, I shall not forget," I replied. "Particularly as Louis is not here. He will not be back in time for dinner, you know, Lady Stewart, in any case; and it is possible I may find a telegram to say he is remaining the night with his mother."

"You are uneasy about her?" she asked.

"Well, we are rather uneasy. I wanted to go over, but we were afraid that it might make her feel that we were unduly nervous, and that is not good for her."

"You are very fond of her," Lady Stewart said.

"Oh, I am a great deal more than very fond of her!" I exclaimed. "If she had been my own mother ten times over I could not love her more dearly than I do."

"That is so rare," said Lady Stewart, a little drily; "with us, at all events."

"Ah, yes, I daresay it is rare with everyone," I replied. And a remembrance of my dear Eddy's mother and the way that she had treated me years ago flashed across my mind. "But, you see, Princess Barzadiev and I were quite devoted to each other

long before there was any idea of my marrying
her son; indeed, I won't say that I married
him to please her, but it was next door to
it."

"You are a very lucky woman," said Lady
Stewart, in a tone of firm conviction. "I think
most of your sisters have great cause to envy you.
I have never met Princess Barzadiev, but if she
is as charming as her son, and so fond of you as
you say, it must be very delightful for you."

"She is all that I say and a great deal
more," I made haste to reply. "Unless you knew
her I could never make you properly understand
the sweetness and light of that dear woman's
perfect character."

"Lucky woman!" cried Lady Stewart, with a
sigh which I fancied revealed to me a good deal
that was not equally fortunate in her own history.
"Ah, here we are at my hotel. My dear Princess,
I have to thank you for a most charming and
delightful drive, and with all my heart, in my
little nieces' names, for this find of yours." She
pointed to the basket of little pots as she spoke,
then she got out of the carriage and Franz opened
the door and followed her into the house, carrying
her purchases with him. On the doorstep she looked
back: "Remember, the same table as last time,
and a quarter past seven. Charming people coming
to meet you!"

As I expected, when I reached my rooms I found
a telegram from Louis saying that his mother was
better, but that he would remain with her for the
night. She sent me her love and begged that I
would not be at all anxious or uneasy; and if I
objected to his remaining at Wiesbaden he would

return by the last train that night. I despatched a message in reply saying that he was on no account to return, that I had been for a delightful drive with Lady Stewart and was dining with her, as he would remember, that evening, therefore that I should be amply looked after and amused.

Having despatched this, I rested for awhile and glanced over the pages of a new English novel; then I changed my cotton dress for a smarter one, and, attended by Franz, went to keep my appointment with Lady Stewart and her husband on the terrace of the Kursaal.

They were both there before me. "You are positively the first. How punctual you are!" she exclaimed, as I joined them. "You know the beautiful Lady Desborough? She arrived in Homburg yesterday, and she is dining with us to-night."

"I have heard of her," I answered, "but I have never met her. But," I added, "I love beautiful people. It is always a pleasure to be in their company."

"Ah, here she comes with Lord Edward Powell. Now, you must let me make you known to each other."

She introduced me to quite one of the loveliest young women that I had ever met or beheld in my life ; then several other guests made their appearance, and our party seemed to be complete.

"Are we all here, my dear?" asked Sir Robert Stewart.

"Not yet, not yet, Robert. A few minutes grace. We may as well be seating ourselves. We are only waiting for a gentleman. Princess, you will sit next to my husband—Lady Desborough, sit on Sir

Robert's other side—yes, that is it. Ah, here is our truant! Now, our party is complete. Lord Clovelly, you are shockingly late! I had almost given you up!"

CHAPTER XXIX

A FACE FROM THE DEAD

IF the heavens had suddenly opened before me, and a thunderbolt had fallen at my very feet, I could not have been more astonished than I was to hear that the name of the new-comer at Lady Stewart's dinner-party was Lord Clovelly. I turned quickly to look at him, that I might see what manner of man the present head of my first husband's family was. Judge, then, of my surprise, my consternation, my horror, I might almost say my dismay, when I saw standing, with his hand clasped in that of our hostess—my husband! Yes, it was Eddy—Eddy himself, in the flesh, alive, well, and apparently happy. I sat staring at him as I would stare at one come back from the dead. I felt that every drop of blood in my body had gone back helter-skelter to my heart; I felt that my face was blanched, my lips drawn over my teeth, my eyes starting from their sockets. I could not have spoken to save my life. I, Princess Barzadiev—Louis's wife —Lady Clovelly—Eddy's wife? Good God! What was I? A thousand conflicting thoughts came beating into my brain in a space of time that could have been no more than a moment. Like one paralysed, like one expecting to go through some terrible form of torture fast and yet slowly approaching, I waited for what would happen next.

"Let me introduce you to Mrs L'Estrange," said Lady Stewart, indicating the lady nearest to her, "and Miss L'Estrange; Lord Clovelly—Lady Desborough. My husband you know—Princess Barzadiev on Sir Robert's other hand."

I saw Eddy bow smilingly, showing just the edge of his teeth, as I had so often seen him do before, and then his eyes fell upon me. If our meeting had been a shock to me, it was ten times more so to him. He looked at me incredulously, half screwed his blue eyes up as if he could not believe the evidence of what they told him, made a step forward, put out his hand, looked back at Lady Stewart. "Who did you say that lady was?" I heard him mutter to her.

"The Princess Barzadiev, an Austrian princess, but an Englishwoman."

I heard her words, although they were spoken in a mere whisper. He put his hand up to the side of his face, and pressed the ends of his fingers against his temples as if trying to force his brain to take in some new idea. Then he came round the table and held out his hand to me.

"Princess Barzadiev and I have met before, Lady Stewart," he said. Then he dropped my hand and went back to the place that Lady Stewart had indicated beside herself as his seat for dinner. I can only say that I never sat through such a meal in my life. I never went through two such hours of mortal pain and anguish, no, not even when I saw my little child lying dead and still in front of me; not even when I received that cruel sheaf of newspapers which told me that I, a young girl, was a widow. Not at any period of my existence, from first to last,

did I ever sit through such a time of intense anguish
as those two hours spent upon the terrace of the
Kursaal at Homburg. I did not dare to look at
him—well, yes, I did once or twice steal just a glance,
but I managed to avoid meeting his eyes. I was
conscious that he watched me from time to time
closely. I, think of it, I, Dorothy Hamlyn, sitting
there on the opposite side of the table to my Eddy,
listening to the tones of his voice, occasionally catching
a glimpse of his face; I, calling myself the Princess
Barzadiev. Heavens! Was this some terrible dream,
or was I on the eve of being taken up by the roots
again and cast out into a world where nobody would
have me?

Fortunately the English lady, Lady Desborough,
was gifted with a tongue; she talked and talked.
Oh, how I blessed that woman for her loquaciousness.
I was conscious that she was chattering away to Sir
Robert, keeping him amply amused, telling him all
sorts of wicked little stories about various people
well known to both of them, and in whom I took
no interest. The man on my other hand had evidently some kind of an affair on with Miss L'Estrange. He did not want to waste a word over me,
and once when he turned with an effort—with an
unmistakable effort—to speak to me, I whispered to
him not to trouble to talk to me, that I was not
feeling very well, and that I would not think him
neglectful if he talked to the lady on his other hand.

So I was left almost alone, except for an occasional
remark from my host, and as course after course went
by, and Franz served me with morsel after morsel
with which I only toyed, I tried to reduce the chaos
in my brain to something like system and order.
But the more I tried to think things out the more

hopelessly confused did I become. Was ever any
woman so placed as I? I was wife to two men,
Prince Barzadiev and Lord Clovelly. Louis was
away—Louis was with his mother; Eddy was on the
other side of the table; and I—what was I? Who
was I? I was wife to both of them! What would
be the end of it? What would they do? To which
should I belong? Oh, dear heaven, was ever a
woman placed in such a position before? I could see
no way out of it. I wondered if Eddy was married
again. Perhaps there was a wife, perhaps there was
a child. He had not forgotten me—oh, no. I had
seen in the first flash of his eyes that he was as un-
changed in his heart as, God help me, I was. My
mind went back over those days of doubt which had
preceded my engagement to Louis Barzadiev, those
days when I had wronged myself, when I had told
him that I had never regarded Eddy as being really
lost to me, that although I had believed him to be
dead, knew—as I thought—that he was dead, yet that
he had never seemed dead to me, that I had always
about me the feeling that some day I should find him
somewhere. And so my instinct had proved to be
true. I had found him again. I had found him, not
in another world, not as he left me, but here, on this
earth. And I had been for more than a year the
wife of another man!

At last the dinner came to an end. I do not mean
to imply that it was an extremely long dinner, for it
was not so, but we seemed to sit an interminable time
over the coffee and ices with which it finished. Franz,
still standing behind my chair, inquired in a whisper
whether I had any commands for him.

"Yes, remain where you are," I replied. "I am
going home immediately."

As soon as the various guests made a move I rose from my chair and went round to Lady Stewart. "Will you forgive me if I leave you now?" I asked. "I don't feel very well, and I would like to go home at once."

"Most assuredly, though I am so sorry, dear Princess," she said cordially. "Do you think the drive was too much for you this afternoon?"

"Oh, no, not at all; I enjoyed it extremely," I replied. "I am a little tired, that is all."

"Who shall go back with you to the hotel?"

"I have my servant here," I replied. "Please do not break up your party."

"Perhaps the princess will permit me to walk to the end of the terrace with her?" said Lord Clovelly, in a quiet tone of intense restraint.

I bent my head. "That would be very kind of you," I said, and I wondered that those standing near did not notice how choked and strained my voice was.

"Yes, do; pray, do," chimed in our hostess. "You are quite sure, my dear, that there is nothing I can get for you?"

"Oh, thank you, no, nothing. I shall perhaps see you to-morrow."

I shook hands with her and with her husband, and with a mere gesture to the rest of the party turned away, Lord Clovelly keeping his place beside me. My servant walked at a little distance behind, but not so near as to be able to hear what we were saying.

So we two, who had parted just five years before in the cabin of a P. and O. boat, turned and walked together down the terrace steps, amid one of the brightest scenes in Europe. As we reached the lower level Eddy broke the silence.

"Doremy," he said, "what is the meaning of this?"

"The meaning—"I turned and looked at him. "Oh, the meaning—I don't know—I don't know. I cannot tell you to-night. Come and see me early in the morning; ask for me at Ritter's. I shall be alone. Prince Barzadiev will not be in Homburg till the afternoon."

"And who is Prince Barzadiev?" he asked.

"I don't know. I am so dazed. I—I feel bewildered. Let me go home and get accustomed to this new state of affairs. I thought you were dead," I said in a voice that sounded like a wail of despair. "I thought that I had every proof of your death. And you?"

"I had no proof of your death, but I could find no trace of you alive," he said gravely, and yet without either reproach or bitterness in his tones. "I traced you to Florestella; I found the child's grave, and there I lost you. I thought you must have died soon after her."

We had reached the end of the terrace by that time, and I stopped and stood looking up at him in the brilliant lamp-light. "Go back to them now," I said in a shaking voice. "To-morrow we will tell each other everything. Don't tell them yet. If the world has to be told what a cruel failure I have made of my life and yours—and—and his, let me get out of Homburg before the blow falls. Only tell me one thing; have you, too, made the same false step that I have done?"

He was holding both my hands in his firm, warm clasp. "You mean have I married? No. How could I marry any other woman than yourself? You were my first, my only love. I have had no temptation to put any other woman in your place."

I felt his words sink into my heart like molten lead; and yet I was so innocent of having in any sense permitted another to supplant him in my affections that I was able to look him straight in the eyes. "When I tell you everything," I made reply, "you will not feel that I was *tempted* to marry again. I think you will exonerate me, and forgive me for what must seem to you now like faithlessness to your memory. But do you go back; let me go home. Come to me early to-morrow. I have so much to tell you."

"Shall I not go back to the hotel with you?"

"No, my servant will take care of me."

"Does the fellow speak English?"

"Not a word."

He stood still a moment longer, holding my two hands hard, and looking down at me with a searching and eager gaze, as if he would fathom the thoughts of my very soul and read there what my trembling lips could not speak. "One question. How long is it since you—you changed your name?"

"Just a year."

"H'm! And—is there—is there a—child?"

I shook my head. "No, there has been no prospect of another child."

I heard him mutter "Thank God!" to himself, and then he pressed my hands again, bade me goodnight, lifted his hat and left me.

I scarcely know what happened next. I went back to my apartments, and when my women had attended me for the night I sat down at the open window overlooking the park with its dark glades broken by rows of twinkling lights, over which the tender strains of a melancholy air came softly on the light evening breeze, and I tried to realise what had happened. It was useless. Think as I would, I could not see light in any direction. Of course, such a situation could not be hidden. In a few days' time every newspaper and journal in every civilised country in the world would be ringing with the story of the English lady who was at one time the wife of an English peer and of an Austrian nobleman. I knew that nobody, not even the two men who loved me, could rightly blame me. And yet what position should I be in? What could I do? I was wife to both, and, it seemed to me, that I could be wife to neither. I had married Louis in all good faith on a clear and honest understanding with him, he full well knowing that my heart was buried, as I thought, in a grave—a soldier's grave. That soldier had come back, full of love! Oh, that was plain to be seen, and my heart had leapt ere it sank at the sight of him. I could not remain with Prince Barzadiev; equally certain was it that I could not go back and take up my old life with my first love. Was ever a woman placed in such a position before? What could I do? What alternative had I to take? Was there a course which would be not unfeeling and unjust to one or other of these two men who loved me? Oh, there was none—none, save to go away to some quiet, out-of-the-way corner of the world where nobody would know my name or my wretched story, and to hide myself from all human eyes; at least, from the eyes of all human things who would be likely to know me. I felt that I had not deserved it, I felt that this new trouble which had come upon me was none of my seeking, had been none of my doing, and yet I must suffer, suffer it to the bitter end.

I looked round, round the spacious room, with its

many evidences of my hitherto serene and contented life, though not the life of my highest earthly happiness. The tokens of that life were all swept far and wide, there was nothing in my apartments that could remind me of that one bronze-faced, blue-eyed man from whom I had just parted. It may seem almost incredible, but the dominant feeling in my heart during that dark hour was one almost of regret that the past had been so different to what I had thought it during all the years that had gone by. I was as much in love with Eddy as ever. Every touch of his hand, every glance of his eyes, every cadence of his voice had the same old power to thrill my whole being through and through, and yet I had no joy in this wonderful, this unexpected meeting; for there stood beside me, during the long watches of that terrible night, a vision of him who had left me on the day before, who had been from first to last consistently kind, courteous and loving, who would, I knew, have sacrificed himself in every possible way if by so doing he could have added to my welfare or to my happiness. My heart all belonged to the old love, but, as I sat by the window and watched the twinkling lights go out one by one, my woman's pity and my reason made me feel that I could give myself to neither of them—these two men who loved me. I felt like some weak, frail, storm-tossed child, trying to reach with either hand to an impossible salvation.

CHAPTER XXX

TWO QUESTIONS

I HAD scarcely finished my pretence of a breakfast the following morning when Lord Clovelly came to see me. I was in my own sitting-room, trying hard to appear as unconcerned and composed as usual, and yet moving restlessly about, now gazing out of the window, now staring at my own wan presentment in one of the hideous pier-glasses, trying to stop the throbbing of my temples by pressing the palms of my hands hard against them, now holding my chin hard in my hand that I might still the horrible trembling of my under-jaw. And through my brain there ran two questions—"Who am I? What shall I do?"

It was still very early, far more early than I usually received visitors, when I heard the door open, and Franz came gliding across the floor to me. "A gentleman is inquiring for Madame la Princesse," he said quietly. "Lord Clovelly. Does Madame la Princesse receive this morning?"

I put my hand up to my chin again, and, with an immense effort, replied quietly and in something like my ordinary tones to the servant's question. "Oh, yes, Franz, I will see Lord Clovelly. You can bring him here."

The long hours of the night which I had spent in fighting with myself had taken half the strength out of me. I felt, as I waited for Lord Clovelly to be brought into my presence, as if I could not, even by the most valiant effort, keep from fainting.

Then I heard the door open again, and the servant's voice say—"Lord Clovelly."

For a moment I positively could not turn round, but at last I did so, and he and I had met again. All the restraint and conventional stiffness of the previous evening had left him. He was no longer Lord Clovelly; he was the old Eddy that I had loved and who had loved me in the years that were gone by.

He put out two trembling hands towards me, and cried in a voice of the keenest anguish,—"Oh, Doremy, Doremy, have you nothing to say to me?"

I had nothing to say. I was dumb, speechless, abashed before him.

"Why — why did you marry the other fellow? Who is this man, this Austrian prince? How came you to marry him? How came you to forget me?"

"I have never forgotten you!" I burst out.

He turned and looked at me. I suppose that something in my tones told him the truth, and set aside all the doubts that had been torturing him during the hours of the night that was past. "Do you mean," he asked breathlessly—"am I to understand —is it true that you are mine still, that you have not forgotten me, that, although you have married, I have never been supplanted in your heart?"

"Nobody has ever supplanted you. I have so much to say that I do not know where to begin. I don't know how to get you told before—before—he comes back."

" Where is he ? "

" He has gone to see his mother, who is at Wies-baden."

" Why were you not with him ? Is his mother like mine ? "

" Oh, no, no! If ever a saint trod the earth, Princess Barzadiev has the right to that name. I married him in a large measure as a payment of my great debts to her. When I first knew her at Flore-stella, when the child died, when I got the news of your death and of Bill's death and of Lord Clovelly's death, there was no thought of my marrying Prince Barzadiev. He was away in Africa, I had never seen him, and he had never seen or heard of me. We did not meet for six months afterwards. There was no thought of my marrying him or anybody. But she, she did for me what no mother could have done better. I lost my child and she lost hers. We two poor lonely women helped and comforted each other with no thought of any closer tie arising between us, and when I was left desolate—Oh, Eddy, you cannot think how desolate I was alone ! Even Nurse went with the rest."

" How went ? " he asked.

" Died. Everybody died in that plague - stricken spot—baby, Princess Elisabeth, the landlord, the land-lady, Nurse Mordaunt. She sacrificed her brave life as dozens of others did in that terrible time. I don't know who died after we left, excepting that one of the sisters wrote and told me about Nurse Mordaunt. I got the news of your death at Venice. Princess Barzadiev took me on board her yacht as soon as her daughter was buried. Oh, she was so good ! She offered to turn back, to take the first steamer from Brindisi, to take me out to India. But what would

have been the good? I had nowhere to go! No
money—well, something like three hundred pounds
—no friends, no home, no husband, no child. I was
stranded, desolate, distracted, stunned by my loss and
by all that I had gone through. And when she asked
me to give the rest of my life to her, to let her take
the place of my mother; when she asked me to take
the place of the dear daughter she had left sleeping
next to our baby at Florestella, what else was I to do?
What better course could I have taken? How was I
to know that such a horrible mistake had been made?
How was I to look forward to anything like this?"

"But, my dear child," he said, looking at me incredulously, "did it never occur to you that I had
money; that I had made a will, leaving all my earthly
possessions to you?"

"No, I never thought of money."

"Did it never occur to you that if I had fallen in
action you would be entitled to a pension?"

"Blood money!" I exclaimed.

"Nay, dear, not blood money, but your right."

"My right!" I repeated questioningly.

"Yes. How was it that you, or nobody about you,
ever thought of claiming that?"

"I never thought of it. . . . I never thought of it
from the moment I had the news of your death until
you now put it into my mind. You see, I was so
stunned. For months and months my brain seemed
as if it would not think or act. I never cried for you,
Eddy, not one tear. I never felt, somehow, that you
were dead; and when, to save Princess Barzadiev's
life, I reluctantly consented—after he had been three
years patiently waiting for me—to marry her son, I
told him then that I had never realised your death;
that I had always the feeling that, if I struggled on

through this world, I should find you somewhere up yonder — somewhere or other. Oh, you must not blame me; you must not reproach me that I did not turn my thoughts, as soon as I knew that I was left to my own devices, to making money out of your death! I never thought of it. They were so rich; money was nothing to them. My love was everything to this heart-broken mother, and her protection was everything to me. It was the only ray of light that fell across my path."

"I am not reproaching you," he said gently. "I only asked you a very natural question. It is a thought that would have occurred to most people; it was the one thing that made me believe that you must have died in that fever-stricken little Flore-stella. I found that you had not even applied to the War Office for official confirmation of my death. It is natural that I should think that nothing but death would have prevented you from making some communication or other with me."

"But I had the proof," I exclaimed. "I saw the proofs a dozen times. First the news that Bill was dead and that you were dangerously wounded; then that you had died of your wounds."

"But that was poor Bill," he put in.

"But he was reported as killed in the engagement."

"No, no; he was brought in as dead, but, as a matter of fact, he lived for some hours after the fight."

"Then I saw afterwards that Lord Clovelly had been stricken down and had died on hearing the news of his son's death. I never saw any contradiction of the report of your death, and everything seemed to confirm its truth. Why," I continued, "we had actually an Englishman staying at Ischelstein who had known poor Bill, and who told me that the present Lord Clovelly was some distant relative."

"And who was that?"

"Oh, a Colonel Wyndham He was attached to the British Embassy in Vienna at the time."

"What, Wyndham of the 1st Life?"

"Yes, I suppose so."

"I met Wyndham only the other day in St James's Street. And you say that he knew you as Mrs Hamlyn?"

"Yes."

"And knew that you were one of my family?"

"Yes."

"Did he mention it?"

"Yes, I told him whose wife I was, how you had died in the same expedition as young Bill, and I told him not to mention me to any member of the Clovelly family. You know, Eddy, they were not kind to me. Your mother was hateful to me, none of your people were in the least nice to me, excepting that poor boy, and I felt that, having lost you, I would rather die than be beholden for so much as a kind word to one of them. And so I told him that, if he saw any of the Clovelly family, he was not to say that he knew a Mrs Hamlyn living in Styria. Oh, Eddy, Eddy, if you could know what I feel like at this moment! To think that I, by my own act, had deliberately blocked the way to our coming together again. You have not reproached me, but, oh, if you could know how bitterly, bitterly, I reproach myself!"

"Reproaches will do no good to either of us," he returned. "They would make the situation

more difficult, and several people very unhappy.
What is the good of them? Besides, there is one
thing that you forget, my Doremy, or that you
have not yet realised, that although you have un-
wittingly married another man, you are my wife
as legally and as honestly to-day as you were five
years ago when we parted at Bombay. What
you have done in ignorance and inadvertence, and
in good faith, has not undone what you and I
did at Simla seven years ago. You are my wife
still, I am your husband. If you had forgotten
me, if you had learned to love the other chap
better, then the complications would be horrible,
but, as I understand it, you have not changed
towards me at all, any more than I have changed
towards you."

"But what of him?" I asked, in a scarcely
audible voice.

"Of Barzadiev? He must be told."

"Yes, he must be told. I have always been
honest with him. I am not going to begin
being dishonest and underhand now. And yet,
to leave him and simply go back to my life with
you, why, it is impossible! I could not do such
a thing."

"If you love me—" he began.

"No, Eddy, no. If I did not love you, it
would be far easier. It is because I do love you,
because I have always loved you—loved you, oh,
with my whole heart and soul, with every fibre
of my being—that I cannot turn my back upon
the man who came in the blackest hour of my
life, who gave me the shelter of his honourable
name, and put his great heart between me and
a world that I was horribly afraid of."

"But you would not, from some mistaken sense of duty, go back to him, remain with him?" he exclaimed.

"Oh, how can you ask me such a question? How can I, in the face of things as they are now, be anything to either of you? Why, I am wife to both—I am wife to neither—I can can be wife to neither! That I love you as I do, as you must see for yourself I do, makes no difference. I have to consider my honour and my good faith before my love, and even before yours."

He broke away from me and began to pace up and down the room. "Who is to tell Barzadiev?" he asked, suddenly pausing and standing in front of me.

"I will tell him; it will come best from me. You had better remain in Homburg until I send for you. I think he will probably wish to see you; at all events, you will not refuse to see him if he does? We must consider him before ourselves, Eddy."

"Poor devil, yes. There, I beg your pardon, Doremy, I ought not to have spoken of him like that; and yet the words slipped out, because, after all, it is the worst for him."

"Before we were married," I said, "I made a kind of bargain with him, that under no circumstances should he ever reproach me with my dead love for you—no, I mean with my love for you whom I thought to be dead, for my love had never died, never! And he told me then that he had never felt such sympathy for any human being in his life as for you. Yes, really, he did say that, and he has lived up to it.

Many a man who knew that my heart was buried in a grave would have troubled me about the past; would have gone on worrying and protesting and asking questions, until he received the assurance that he was the most loved of the two. He has never done that: he has been true to his word from first to last, from beginning to end. I love you the best, but my respect and my affection for him are almost too sacred to speak of, even to you."

He stayed a long time with me, talking over all the possibilities that the future might hold, making suggestions, finding out loop - holes by which I might go back to him with something like honour; but one by one, I disposed of them all. One might have thought that I was eager not to set the time back and sun myself once more in a glory of happiness, but it was not for that reason that I so strenuously held out against each and every suggestion that his brain could devise.

"I can do nothing, arrange nothing, and consent to nothing until I have told him all," were my last words.

It may seem strange, but it was by the greatest effort that I once or twice spoke to my husband by his Christian name. My instinct was to treat him as a stranger, to call him "Lord Clovelly." I had a curious sense about me of reserve and strangeness. He, on the contrary, slipped back, after the first few minutes, into precisely the old terms of speech and endearment.

"Doremy," he said, when we parted, "you have not kissed me."

Instinctively I drew back. "No, don't ask me

to do that until everything is settled. I shall get through my task more bravely if I have been fair and honest towards the man who believes that I am his wife."

He understood me, and, bending down, kissed my hands. "You will send for me?" he said.

"Yes, as soon as there is anything to tell you."

"And you will remember that I have been mourning you, regretting you, hungering for you during five long years?"

"I will not forget it," I replied.

So he went away.

Franz came, bringing me flowers which some man or other had brought for me, and then told me that luncheon was served in the adjoining room. I sat down and looked at it, but I ate nothing, for a single mouthful would have choked me. Franz was politely distressed.

"I am not very well. I cannot eat," I told him. "Take it away, don't trouble me with it."

So I went back and wandered up and down the *salon*, waiting restlessly, and yet impatiently, for the time when Louis would return. What should I say to him? How should I find words in which to tell him? What would be the end of it all? Was I glad? Was I sorry? I did not know.

I looked forward—all was black, black as night; dark, lowering, impenetrable clouds seemed to have come thick and fast upon me, and only one thing was inevitable—that again I was to be the sport of fate; the ball of chance and mischance, tossed from one to the other without any will-power of my own. I was to be taken up by the roots

and hurled out into the world yet once again.
What would be the end of it all? Who was I?
Lady Clovelly, or the Princess Barzadiev?

Those were the two great questions which
troubled me,—" Who am I? What shall I do?"

CHAPTER XXXI

LEFT ALONE

IT was nearly four o'clock when Louis returned from Wiesbaden. He came into the *salon* with a laughing reproach upon his lips. "Are you really here and alone?" he asked. "How was it, then, that you did not come down to the station to meet me? You are beginning to neglect me, Dorothy."

I turned to meet him. Some instinct told him that something had happened. He made a step towards me. "Dorothy, my dearest! What has happened? Something has gone wrong with you. You are ill."

"Yes," I replied, "something has happened; something has gone wrong, something is amiss. I don't know how to tell you what it is."

"But how—what is it—what can have happened? I only left you yesterday. Tell me quickly. Don't spin it out—don't break it to me."

"I don't know how to tell you," I cried, trembling in every limb. "I cannot break it to you. I can only tell you the truth—brutally, and almost unfeelingly."

"But what is it?" he asked anxiously.

288

"I went to dine with the Stewarts last night on the terrace of the Kurhaus."

"Yes," impatiently.

"And among the guests was—Lord Clovelly."

"Lord Clovelly? What, the head of the Hamlyn family?"

"Don't you understand?"

"No. Do I understand what? Had you never seen him before? Was there anything extraordinary about him?"

"Yes," I said, "I had seen him before. Don't you see what I mean? I—I—had believed him to be dead."

"What!"

"Yes, it is quite true."

He looked at me incredulously. "Do you mean that Lord Clovelly is your first husband?"

I had no words in which to reply. I only looked at him, but my eyes told him the pitiful truth.

"Then you—I—what am I? Who are you? What does it all mean? My good Dorothy, am I dreaming?"

"What does it all mean? It means that I have been deceived, not wittingly, but by an extraordinary chain of accidents and of evidence that seemed too circumstantial to doubt. It means that I in my turn deceived you; that I have been the victim of the most cruel mischance, and you of the most cruel fate that ever befel any man."

"But you are the wife of both of us?" he cried.

"I am not your wife, Louis," I answered pitifully. "I am his lawful wife, his legal wife."

T

"You are not mine? You are not Princess Barzadiev? He can take you away from me?"

"It is not a question of taking me away. It is rather a certainty that I can be nothing to either of you."

"And he has never married?'

"No."

"And he loves you still? Oh, of course, he does. I need not ask such a question. Who that had known you once, and possessed you, could cease to love you, could cease to regard you as the pole-star of his existence? What did he say? What did he do? Why don't you tell me everything?"

I sat down upon the nearest couch, and drew him to sit beside me. In truth, my limbs were shaking so that I could no longer stand. So there we sat together, and I told him as far as I could do everything that had happened the previous evening, and during my conversation with Lord Clovelly that morning.

"You will remember, Louis," I said, when I had told him the whole tale from beginning to end, "you will remember that day at Ischelstein, when I reluctantly consented to become your wife, that I told you that I had never been able to shake off the feeling that I should find my husband again somewhere — some day. I thought that he was dead; I thought that it would be up yonder that I should find him. I had no hope, no suspicion, that he might be still alive and looking for me, and yet I had never realised that he was dead. I had left him strong and well, in the very pride and bloom of his manhood. He had never seemed dead to

me, as he would have done had I seen him die
with my own eyes. You remember my saying
that?"

"Oh, yes, I remember everything."

"For years he has believed me dead, as I thought
him. As soon as he was free of the Service he went
to Florestella to seek tidings of me, to be met on
all hands by tales of death, disease, disaster and
woe. The landlord of the hotel where we stayed
—he was gone, his wife, the nurse, the doctor also
—one by one those who had known me had died
in that plague-stricken spot, and there was no
record of my stay beyond my name in the hotel
books as having gone there on a certain date,
and my little child's name in the books of the
graveyard, where she lies sleeping. There was no
trace of my leaving Florestella. How should there
be, for, as you know, I left on board the *Kaiserin
Elisabeth.* I left under the shelter of your mother's
passport, and my own name never appeared. Nobody asked, nobody cared to know where we were
going. We were going on to the yacht. There was
no time for little formalities such as tracing the
personality of every person mentioned in the passport; the authorities were only too glad to see the
last of us, for fear that a woman of your mother's
rank should die in Florestella and have her name
blazoned all over Europe, her name and her tribulation. They were only too anxious to hide everything, only too eager and willing to help us to take
flight. So, as he could find no trace of me, he believed that I, too, was dead, especially as I never
sought any official confirmation of his death. It
all came through the mistake which arose between
his name and his cousin's in the despatches con-

cerning the killed and wounded. Almost his first question to me was to ask why, believing that he was dead, I had not made good my claim to his property and to the pension to which I should have been entitled in the event of his death? I never thought of it. I told him so. With regard to his property, well, I was so stunned, so broken by my losses, that I never gave so much as a thought to it. And money never seemed to enter into your mother's calculations one way or the other. As for a pension; why, it would have seemed like blood-money! I ought to have thought of it. If I had been a little older, I probably should have thought of it; and we should have been spared— you would have been spared all this pain, this dreadful revelation and upheaval which has come upon you now."

He made a fierce gesture of his arm, as if I need say nothing more about that. "Don't reproach yourself," he said brokenly. "You acted in all good faith, and we persuaded you, my mother and I, against your will. I shall tell Lord Clovelly that when I go to see him."

"You are going to see him?"

"Yes; I shall go now. I think that I had better send for my mother. She will know what to do for you. I cannot have you go out into the world friendless, with nobody who understands your nature. Or have you made up your mind that you will go back to the husband to whom you rightly belong?"

"No," I said, "no, I shall not go back. I told him so. I have in a sense wronged you both, failed you both, failed myself most of all; but I will be just and true to each of you, whatever it

costs me. If your mother would come to me—
perhaps she won't—it would help me through this
terrible time, even if it was only for a little while.
I would be so grateful."

"I will send for her. I will only ask you one
question before I go to despatch a message to her
and seek out this—this rightful husband of yours.
You have been contented, almost happy with
me?"

I turned and put my hands into his. "Louis,"
I said earnestly, "if it is any comfort for you to
know it, I have been more than contented as your
wife. I cannot help loving him best, because he
was the first, and you cannot undo what is done,
but I would rather that things had been as I
believed them to be all along—and yet— Oh, no,
no, it is not quite the truth to tell you that; I
could not help my heart leaping at the sight of
him. It is best to be honest with you; you have
made me happy, you have made me content, you
healed my broken heart as nobody else in the
world could have done, and all that I can do for
you, all that I have been able to do for you, has
been to ruin your life."

"We won't talk about that," he said bravely.
"If you have ruined my life, Dorothy, it is by no
conscious act of yours. I cannot allow you to
speak of yourself so. To me you are, as you
have always been, the best and dearest woman
that the world holds. Don't abuse yourself. It is
not necessary. I go to send for my mother."

He kissed my hands as the other one had done,
and I was once more left alone, and for the next
hour I remained alone, and in a dazed state of
wretched waiting. One of my women came and

brought me some tea, which I drank with feverish thirst. Then Louis came back again, told me that he had seen Lord Clovelly, that he agreed with him that the princess was the only person who could succour me at that time. "He is a fine fellow, that husband of yours," said Louis, with a generosity which was all his own. "I don't wonder that you were so reluctant to put anyone in his place. He agrees with me fully that you could not go back to him at present; and yet, as I told him, it falls terribly hard upon him to find his wife after so long a time, and to have no joy in the reunion. I feel as if when my mother comes that she will be able to see some way out of the difficulty, some way by which you can eventually go back to him. After all, why should three lives be wrecked where two, at least, might be perfectly happy?"

"I will abide by what the princess advises," I said in a low tone. "What she tells me to do I will do. I know that she will advise me rightly. You will meet her when she comes?"

"Yes."

"You will tell her everything? You won't leave it to me? It was bad enough that I had to break it to you. You will tell her for me? You won't let her blame me? She will understand my situation."

"My mother will understand you," he replied. "She will be here at nine o'clock. But you will remember that she is frail and delicate—but there, I need not tell you how to treat her."

I did not see either of them again that evening, I mean either Prince Barzadicv or Lord Clovelly. At the usual time I went and sat down at the dinner table, and forced myself to take some soup and wine, for I was fast becoming faint and exhausted, and at nine o'clock my dear princess-mother arrived.

CHAPTER XXXII

WAITING—AND THE END

FOR the first time since the news had come to me I was able to give way and lean upon somebody else. Neither in the case of Prince Barzadiev or Lord Clovelly had I dared to show a sign of the white feather, because I felt that any sign of weakness on my side would double the pain and anguish that each was suffering; but when my dear adopted mother came — came with all her woman's heart in her dear eyes, came with arms outstretched and caught me close to her tender heart, I knew that I had found a haven which had never failed me and which would never fail me in this world.

"My poor child! My dear, dear Dorothy!" she cried in accents of the most tender pity, "I shall never cease to reproach myself for this new trial which has come upon you. Louis has told me everything. My poor child! One cannot feel sorry, and yet, the pity of it all is so great. Oh, my dear, to think of the years of your young life wholly wasted—to think that we who loved you, we who had no wish but for your best and truest interests, should have persuaded you into a step which has brought ruin and disaster upon all of us. Yes, I know—Louis has told me. There is the poor husband not daring to rejoice in having found you again, and my poor boy, who has lost you. It is only I who can remain feeling towards you as in the beginning."

"And you do, Princess? You do, Mother?" I cried.

"Oh, my dear, of course I do. It is sad for both of them, but it is far sadder for you. But you are right—you could not go back—not as things are at present. My dear, you have always the right instinct, and your instinct was right when you held out so long against marrying Louis. We ought to have trusted that instinct of yours, it was unerring; but since we would have our way, he and I, we must stand aside now and think only of you. Louis is a man—it is a great trial, the greatest and most terrible that could have come upon him—but he is a man, and men must be strong and bear. For the other, he must wait for you a little longer, until your own feeling shows you what you ought to do, what is the best and the most right for you to do. And for me, darling child, I am at your service. We have stood by each other too long, you and I, Dorothy, to desert each other now. We will go away, you and I—we will leave these two strong men to fight out their trouble by themselves, and you and I will protect and help each other."

"But, dear Mother," I said, "will you answer me one question—Who am I?"

"My dear," she said, "there is no question as to who you are. You are Lord Clovelly's wife—you are Lady Clovelly. Your marriage to my

son was an accident. It is null and void; it is
no marriage. Louis will have to see his lawyers;
he will have to have everything put upon a proper
legal footing, for the sake of yourself and your
future, and of his family. But you are Lady
Clovelly. When we go away from this, you must
bear that name; it is your own, and the whole
world will have to know it; the whole world must
know it, ought to know it. It is imperative that
the world knows it," she added with great decision,
"and there is nothing to be ashamed of. It is a
misfortune for which the whole civilised world will
pity each one of us. But there is no blame that
can be attached to you. If there is any blame
it is attached to me—to Louis—for we two persuaded you—nay, we did more than that, we over-
persuaded you to take a step against your instinct,
against your better judgment—I might say almost
against your natural inclination."

"And what will become of Louis?"

"My dear, we will go, you and I, to some quiet
place where we can await events as they arise. I
will take some château in a neighbourhood where
we are not known, and we will stay there until
everything has been put right with the lawyers.
That is necessary; that is your plain duty so far
as Louis is concerned. After that, we can shape
our plans according to our wishes, and according
to what seems wisest to us both at the time. Louis
will make his own plans. You and I know him
well enough to feel that he can be trusted to make
them wisely and to follow them bravely."

I knew that her words were wise, as I knew that
her heart was right, and it was comfort unspeakable
that I, who was right in the course which I had

marked out for myself, should have this brave, patient and tender woman to walk beside me and hold my hand along a way which was bitter, a way which was apparently hopeless. I felt more brave, more patient, more safe. I felt as if I had strength and courage to live on to the end, whatever that end might be.

We left Homburg the next day, she and I, travelling by easy stages as far as Munich, in which place it seemed to the princess that we could most readily find retreat for a time, and yet be within reach of the lawyers in Styria. I saw both Louis and Lord Clovelly before we departed. To the one I said good-bye, practically for ever, to the other I could only say that for the present I felt that it was best that everything should stand in abeyance.

"But the princess tells me that you will take your own name again?" he said.

"Yes, I will do that," I replied. "It is my name, and, of course, I have no right to the one under which you met me the other evening."

"And, Doremy," anxiously, "you are not going away, leaving me quite without hope? You will come back to me some day?"

"I don't know," I replied. "I can say nothing definitely. I must have time to let things arrange themselves a little. Not even for you can I do anything which will pain either of those two."

So we parted, and the princess and I set off on another stage of life's journey together. At Munich we settled for an indefinite time, the princess having secured a beautiful villa just on the outskirts of the town. We passed, on the whole, a very dull and dreary existence, for we saw no visitors, and our only interests lay in the news which came to us through the newspapers and the post. Eddy wrote to me every day, giving me the fullest details of his life, his hopes, his thoughts, his doubts and fears. Louis never wrote to me at all, but he very often did to his mother, and several times lawyers came to and fro with papers that it was necessary I should sign.

Then Louis wrote and told his mother that he had made up his mind, as he could not bear the desolation of Ischelstein, to go to North America on a big shooting expedition. "Nothing is so likely," he wrote, "to take me out of myself as complete change of scene and of occupation. I know that my dear love is safe with you, and, if you can spare me, I shall make my preparations for leaving immediately."

It is needless to say that the princess not only consented, but she willingly concurred in this decision. And so time went on until nearly a year had gone by since the last and greatest upheaval of my life had happened.

After this our life together was even more dreary than it had been before. From time to time, though at very irregular intervals, Princess Barzadiev had news of Louis, and at last he wrote to her making a definite suggestion on my behalf, which was to me the strongest possible confirmation of the noble and unselfish love which he bore me.

"I wish that you would say to Dorothy," he wrote, "that every day I live I feel how hard it is upon Clovelly that he should be kept away from her. After all, there is no reason that the man who has the best claim to her, the first right, and a love for her equal to my own, should be kept at arm's

length out of a feeling of delicacy towards me.
Will you show this letter to Dorothy? I think that
she will understand me when I say that I do not
make this suggestion from lack of love, but rather
the contrary."

"I have been waiting for this," said the princess,
when I had come to the end of her son's letter. "I
knew that Louis would see things sooner or later
in their true and right relation. It is not just to
Lord Clovelly that you should be kept apart any
longer. You love each other, you have always
loved each other. My son is perfectly right in all
that he says. If you will allow me, I will send for
Lord Clovelly and give you to him myself, in
Louis's name.

"Oh, no!" I cried. "Why should I put you to
such pain?"

"Nay, dear child," she said, "you forget that I
am Louis's mother. It will be one of the proudest
moments of my whole life."

.   .   .   .

So we came together again, Eddy and I, by the
wish and at the hands of my adopted mother,
Princess Barzadiev. He came to Munich to fetch
me, and from there we made a long tour, passing
through many lands, making few acquaintances,
living wholly and solely for each other.

I wrote to my dear princess constantly, and learned
from her that Louis was back at Ischelstein, and
that he was bearing his life more bravely than even
she had anticipated.

Then, when there seemed to be some prospect of
an heir to the old West country name, we turned
our steps towards England, and in due course of
time a little son was born to us, whom we named

after that brave and unselfish soul who had loved me
so dearly and yet so unfortunately.

I will not say that my life was without shadow.
I was happy—oh, yes; and yet there were days in the
year, sacred anniversaries, in which I felt that my
husband had no part. There were times when he
lavished all the wealth of his love upon me, when
I felt that, although his love might equal, it could
never outshine that other which stood alone outside
the zone of my life.

So the tranquil years rolled on, and with every one
my adopted mother found her way to Clovelly, and
sojourned with us for a little while. Every time
that she came I hoped that she might bring the
news that Louis had found happiness elsewhere; but
he never did so. He passed to and fro in different
parts of the world, sometimes going to the wildest
and most outlandish spots in search of big game,
sometimes spending a season at Ischelstein; but he
made no effort to remodel his life in a domestic sense,
he never seemed to think of filling the place which I
had held with another.

One by one little human flowers bloomed out in
the old west country home, little golden-haired
blue-eyed creatures, all Hamlyns every one of them,
bright little souls, who called Princess Barzadiev
granny, and must have made her heart ache, though
she hid the fact like a martyr. Only once did she
ever betray to me anything of what must often have
passed through her mind. "Ah," she said, "if we
had only one of these at Ischelstein!"

So the strange story of my life drew to a close,
and became lost in the obscurity of a perfect and
idyllic happiness.

It happened one golden August day when we were

alone at Clovelly, excepting for the children in the
nursery, that I received a letter from my princess-
mother. "I am greatly afraid, dearest child," she
wrote, "that I shall not be able to pay my visit to
you this year. I am uneasy about Louis. Since his
return from his last trip to South Africa, he has
seemed singularly unlike himself, and I should not
like to leave him as he is at present. He is not ill,
but he is troubled by a kind of low fever, which is
intermittent and strangely persistent. When I say
he is not ill, I mean that he is not laid up. He
goes about very much as usual. The doctors have
recommended him to try several places in order to
get rid of this South African legacy. We are starting for the high Alps early next week. He laughs
at my fears, says that I ought to have seen him
when out lion-hunting and speechless from ague. I
am very glad that I did nothing of the kind. I
have no wish to see him in any worse health than he
is at present. The doctors tell me that I am not to
be uneasy, yet there are times when he reminds me
so much of my dear Elisabeth that my heart fails me
altogether."

I think that my husband saw from my face that
there was no good news in the princess's letter. He
took it from me, and read it, with only two words of
comment as he laid it down again. "Poor chap!"
he said.

That was the beginning of the end. The princess
and her son moved during that winter persistently
from place to place. She wrote to me continually,
always telling me the same thing—that Louis would
not own to being ill, that he always laughed at her
fears.

And then, during the cold spring days which

followed, I received at last a telegram, which simply said—"My dear Louis left me at noon. Pray for me."

So the struggle was over; and my story comes to an end.

THE END